THE MOONS
OF SUMMER

THE MOONS OF SUMMER

BY

S.K. EPPERSON

DIF

DONALD I. FINE, INC.
NEW YORK

For Donna

THE MOONS
OF SUMMER

CHAPTER
ONE

GUY DRISCOLL SAT on the new wooden glider on his front porch and attempted to see into the house next door to his. His daughter Adele was in that house, and his mind refused to stop wondering what she could be doing. The man who lived there, Adam Dupree, was a bachelor older than Guy. Adam owned a small black poodle with a high-pitched bark, and the poodle was the first friend Adele had made since moving to Colson, Kansas. Adam was her second friend, and though he seemed tame and harmless, if not a little quirky, Guy was at a loss to understand the relationship.

What it came down to, he supposed, was the fact that he didn't trust his daughter. Guy didn't necessarily think she was over there in bed with the man, but knowing Adele, as Guy was beginning to, it wasn't entirely out of the question. At sixteen, his daughter appeared to have more sexual experience than Guy did, and it was an uncomfortable knowledge to have about one's child. In the six months Guy had been in custody of Adele, the girl had been pregnant twice by two different males and had been on her way to a second abortion when she was struck by a Chicago policeman in an unmarked car on Lake Shore Drive. She asked for and received the abortion while she was in the hospital.

It was time to get her out of Chicago, Guy had decided after a long session of guilt and recrimination and cursing her dead mother. He had been divorced from Jill for six years before her death from breast cancer, but Jill's hatred of him obviously lived on in Adele. Adele wanted nothing to do with her father, and she chose to live on the street rather than share a house with him. When Guy finally asked her what the hell her problem was, she had looked at him and said, "Mom told me there's something wrong with you. You never touched her, and as far as she knew, you never touched anyone else. She warned me to be careful when I was with you."

Guy was disgusted beyond belief that Jill would actually say such a thing to their daughter. Later he would learn it was typical of Jill. He assured Adele that he was as normal and healthy as any busy managing editor of a major newspaper could be. It was simply that he had no time to invest in personal relationships. He didn't mind being alone. He wanted to go on and tell her that life with the poisonous woman who was her mother would leave any man insane and impotent, but he refused to resort to the same vituperation Jill herself had used. He hadn't touched Jill because he often found himself unable to even be near her. He had stayed with her as long as she wanted him to stay. When she said go, Guy went.

A peal of laughter reached Guy's ears and he sat forward on the glider, straining to see past Adam Dupree's screen door. The little bitch, he thought. Then he felt guilty for the thought and attempted to erase it from his mind. You didn't call your own daughter a little bitch. Even if she was one. You loved her and provided for her. You gave up the best newspaper job in the city of Chicago for her and moved her to a small town where you hoped she'd pick up some values and morals and maybe do something nice with her hair.

Guy smiled bitterly to himself. If Adele knew of the sacrifices he had made for her, she certainly didn't care. He was now a lowly general assignment reporter and sometime columnist for the Colson *Beacon*, a local daily approximately one-eighth the size of the paper he had run in Chicago. He was treated poorly by the other employees of the paper, many of whom feared for their jobs when they heard Guy's background, but he did his best to get along. Most people acted as if they didn't believe him when he told them he had left Chicago for his daughter's sake. Several looked at him like he was crazy. There had to be another reason, they rationalized. There had to be some dirt he didn't want dug up. People didn't do things like that for their kids anymore. They didn't give up six figure salaries to move to Kansas and be a GA on a paper like the Colson *Beacon*. Not for their kid, they didn't.

Guy did. Which wasn't to say that he didn't regret it. He couldn't think of anything else to do with her at the time. Guy had been born and raised in Colson, and since he considered himself to be a relatively decent person, with no major faults and only a few sins to his past, he was trying for the same kind of influence for his daughter.

As another peal of laughter drifted across the porch and reached his ears, he decided he was failing miserably.

What the hell, he told himself. He always meant to come back to Kansas anyway. After the death of his parents when Guy was twelve, an aunt from Chicago had come and taken him away. His parents had been aged and most of his relatives were scattered over the eastern half of the United States, so Guy had little choice in the matter. He loved his life in Colson, though, and he never forgot where he came from, or the parents who loved him. During the all too frequent moments of stress at his job in Chicago, a vision of a vast Kansas field rolling with the wind had always held the power to soothe him.

There was no vast field off his porch now. Just a three bedroom bungalow behind him and a cracked and rutted road in front of him. It wasn't what he had imagined for himself and Adele. And he did miss Chicago. His old life. He missed the

Kennedy Expressway, the South Side, and the West Side. He missed worrying over the crime around Cabrini-Green, and shaking his editor's head over the affluent Gold Coast. He missed the "glass house," a tag for his old office, and being able to sit down behind his computer and collect a day's worth of messages with the touch of a key. He missed being a respected and influential man.

When a gunmetal gray Nissan Sentra parked at the curb in front of his house, Guy frowned and stood up from the glider. He walked forward to place a hand on the railing and saw a woman with sunglasses, white blouse, khaki trousers, and a serious face approach the house. In her hand was a wadded-up newspaper.

"Hello," Guy said in greeting.

"Are you Guy Driscoll?" she asked.

He nodded and eyed the careless light brown ponytail that fell over her right shoulder.

"You wrote this without even asking me what happened. Why would you do that?"

"Wrote what?" Guy asked. He had several pieces in that day's edition.

The sunglasses came off. Her eyes were dark blue and full of anger. Her voice was ice. "The column on the Vernon Diest incident."

Guy was listening, but he wasn't hearing her. He couldn't seem to stop staring at her. Tiny beads of perspiration covered his upper lip as he struggled to make himself comprehend what she was saying to him.

"I'm sorry . . . what has that got to do with you?"

"I'm Michael Bish," she said, "the officer you wrote about. You didn't ask me what happened. You didn't hear my side of the story. The police department, the county attorney, and the Kansas Bureau of Investigation had already cleared me when you wrote this. Now the public is asking for the grand jury you suggested, based on what you wrote. The switchboard at the police department has been jammed with calls all morning, and to appease the masses I've just been suspended *without* pay, pending the results of a second investigation.''

Guy knew he was staring again, but he couldn't seem to help it. He watched her mouth and the way her lips moved over her teeth as she spoke. He watched the way her nostrils flared, and the way the skin at the bridge of her nose crinkled as her brows met. The blue in her eyes went on forever, dark as the midnight sky.

"You're Michael?" he managed finally.

"Surprised?" she asked. "Were you expecting a large white redneck male?"

"No, Miss Bish, I—"

"That's *Mrs.* Bish."

Guy's stomach did a dull flop of disappointment. He willed his mind to clear and his hands to stop shaking.

"First of all," he began, "let me apologize for any harm the column may have caused you. Secondly, your department wouldn't let me talk to you even if I'd asked. Thirdly, let me ask why you're afraid of further investigation?"

She stepped up onto the first porch step. "I'm not afraid of further investigation. What I'm afraid of is the publicity. You of all people must know the public's perception of law enforcement officers."

"Why me of all people?" Guy asked.

"You're from Chicago, aren't you? I'm sure the people in Chicago just love their cops. They shoot one a day, don't they?"

Guy's mouth curved. "Not quite. But I get your point. The question is, what do you want from me?"

"My salary for the next month will do for a start."

Guy spread his hands. "Look, I'm sorry. I—"

"You certainly are."

"Hey, be nice," he said, irritated.

"Like you were?" she retorted, holding up the paper in her hand.

"I didn't know who you—I didn't know anything about

you. The fact that you're a woman actually makes several of my points moot, if you hadn't noticed. It makes me look like the original cub reporter, and that should give you some satisfaction."

"Oh, it does," she assured him. "It's the only thing that kept me from being outright fired, Mr. Driscoll. That and the fact that people in Colson are still watching you with cautious eyes. They don't know whether to believe you or not, but some people were angry and curious enough to ask for that investigation. The rest of them want you to take your *Chicago Manual of Style* and shove it up your ass."

Guy's fingers curled on top of the rail. "Suppose you tell me your side of the story right now, Mrs. Bish. Believe me, I'm all ears. Exactly why did you shoot Vernon Diest in the back on the night of January the eighth?"

Michael Bish raised her fist and threw the wadded-up newspaper at him. "You figure it out."

CHAPTER TWO

MICHAEL WAS STILL SMARTING with anger as she drove away from the gray and white bungalow. The way he had looked at her made her even angrier. Someone you just met, someone you'd never seen before wasn't supposed to look at you like that. Guy Driscoll wasn't anything like she had expected. He didn't look like her idea of a tough editor type. He was shorter, for one thing, five feet eight at the most, she guessed. And his face was young-looking, almost a babyface. With his meticulously combed brown hair and clean-shaven cheeks he reminded her of a schoolteacher, or a parson.

The giveaway was his eyes. They were a startling shade of green, and they hadn't missed very much, Michael saw. There was definite craft there as he gave her the once-over and then came back to scrutinize her features as if he were administering a lie detector test. Michael should have told him what he wanted to know. She should have told him what happened the night she shot Vernon Diest. He might have decided to write another editorial and try to sway public opinion the other way.

And then again, he might not. Michael gritted her teeth in frustration and looked at her watch. She was late for the hospital. She had told Oliver she would be there by four o'clock, and now it was almost four-thirty. The fact that Oliver was in a coma made no difference. Michael believed her husband was aware of everything that went on around him, even the time. She treated him as if he were, and she believed that once or twice she had seen him respond. The doctors assured her that she was mistaken, but Michael refused to accept it. She knew what she knew.

The bullet lodged in his brain for the last nine months had not killed her husband, it had merely removed him from her reach. She couldn't converse with him, but she could read to him, touch him, hold him, and let him know she was there. Michael believed he knew when she was there. She thought she sensed a difference in his breathing, a relaxation in his facial muscles. He seemed more peaceful when she was by his side.

Accidentally shot and wounded by his partner, Oliver's condition was considered inoperable. Should any attempt be made to retrieve the bullet, the resultant hemorrhaging would kill him instantly. After the first night, the doctors had been grave in their estimations of his longevity. A week, they had said, maybe less. The bullet could shift at any time. Even a fraction of a millimeter could kill him. But Oliver lived on, and the hospital had become Michael's second home.

Now, she supposed, she would have more time than ever to spend with her husband. Oliver would be upset to hear of her suspension even if he were conscious, so she decided against telling him what was going on. Oliver and Michael had met in the police academy and dated through graduation. It was only after both had been hired by the Colson Police Department that they decided to wed. They had been married three months and ten days when Oliver's partner reportedly dropped his gun in the police department parking lot. The discharge struck Oliver at the base of his neck and angled up into his brain. Michael never saw the man she married again.

Though she still loved her husband, the love had gradually

changed. Where once there had been passion, now there was a great maternal tenderness, as though Oliver were her child and needed caring for. When Michael's father and sister suggested she spend some of her free time away from the hospital, Michael had become angry. She couldn't leave her Oliver alone. The nurses wouldn't care for him the way she did; they were rough and careless when they turned him, and they never massaged his muscles the way they needed to be massaged. Eventually, after months of the same routine, Michael had relented—and suffered guilt every moment she was away from his bedside. She was getting better about leaving him, but it was a slow, painful process.

That day she said hello to all the nurses and doctors as she walked through the hospital and was surprised to see her older sister, Sean, waiting for her in Oliver's room. Sean stood as Michael entered and the two women briefly hugged. Sean opened her mouth, but Michael put a finger to her lips and turned to the figure in the hospital bed.

"I'm here now, honey," she said. "I'm late, I know, but I had to stop and talk to someone who writes for the paper."

"You did?" Sean blurted. "What did he say?"

Michael looked at her and asked her to keep her voice down. "What did you expect him to say?" she whispered.

"That he was sorry," Sean said.

Michael's nod was grudging. "He said that. But he didn't sound sorry. And you should've seen the way he looked at me. It gave me goosebumps."

Sean lifted her brows. "How? How did he look at you?"

"I don't know. I can't explain it exactly. All I know is it made me feel strange."

"Was he rude?" Sean asked.

"No. He told *me* to be nice," Michael said with a shake of her head.

"Was his daughter there?"

Michael frowned. "I didn't know he had one."

Sean nodded. "She's in my homeroom at school. A bit

more mature, shall we say, than the natives. Seems to be a bright girl, though. Hey, I came to see if I could buy you dinner, and to ask you a favor."

"No dinner," Michael said, "but ask away."

"Are you sure? What did you eat today?"

"I'm fine. What do you need?"

Sean sighed. "Some help at the school tomorrow night. I don't have enough people to help with the used book sale. I thought I would, but naturally I don't, so could you please come down and help take money and answer questions?"

"Will I know the answers?" Michael asked.

"Sure. Where's fiction and where's reference and that sort of thing. All right?"

"Okay. What time should I be there?"

"As early as you can. Between four-thirty and five would be great."

Michael briefly closed her eyes and wondered if this was another of Sean's plots to get her out of the hospital. She opened her eyes again and looked at Oliver in the bed. Then she looked at her sister, smaller and prettier than Michael, with large, dark eyes. She reached over to squeeze her hand. "I'll see you tomorrow night, Sean."

"Great," Sean said, and she kissed Michael on the cheek before leaving the room.

Michael watched her go, envying her the cozy home and healthy husband she possessed. Sean had what Michael considered to be a perfect life. She was a teacher, and her husband, Gordon, ran a print shop. They had no children yet, but they intended to start a family soon. Gordon would trade in his two-seater for a station wagon, and Sean would teach part-time for the first few years. It sounded like a perfect plan.

"We had the same plan, didn't we?" Michael said to Oliver. Michael had intended to leave the force as soon as she became pregnant. The stress of the job would be too much for the baby and probably too much for Michael by that time. She and Oliver had entertained so many fantasies about the family they would some day have.

Michael sighed and got up to check the chart beside Oliver's bed to see when was the last time he had been turned. She found no notations on the chart. She removed the page and turned it over, curious and then suddenly angry. This was the second time they had done this. The second time in less than a week the nurses had completely ignored him and gone on with other hospital business, leaving Oliver to simply lie there. She checked his catheter bag and found it full. Michael snatched the bag away and attached a new one before writing down the fluid contents. After emptying the bag, she marched down to the nurses station of the small hospital and stood at the desk. There was no one in sight.

Suddenly the emergency door at the end of the hall burst open, and Michael turned to see nurses and doctors with grim expressions wheeling a gurney with a sheeted form on top into the emergency room. Behind them came a white-faced Guy Driscoll. He followed them into the emergency room and was led outside again by a firm-handed nurse. She pushed him down onto a seat and pointed to the coffee machine before returning to her colleagues. Driscoll sat back and stared at the door. Then his head sank into his hands.

Michael stood watching him, afraid to move lest he look up and see her standing there at the end of the hall. She felt like an intruder, an unwilling witness to whatever he was going through at the moment. A part of her said it served him right, whatever it was, for the trouble he had caused for her. Another part of her said she was being selfish and coldhearted. She forced her legs to move in his direction. His head lifted and he saw her coming. The flicker of surprise in his eyes was quickly replaced by wariness. Michael stopped before him and crossed her arms over her chest. "Is it your daughter?"

His look narrowed, and before he could ask how she knew, Michael said, "My sister is a teacher at the school. What happened?"

Guy turned his head. "She found some pills in the neighbor's medicine cabinet. He said she took all of them."

"I see," said Michael. "Is this the first time she's tried to kill herself?"

He looked at her. "What business is it of yours?"

Without a word, Michael turned and walked back down the hall, feeling his eyes on her all the way to Oliver's room. Inside, she went to Oliver and picked up one of his limp hands. She held it close to her chest, and after several long moments she simply began talking, telling him everything that had happened and all she had been through since the night she shot Vernon Diest. When she finished she released his hand and bent down near his face. "The man who wrote the column is here in the hospital now. I didn't want to tell you, Oliver. I wasn't going to, because I know how you'll worry. But I had to tell someone. I had to talk about it. It shouldn't be too hard to find another job. I'll probably have to. Once they suspend you without pay, they've already made up their minds.

"It's as if no one *wants* to believe me about Vernon Diest. Sometimes I still can't believe it myself. But he did have a gun, and he was going to shoot me. He turned away when his pistol jammed, and that's how I . . . shot him in the back."

She paused as her eyes welled up. "I know it sounds horrible, Oliver. It does. But it's what happened. I was never more scared in my life than when he pointed that pistol at me. Remember how we always talked about what we'd do if someone pointed a gun at us? Well, you can't think about anything when it happens. Your mind goes blank and instinct takes over. My hands were up and firing before I even realized what was happening." She stopped and sighed again. "And now I'm paying for it. For keeping myself alive. And Vernon Diest is suing everybody."

"What happened to the gun?" a male voice asked behind her, and Michael whirled to see Guy Driscoll standing in the doorframe with his hands in his pockets. "Diest's pistol," he said. "What happened to it?"

Michael's mouth trembled in anger. "Get out of here. You have no right to be in here. Get out."

"What happened to the pistol?" Guy repeated.

"I don't *know*," Michael flared. "It disappeared. How dare you stand there and listen—"

"I wanted to apologize. When I came in I overheard you talking. Is this your husband?"

"What business is it of yours?" Michael coldly mimicked.

Guy met her glare for a moment, then he inclined his head and stepped out of the doorway.

CHAPTER
THREE

VERNON DIEST POKED THROUGH the books in the sale at a leisurely pace, taking his time over the titles and occasionally reading through a few pages before replacing a book on one of the long tables set up in the school's gymnasium. He felt the eyes of Michael Bish on him as he moved through the rows. It made him smile to know she was so aware of him. He had been aware of her for a long time. Since her mother's funeral, six years ago, he had been aware of Michael Ogilvie, now known as Michael Bish.

He could still see her, sitting there in the family section of his chapel with her father and sister, all of them wearing black and sobbing for the mother Vernon had done such a wonderful job on. The heart attack had done awful things to Mrs. Ogilvie's face. It gave her a pinched look that Vernon did his best to smooth out but was ultimately unable to be rid of. He worked around it, giving her a sweetly frowning face that he compared to pictures he had seen of the Virgin Mary.

The family was reservedly pleased with the results, and the corpse had been a success at the funeral, with nearly everyone remarking how oddly peaceful the woman appeared. Vernon knew they weren't just saying this to be nice. He could tell when people were lying, and this time they were not. He had outdone himself on the Ogilvie woman.

His tender smiles of concern for Michael went unrewarded, however. She refused even to look at him, before, during, or after the service. He didn't exist in her world of pain. He was just the man who made up corpses and sent them down the road to be buried. No matter what he did to be noticed, Michael was unaffected. Frustrated, Vernon had given her mother's corpse a punch in the stomach when no one was looking. It made him feel better, but not much.

The next time he saw her was when he took matters into his own hands and went to her home. There were flowers that hadn't been picked up, so he had brought them to the family rather than disturb them with a call. Michael thanked him and disappeared somewhere inside the house, leaving him to talk to her father. Dejected, Vernon departed.

For a time he forgot about her. When his own mother died of cancer he was undone for several years, and running the mortuary and the Diest mansion on his own was harder than he had anticipated. The three-level stone landmark in the center of town was the oldest building in Colson, built by his great-great-grandfather and operated these many years by Diests of each generation. Now there was only Vernon, the last of the Diest line. He had never married. He had never been on a date. He had never asked anyone.

He lived alone on the third level and operated the mortuary on the first level. The second level was for the storage of caskets and Vernon's files. Many of the rooms went unused and were closed off. The population of Colson was a healthy one, with a low death rate for its twenty-five thousand citizens, many of whom were Seventh-Day Adventists, who ate no meat. Because business was slow, Vernon couldn't afford to heat more than four or five rooms in the house at a time. But rather than let people know the depth of his penury and possibly form opinions of his worth as a man, Vernon chose to be seen as a quiet, contemplative ascetic who cared little for the creature comforts craved by others.

There was no reason to question Vernon. His family was one of the oldest in the community. No one wondered how he came by his money—or didn't. On paper everything looked wonderful. On paper Vernon was a wealthy man, with the huge house, the business, and three vehicles in his name. And there was the trust his father had left him, rumored to be seven figures. It was a lie. His father had left him two hundred thousand dollars to be doled out in monthly one hundred and fifty dollar increments and not a penny more. On paper, Vernon was in fine shape. In reality he was a struggling pauper. In bad months, when no one died and no fatal accidents occurred, Vernon moved into the chapel and viewing rooms. The less light, electricity, and heat he used, the less money he spent. He slept in one of the bigger caskets and ate bread and cheese sandwiches. When business picked up again, he returned upstairs. Though irritated with the discomforts, Vernon couldn't imagine living any other way. Members of the Diest family had cared for the dead of Colson since the town's inception. If Vernon were to find some other way to make a living, it would mean the end of a dynasty. And it would mean Vernon, the last of the line, was a failure.

There was no way it was going to end with Vernon. He swore to keep the mortuary and the mansion alive, even if it meant killing someone to bring in business. It was a joke at first, something he toyed with in dark amusement, but the lean months made the prospect darker, and a bottle of Jack Daniels one long night made it deadly serious. If it had been anyone in the car that night but Michael Bish, Vernon knew he would have chickened out and gone home to sleep off his drunken scheme. But the woman who had so coldly rejected him was there, dressed in a police uniform, badge on her chest. From her car she had waved for him to pull the van over. Vernon realized his intoxicated state was about to be revealed, and in a state of panic he left his van as she left the patrol car. In his hand was a pistol.

He often thought it would have been a beautiful, spectacular funeral. He would have made her look like an angel. But the pistol jammed. The first time he had ever handled the fool thing, and it seized-up on him. He had been lucky Elma was with him in the van at the time. Michael Bish never saw Elma slip out and take the pistol from Vernon's fingers after the shooting was over. Michael was too busy calling for an ambulance.

Elma was Vernon's stepsister, daughter of the man Vernon's mother had married five years before her death. Elma was a deaf mute, and stupid like her father. The man had run off after Vernon's mother died, leaving the dumb female with Vernon. He paid no attention to her, but she always seemed to be there, watching him with her adoring brown eyes. The only reason he allowed her to stay was because she could fix hair. Vernon had never been good at fixing the hair on his corpses, but Elma had a flair for it. He wasn't sure where in the house she lived, what she ate, or even which bathroom she used, but she remained presentable and that was all that mattered to him.

He supposed she was staying somewhere on the second floor, where he wouldn't see her. Vernon kept his files there, his notes, his bills, his important papers, everything in triplicate. He kept dry cleaning receipts, grocery receipts; and he kept every letter, card, or postcard he had ever received. If he ever needed anything, he reasoned, he would know where to find it: on the second floor. There were a dozen rooms up there besides the room his files were kept in. Elma could live in any one of them.

She had been with him that night in the van, and he hadn't even known it. She was always slipping around, always appearing where he least expected her. Vernon had been angry, but was ultimately relieved when he saw her slip the pistol into her jacket and dart away into the night. That made it his word against Michael's, and since her gun was the only one at the scene, things looked pretty good for Vernon. He was certain to win his lawsuit against the city. And if he had heard correctly, there was an attempted suicide taken to the hospital last night. That could mean more good news. For even if the patient survived this try, one attempt was usually followed by another, so there was still reason to hope. A young body always brought mourners flocking to the chapel. The parents spent more money on services than usual, and requested all manner of special touches for their lost lamb. Vernon was there to provide whatever was needed.

He looked up from a book on horticulture to find Michael Bish still staring at him. He lifted one brow and looked pointedly away from her, telling himself what a shame it was that she had so overtly rejected him all those years before. She was a striking woman, after all. But Vernon considered himself a striking man, with no need to beg after the affections of women. All the Diests had been handsome to a fault, and Vernon was no different. With his coal black hair and ebony eyes, he drew the gaze of more than one woman in the crowded gymnasium. His height and the width of his shoulders matched that of any athlete in town. It was too bad he couldn't exercise more, but he wasn't really the outdoors or exercising type. He still managed to stay in relatively good shape and was often mistaken for a man younger than his thirty-six years.

Suddenly tired of his game, Vernon abandoned the tables of books and walked slowly toward the exit. Before he could reach the double doors, a voice hailed him. He turned and saw an unfamiliar man walking toward him. Vernon stood and waited. The approaching man held out his hand.

"My name is Guy Driscoll. I write for the Colson *Beacon*. I was hoping you could spare a few minutes."

Vernon remembered the name. He briefly shook the hand and released it. "You wrote the column."

"Yes, I did. Since then I've heard more of the details. Would you consider talking with me?"

Vernon studied the man before him. Guy Driscoll studied him back. The unwavering gaze made Vernon faintly uncomfortable. He said, "I'll think about it," and pushed past the other man.

"Call the paper when you make up your mind," Driscoll said to him, and Vernon lifted a hand but didn't turn around.

He didn't know what he would gain from another interview. Driscoll's column had done all the damage Vernon required. He didn't have to talk to anyone.

But maybe he should. To help his court case. It would look good if he appeared cooperative.

Vernon was undecided. As he passed through the exit he felt Michael Bish's cold gaze on him again. He smiled bitterly to himself and thought maybe a chat with Guy Driscoll wouldn't hurt after all. He could inject a human element this time, tell Driscoll all about the pain he had suffered in his back and the excruciating physical therapy he had endured, all because of the paranoid woman cop with the comatose husband. Hadn't she accused David Eulert, her husband's partner, of attempted murder after the accidental shooting? Vernon had read all about it in the paper. The poor man quit the force and left town all in one day. If Vernon could bring Michael's state of mind, perhaps even her sanity, into question it would make things that much more interesting.

Any woman who rejected Vernon Diest ought to have her sanity questioned.

CHAPTER
FOUR

GUY WALKED OVER to the table where Michael sat and stood beside her. When she looked up at him, he said, "I asked Vernon Diest to talk with me. He said he'd think about it. I'm going to tell him your version of the events and ask for his response."

"He'll call me a liar," Michael said.

"Why would he?"

"Why would I shoot him?"

"You tell me," Guy said.

"He pointed a pistol at me. I drew my gun and fired."

"Where's the pistol?"

"I don't know. It was there. I saw it. I didn't expect it to *not* be there when the ambulance arrived." Michael drew a deep breath and clasped her hands together. "How's your daughter?"

"She's all right. She gets out tomorrow."

"What are—" Michael paused and rephrased her question. "If you don't mind my asking, what are you going to do with her?"

"I don't know. Take her home. Have you had problems with Vernon Diest in the past?"

Michael looked surprised. "Me? No. I barely know the man. He's the mortician. He runs the mortuary and the chapel and he buries people in Colson Cemetery. He buried my mother six years ago."

"What else do you know about him? Is that the only time you've ever dealt with him?"

"I don't know anything about him," Michael said. "I can't remember ever speaking to him or anything else."

Guy's green gaze was steady. "Why would he want to shoot you, Michael?"

She met his look. "I've been asking myself that same question every day for the last three months. All I can tell you is from the moment I pulled him over—"

"You pulled him over because he was driving too fast. Is that correct?"

"Yes. He was doing forty-five in a thirty zone. When I left my car to approach his van he suddenly opened the door and got out. He pulled a pistol from his jacket and pointed it at me. I think it jammed because he was tense and didn't quite know how to use it. The only explanation I can come up with is that he wasn't alone in the van that night. I didn't see anyone else, but someone could have been with him. There's plenty of room. I'm told that he sometimes carries bodies back there."

"Bodies?" Guy echoed.

"Bodies he picks up from the hospital and such. Dead people."

"He doesn't use a hearse for that?"

"Not always. He told my father that hearses depress people."

Guy nodded. "So you think someone in the back of the van took the pistol. Will that be your story for the Kansas Bureau of Investigation?"

Michael's brows met. "My *story*? I'm not—"

"Hello," Sean said as she approached. She looked at Michael and then at Guy. "You must be Guy Driscoll, from the paper. I'm Sean Parkinson, Michael's sister."

Guy took the hand she extended and gently shook it. "Nice to meet you, Sean. I'd better be getting on to the hospital." He looked at Michael. "Do you spend your nights there?"

Michael looked away and refused to answer him. Guy nodded to Sean and walked out of the gymnasium. As he left he could hear Sean whispering fiercely to her sister. Michael's answering whisper was just as fierce. Guy felt his shoulders drop as he left the school grounds and walked to his white Volvo. He hadn't expected to find Michael at the book sale. He had known Vernon Diest would be there after driving by and spotting the familiar black van with Diest Mortuary and Chapel painted on the side. Was that why Vernon had been in attendance? he wondered. Had he known Michael would be there?

An uncomfortable shifting in his stomach occurred as he thought of the way she had looked at him a few moments ago. She had looked at him the way Adele looked at him most of the time now, like she wanted to believe in spontaneous combustion and was keeping her fingers crossed that it would happen to Guy at any moment. Guy was tired of being looked at that way.

In the hospital he found his daughter awake in her bed and reading a dog-eared copy of Mario Puzo's *The Godfather*. She looked up from the page when he came in, but she soon went back to reading.

"I brought the blouse you wanted," Guy told her.

"Thanks," she said, not looking at him.

Guy hung the blouse near the door and sat down. As he watched her he found himself thinking she didn't really look like either Jill or him. Adele looked like Adele and no one else. Her features were all her own.

"You feeling okay?"

"Fine," she said. Then she looked at him. "Adam called a while ago. He said you told him not to come up. Why?"

Guy shrugged. "Because you'll be home tomorrow. I didn't forbid him to see you, if that's what you're thinking. It's not Adam's fault you took his pills and tried to kill yourself in his house."

Adele smirked and shook her head. "Wow, Dad. That's some heavy psychology there."

Guy ignored her. "Where did you get the book?"

"It was in the drawer. Somebody left it here, I guess. It's pretty good."

"Yeah. I read it when it was first published."

"You did?" Adele seemed surprised.

"Sure," said Guy.

"Doesn't seem like something you would read," Adele commented.

"Why not?"

She lifted both shoulders. "I don't know. It's just pretty involved, you know. Lots of killing and sex and gore."

Guy nodded. "I couldn't put it down." He waited until that soaked in before saying, "Adele, I want you to talk to me. If I could have done something to prevent what happened yesterday I want to know what it is."

Adele blinked. Her voice was as blank as her eyes. "There's nothing you could have done. I saw the pills, and I watched my hand reach up and grab hold of the bottle. The next thing I knew I was emptying them down my throat and gulping water from the tap. *I* couldn't stop myself, so what could you have done?"

"But why?" Guy asked, leaning toward her. "That's all I'm asking. I just want to know why. Do you want me to take you back to Chicago? Is that it?"

Adele shook her head. "No. I don't want to go back there. I have no one there. No one has me. I'm gone from Chicago, body and soul."

Guy listened and felt helpless. He didn't know what to do when she talked like this. He extended a hand to brush her dark brown hair from her eyes and saw her cringe away from him.

"Please, Adele. Don't do that. Can't I just touch you?"

"Nobody touches anybody anymore, Dad. We all remain distinctly untouched. Have you noticed?"

"No," he said. "I haven't noticed. You're my daughter and I love you. I want to comfort you, but I don't know how. Tell me how to comfort you without touching you."

Adele smiled and laughed a tiny little laugh that sounded suspiciously like a sob to Guy. He looked closely at her but saw no tears in her red-rimmed eyes.

"All those hugs, Daddy. Remember the way you used to hug me after dropping me off on Sundays? Those short little squeezes that were supposed to reassure me of your love but served only to prove to me how apart we were. Your body was with me, but your mind was always somewhere else. You were putting together future papers the whole time we were at the movie, or the whole time we ate out. You were working on future headlines and slugs and future Sunday features. And now I'm supposed to be delirious with joy that you've given up your heart-attack act to move to Kansas with me and settle down to small town simpletude."

Guy started to tell her that there was no such word as "simpletude," but he could see she knew it. Instead he said, "So you're telling me that all my efforts have been for nothing. That it doesn't matter what I do, because it's too late for us. Is that it?"

Adele looked at him and heaved a long breath. "Yes," she said. "That's it." She cleared her throat then. "But I'll be a good girl. I'll get out and go back to school. I'll do my homework and get good grades. I'll even let you hug me and tell me you love me. But we'll both know the truth, won't we?"

"And what is that?" Guy asked, his throat dry. He searched her dark eyes until she coldly answered him.

"That you never wanted me to begin with. But you're stuck

with me now and in a hell of your own making. Isn't that right, *Daddy*?"

Guy went on staring at her. "Did your mother tell you that? That I didn't want you?"

"She told me everything. But look at it this way, it wasn't anything I didn't already know. Now, if you'll get out of here and leave me alone, I'm going to try and finish this book. I've never finished one before, so it'll be a challenge for me. Call it part of my new leaf." She lifted the book and trained her attention on the open page, leaving Guy to sit and watch her. After five minutes, he got up and walked out of the room. He started down the hall, then he turned back and went the other direction.

There was a nurse in Oliver Bish's room. She was attempting to turn the man in the bed. Guy went to help her and together they accomplished the task. When they were finished she turned to Guy and asked if he were a relative. Guy said no, and he explained that he was a reporter with the Colson *Beacon*.

"I was curious about Mr. Bish's condition."

The nurse exhaled through her nose and lifted a hand. "There's no change, certainly. He's been comatose from day one."

"And how long has that been now?"

"Oh, lord," the nurse said. "I'll have to look at the chart. I think it was last July or August that he came in here. It's been nine months, anyway. His poor little wife comes in here every day, bless her heart. She hasn't missed a day yet. Are you going to do a story on Oliver here?"

"The thought crossed my mind," Guy fibbed. "What's his prognosis?"

The nurse shook her head. "He could go on like this for another year, or he could die tomorrow. With cases like this, where there's a bullet lodged in the brain, you never know. He's not coming back, and that's for sure."

Guy thanked the woman and left her taking Oliver Bish's

temperature. He thought about going back to the book sale to look for something to read, but the idea of facing Michael Bish again prevented him from following through. Married or not, he still shook and strained for breath when he was around her. He'd never felt anything like it in his life, and he didn't know what to do about it, especially in view of her circumstances and the way she felt about him. He decided the best thing to do was get away from it and from her . . . not to mention the daughter who despised him. The only way Guy knew to do that was to go to work.

He drove to the offices of the paper and parked out back behind the building. Inside he saw the copy editors hard at work for the evening, and he spoke to two of them in greeting as they looked up from their terminals. They waved and buried their noses once more as soon as he passed them. Only one of Guy's articles was being polished off for the morning edition, but he had a long-term assignment that he was working on for a future Sunday edition. He would do some work on the piece and possibly kick around some new ideas while he was there.

Once he sat down at his desk, he saw a memo stuck on his memo holder. He snatched at the note and saw that it read, "Vernon Diest wants to talk. Call him tomorrow." Guy wadded up the note and threw it into the wastebasket beside his desk.

CHAPTER
FIVE

MICHAEL AWAKENED SUNDAY MORNING and walked into her kitchen to prepare some tea. Many of Oliver's things were still scattered around the house, and she left them where they lay, always picking up around them, so that if anyone should come over it would appear as if two people lived in the small ranch style house. If she wanted to, she could look out her kitchen window and see Guy Driscoll's house. He lived on the block behind her, three lots to the south. Since the first warm days of March she had seen him out in the yard at odd times, either mowing the lawn or trimming the hedges along the back fence. On some plane she had always been aware of him. Only now did she have reason to be aware. She had seen his face and knew who he was.

That morning as she stared trancelike out the window she saw him emerge from his back door with a cup in his hand. He wore only pajama bottoms and he stood very still, as if listening to the June morning. Michael eyed his figure for several minutes before forcing herself to turn away. He didn't know where she lived. He didn't know she could spy on him. She thought about the daughter and wondered why she had never seen her. She wondered why the girl had tried to kill herself, and what had happened to her mother. She wondered why Guy Driscoll had brought his daughter here, and if she had been in trouble back in Chicago.

She shook her head and left the kitchen to walk into the living room. She opened the front door to look for the paper and saw it on her driveway. Michael skipped outside in her short T-shirt and dashed back inside again, hoping no one had seen her. She opened the paper and sat down on the sofa to look at the front page. Later she would retrieve a Kansas City *Star* and a Wichita *Eagle*, but for now she studied the Colson paper. It was a habit learned from her father, to read the paper from front page to last and find out what was happening in the world. Oliver had never read anything but the comics and the sports page, and Michael had often teased him about it. These days she took the sports page to the hospital and read it to him.

Guy Driscoll's byline caught her eye, and she read his article on Colson's water problems twice before putting the paper away from her. He was good. She wasn't a newspaper person, and even she could see he was too good to be doing what he was doing in Colson. Which only added to the mystery of why he had come to their town. Was he working undercover for his newspaper in some investigation into small town corruption?

She doubted it. The jerk had cost her a job, possibly even her career, and Michael didn't think anyone working undercover would bother with someone like her. He was here for his own reasons, whatever they might be, and she really didn't give a good damn about them. He had maligned her without speaking to her, without even meeting her, and engendered more passion in her offended breast than she had felt in months. She didn't know whether to thank him or kill him.

With Oliver, she thought, had gone her ability to experience passion. When he died, she told herself, she would no longer be able to love the way normal women do; she would be mentally and physically numb by the time Oliver died, so the effort of a new relationship wouldn't be worth the trouble. At the age of twenty-nine, Michael had resigned herself to life without a man.

It wasn't that she didn't want a man—she did. There were nights when she lay awake and staring, craving the touch of a hand or the feel of lips on her body. But she was certain no man would ever do for her what Oliver had, and she was equally certain she would never love anyone the way she loved Oliver. This knowledge prepared her for a life alone, regardless of any prompting by her father and sister, and regardless of the way a stranger from Chicago looked at her.

Michael swallowed and picked up the paper again. It was time to look through the want ads and see if any jobs were available. She knew she would need one. The public would never allow her to be a police officer again—not unless Vernon Diest's pistol were found. If at all possible, Michael wanted to avoid a return to office work. Before entering the police academy she had worked for the Colson Chamber of Commerce in an executive assistant capacity, which meant she did nothing all day but talk on the phone and type letters. Work as a police officer had ruined her for any position where she would be tied to a desk. She wanted to be out and about, where she could breathe the air and wear anything in the world but nylons and heels.

The phone on the table beside the sofa rang and Michael reached over to pick up the receiver.

"How are you this fine Sunday morning?" her father asked in reply to her hello.

"Fine, Dad. How are you?"

"Wonderful. Sean said you helped with the book sale yesterday. I was wondering if you could do a like favor for me."

"What's the favor?"

Benjamin Ogilvie was a retired aircraft mechanic who now ran a lawnmower repair service. Michael doubted she would be able to help him with anything at his shop.

"I plan to run over to Springfield, Missouri, soon and I'll be needing a house sitter. Someone to watch things while I'm gone. Are you interested?"

"Sure. Just let me know when you're leaving and I'll come over and pick up a key."

"Good. How are things going? Will your savings hold out, or do you need some help?"

"I'll be all right for a while," Michael told him. She didn't have a bankroll, but she wouldn't starve anytime soon. If not for Oliver's health insurance she'd be on the street.

"What's in Springfield?" she asked.

"That pro shop I was telling you about. I'm going to run over and pick up some fancy fishing lures. Speaking of Springfield, did I tell you David Eulert is working there now? He got on with the sheriff's patrol."

Michael's flesh turned cold. David Eulert was Oliver's former partner. The man whose gun had destroyed her husband.

"Who told you that?" she asked her father.

"David did. He was in the shop last week, picking up his father's mower. He's in Colson on vacation."

"What else did he say?"

"He asked about you. I said you were fine."

"That was kind of him," Michael said stiffly.

"I thought so," her father commented. There was silence on the line, then, "Michael, it's time to drop this nonsense about David shooting Oliver on purpose—"

"I didn't bring it up," Michael responded. She looked at the clock on the wall. "I need to be going, Dad. I'll see you later in the week." She hung up before he could protest.

So, David was working for the sheriff in Springfield. And Michael was suspended without pay in Colson. It didn't make sense to Michael. It didn't seem fair.

She finished a quick read of the paper and then stepped into the shower. While she dressed, she ate two pieces of toast and a banana. As she was dusting the crumbs off her blouse in the kitchen she found herself looking out the window at

Guy Driscoll's house again. There was no sign of him. She grabbed her purse and keys and stepped outside. As she pulled the door closed behind her, she saw him. He came jogging up the street in front of her. She tried desperately to open the door again, but it was already locked and she couldn't get the key out in time. She thought of turning her back, but she knew it was no good as the sound of his footfalls neared. She could already feel him looking at her. Michael steeled herself and walked unhurriedly to her car in the driveway. As she looked up she saw him watching her, but his eyes gave away nothing as he approached.

Her mouth came open, ready to deny that she lived in the house behind her, but Guy Driscoll didn't stop. He merely nodded his head to her and kept on running. Michael stared after him, at the muscles pumping in his calves and across his back underneath the white T-shirt he wore. She had never seen him jogging before. But then she had never been home at this time on a Sunday before. She had always been out on patrol. He could jog this time every day and she would never have known it.

She opened the car door and shoved her purse inside before sitting down behind the wheel. So now he knew where she lived. That was no big deal, as far as Michael could tell, because the way he had looked at her just now was nothing like his previous behavior. This look had been as impersonal and disinterested as a person could get, and that was just fine with Michael.

At the hospital she went into Oliver's room and was in time to help turn him. The nurse looked at her when they were finished and said, "This really isn't necessary. The special mattress beneath him will prevent bedsores."

"It's necessary," said Michael. "It lets him know we're doing something. It tells us we haven't given up."

When the woman left she opened the paper and read the sports page to Oliver. As she finished, an impulse struck. She told Oliver she would be right back, and she got up and left the room to ask the nurses where she could find Guy Driscoll's daughter.

The girl's room was empty. Or so Michael thought after peering inside and seeing no one. She stepped through the door and suddenly found herself face to face with a dark-haired, dark-eyed teenager dressed in jeans and a backless hospital gown. The girl came out of the bathroom and pointed an accusing finger at Michael.

"I don't need another counselor. Just get out of here. And tell them to give me back that book. It was right here by my bed last night and the bitches took it."

Michael lifted a brow. "I'm not a counselor. What book are you talking about?"

"*My* book. *The Godfather.* It was right here and now it's gone." She stopped suddenly and looked at Michael. "If you're not a counselor, then who are you? Another gawker come to see the amazing suicidal girl?"

"No . . . well, yes, actually, I did come to gawk at you," Michael admitted. "But not because you attempted to commit suicide. I was curious to see if you're anything like your father."

"Really?" Adele smiled. "And what would you know about it? You know him well, I suppose. I mean we've been here, what, all of three months now?"

"You're right," Michael said, becoming annoyed. "I don't know him at all. Forgive the intrusion."

"I will if you tell them to give me back my book. I mean it. I want it back. They had no right to take it from—Adam! Oh, God, I'm so glad you're here."

Michael turned to see a tall, long-faced man standing behind her. His lips turned up in the corners at sight of Adele Driscoll, but beyond that there was no other sign of emotion in his face. Adele held her arms open and rushed to embrace the older man. Michael stared as Adam clumsily patted her on the back and touched the top of her head. The man was old enough to be her father. Maybe even her grandfather,

Michael thought. But no, she saw as she looked closer. She knew Adam, or rather, she had heard of him. He was fortyish, but looked older, primarily because of his shuffling walk and wrinkled chambray shirt and cotton pants.

"I can't stay long," he told the girl in his arms. "Baby is in the car. Your dad said you were coming home today. Is that right?"

"Yes," Adele said against his chest, and she looked up to see Michael edging slowly toward the door. "Get out of here," she ordered. "And tell the nurses I want that book!"

Michael left and went to the nurses station. When she asked after the book a plump nurse with a freckled face put a hand on one padded hip. "That's *my* book. I left it in her room by mistake one night. I'm still reading it."

"I suggest you ask her father to buy her another copy then," Michael said. "She seems rather attached to the book." And to Adam, Colson's version of Boo Radley.

Michael didn't envy Guy Driscoll his problems, and she had the feeling there were many of those. That was something they had in common, she decided as she walked back to Oliver's room. No one would envy either of them their problems.

CHAPTER
SIX

VERNON SAT AND STARED at the phone in his office most of the day Sunday. He had left a message for Guy Driscoll to call him, so why on earth hadn't the man called? Didn't newspaper people work on Sundays? Vernon was certain they did. They worked every day, didn't they? They had to, since a paper came out every day. Evidently, the man was negligent about checking his messages. He thought of calling and leaving yet another message, but he didn't want to seem too eager to talk. He wanted it to appear as if his interviewer had to pull the things he intended to say out of him, as if he were reluctant to say anything. Vernon was no dummy.

Unlike Elma. He still couldn't believe what she had done last night. The stunt she had pulled. Who did she think she was? The grand lady of the mansion? Vernon had come home from the book sale last night to find her wearing one of his mother's good dresses and swirling around the table in his dining room like she owned the place. She had set the table for two and was lighting candles when he arrived. In the center of the table was a clipped copy of Guy Driscoll's column on Vernon's shooting.

Vernon had looked in the kitchen and found nothing but a pan of rolls on top of the oven.

"What a wonderful meal you've prepared," he told her snidely. "Is this your idea of a celebration dinner?"

Elma had looked at him and blinked, her expression hurt.

"Take off that dress this instant," Vernon had ordered, and after a moment of hesitation, Elma did just that. With quivering lips and trembling fingers, Elma removed the dress. Vernon stared, his jaw slightly open as her thin, naked body was revealed to him. The woman was thirty-two years old, maybe older, and she didn't know better than to strip herself naked in front of someone?

"Good God, Elma." Vernon grabbed her arm when she turned to run away. "What's wrong with you? What do you think you're doing?"

Elma looked confused. He had ordered her to take off the dress and she had taken it off. What did he want now?

She tried to cover herself, causing Vernon to grow even angrier with her. He bent down and scooped up the dress from the floor. "Put it back on, dammit. Don't just stand there like a stupid fool." As he shoved the dress at her his hands brushed against her bare breast. Vernon felt a tingle in his loins and jerked his hands away in shock. No. He would never degrade himself with this . . . person. This lowly idiot. He was better than that. He was above simple lust.

He forced himself to back away from her. Her large brown eyes were full of hurt as she watched him. "Put the dress on and get out of my sight," he said. "I don't want to look at you, Elma. I don't want to know you're here. Nothing has changed because you took the pistol and ran away from the van that night. I want you to know that. The only reason you're still here is because of your cosmetic abilities, and believe me, I can always find someone to do hair as well as you can, so don't consider yourself irreplaceable by any means."

A tiny squawking sound had come from Elma then, a sound of anger and pain and embarrassment. She had clutched the dress to her tiny bosom and run from the room. Vernon hadn't seen her since. He had gone upstairs first thing that morning and locked the room that held his mother's things, but later he considered that to be unnecessary and he went and unlocked the room again. Elma had learned her lesson. A pan of rolls, for chrissake.

What had she thought? he wondered. That they would be friends now? That because she had absconded with the pistol that night Vernon would feel indebted to her and allow her to become a part of his life? Vernon shook his head as he continued to stare at his phone. The very idea. But he should have known there would be consequences. Nothing came for free, and Elma wasn't entirely unselfish. For some time now he had been aware of changes in her. He had denied them to himself, to be sure, because Vernon was never one to appreciate change. But he had sensed Elma growing bolder, taking firmer steps around the house, as if to remind him of her existence. Vernon wasn't likely to forget it anytime soon.

He wondered if he should try to do something about her. Silence the deaf mute for all eternity and preserve himself against her plans.

But no. There was no money in harming Elma. He would gain no corpse for burial because he would have to somehow hide it. And people would eventually ask questions. Though they cared nothing for her now, should she turn up missing, someone somewhere down the road would be curious and start asking him whatever had happened to the deaf mute woman who lived in the house with him. Vernon couldn't exactly feign ignorance, though it was a very large house. No one would believe he didn't know something.

He had no alternative but to wait and watch and try to determine what she intended. If blackmail was her scheme, then perhaps he would reconsider getting rid of her. But he didn't think blackmail was in Elma's cards. She would obviously have trouble communicating. Vernon knew she could read, but he had never seen her write even her name. He had always assumed she knew how, but perhaps he had been wrong. Nor did she sign, though Vernon had assumed she could do that as well—didn't all deaf people know how to sign? He had always simply looked at her while speaking, thus enabling her to read his lips and follow his commands.

If blackmail was what Elma intended, she would have a difficult time of it. Vernon suspected otherwise, however. He suspected that Elma wanted something from him. Something personal. It was in her eyes when she looked at him. A simpering kind of yearning that made his stomach churn with nausea. Vernon wasn't stupid. He knew when a woman wanted him. Elma had looked at him with adoring eyes from the moment her bastard father brought her inside the house. While Vernon's mother was alive, Elma had frequently played dress-up with her clothes and jewelry, putting on things and spinning around the room while Vernon's mother laughed and clapped her hands with delight. Vernon had been sickened by his mother's attachment to the girl. She played with Elma as if she were a pet dog.

After his mother died and her father left, Elma disappeared inside the house for a long time, and Vernon forgot about her. Even when her father returned, as he had on various occasions, drunk and reeling, Vernon didn't think of Elma. Not until the day he went to the second floor to find a certain make of casket and found her sitting like a stone in a patch of sunlight. He had been startled to see her there, and before he could stop himself, he went forward to touch her, just to make sure she was alive. At the touch of his hand her lids fluttered and her eyes opened. She looked up at him and smiled a beatific smile, as if she were a princess awakened by the touch of a prince. Afterward, Vernon saw her infrequently, she always smiling at him, he always hurrying away from her.

And now they had come to this. This point where he knew she believed she had the upper hand and was ready to make some demands on him. Well, he was ready for her. He could handle Elma. She was nothing but a deaf mute dummy, after all. Nothing but a simple woman who knew no better than to undress in front of a grown man. Standing there naked and looking at him like she wanted him to hold her. He'd hold her, all right. He'd hold her silly damn head under a tub full of water if she didn't straighten up. But of course that would mean he'd have to touch her, and after his experience last night, Vernon didn't want to do that again. It was best to keep his distance.

By three-thirty he was tired of waiting. He called the paper and asked for Guy Driscoll. He was told Guy wasn't available and wouldn't be in until tomorrow. Vernon asked for a home number and was denied. "We can't do that," the woman told him. "If you'll give me your name and number I'll see that he gets your message."

Vernon hung up.

A moment later he picked up the phone and dialed the hospital. Time to check on the status of the patients. He had an inside friend there, a woman he had gone to school with, who told Vernon what he wanted to know. When she came on the line he greeted her cheerfully and smiled at her warm response.

"How is everyone today? Any possibilities?"

"Sorry, Vern. Not a one."

Vernon cursed softly to himself. He hated to be called Vern. "What about the suicide?" he asked. "Is she still sulking?"

"And how. She'll be in here again, I figure. Or out there with you. Too bad, really. Her father seems like a nice person. He's that newspaper man from Chicago who writes for the *Beacon* now."

"Is that right?" Vernon asked with interest. "It's his daughter?"

"An only child, apparently. Mother's deceased. She obviously has no friends in school yet, because no one but her father has been up to see her. Well, the neighbor came this morning, but he stayed only for a minute. Mrs. Bish looked in on her as well, but I think she was only being nosy."

"Mrs. Bish? Michael Bish?"

"Yes, she was—oh, that's right. I'm sorry, Vern. I shouldn't have mentioned her name to you. She's the one who shot you, isn't she? I'm telling you, the nurses here are still atwitter. It was so nice to have such a good patient on the floor. They're all still talking about you. Kate said she was thinking of shooting you in the leg so you'd have to come back and see us again. Isn't that a laugh riot?"

Vernon forced a stiff chuckle. Then he asked, "Why would Michael Bish look in on the girl? Does she know her?"

"Oh, no. Like I said, she was just being nosy. You know the morbid fascination people have with suicides. And after that piece Guy Driscoll wrote in the paper, I wouldn't be a bit surprised if Michael had gone in to complain to the daughter about being suspended from her job. It sounds like something that headstrong Ogilvie bunch would do. I'm telling you I've never seen women so mean and bullheaded in my life. I'll never forget the day Michael gave me a ticket for driving too fast in a school zone. And her sister, Sean, is just as bad. She gave my son four hours of detention last week for the horrible crime of forgetting to bring his book to class. He's forgotten it a few times before, but they have extra books there in the classroom, don't they? They did when we went to school anyway. I tell you their father is responsible for raising them to be so hardheaded. If—"

"I'm sorry," Vernon interrupted. "My other line is ringing. I'm going to have to hang up now. I'll call you later on in the week, all right?" He said goodbye then and hung up. He didn't have another line, of course, but she didn't know that. She got so carried away sometimes, going on and on until he wanted to scream at her to shut up. But he *had* learned a few interesting tidbits of information.

The suicidal girl was Driscoll's daughter, and Michael Bish had gone in to see her.

What did that tell him?

Vernon wasn't sure. It was possible that it didn't mean anything, that Michael had simply been being nosy, as his informant had suggested. Or it could mean she was plotting something against Driscoll for screwing up her life. Or it could mean she was interested in the girl, for what purpose, Vernon had no idea.

There was just no telling what it meant. And perhaps that was why Guy Driscoll hadn't called him back. He was busy with his suicidal daughter. Had his friend said she was leaving the hospital that day? He couldn't remember.

Vernon sat and stared at the numbers on his phone. He couldn't pay for the one line he had, let alone two. And he was into overdue notices on the electric and gas bill again. His lawyer had informed him that his suit against the city could go on indefinitely. There was no money coming in anytime soon. He was right back where he started.

All he could do was pray for death to come to Colson. To one of the older folks or one of the young, he didn't care. Vernon put his head in his hands and wished for a miracle. And if he couldn't have a miracle, well, then maybe he could figure out how to help a certain suicide along.

It came to him then, an idea, something he would have laughed at and considered another little private joke if he had not already stepped over that line. He lifted his head from his hands and stared unfocused as his mind raced. The first shooting had been viewed by some as the irrational act of an unstable woman. What if it were to happen again?

What if she gunned down some other poor unfortunate soul, this time killing the person? It would be the desperate act of a clearly unbalanced person. A heinous crime no judge could ignore. Michael would be sent away, the lawsuit would be as good as won, and Vernon would have a corpse to prepare.

He clenched his hands and wondered if he had the guts to

go through with it. Maybe he should buy another bottle of Jack Daniels.

No, it might ruin his aim.

Vernon got up and went to get a bottle anyway.

He had to do it. He had to pay his light bill before the fifteenth.

CHAPTER SEVEN

GUY STARED AT HIS DAUGHTER in amazement as she informed him of her plans. His knees felt suddenly weak, unstable, and he sat down hard on the sofa in his living room. Adele heaved an exaggerated sigh and cocked one hip. "Oh, Christ, don't look like that. It's not like you have a choice, Daddy. You bring me back and I'll head out that door the first chance I get. Besides that, I'll *be* right next door. Adam says you can come over any time you want. He likes you."

"Adele . . ." Guy was at a loss for words. He did not know what to say.

"It's not like we're getting married or anything, so you don't have to worry about shocking any of the relatives back east. We'll just be living together."

"Adele, he's . . ."

"Save the speech, okay? I know how old he is. He's two years older than you. But he's still incredible in bed." She smiled as Guy's face paled. "Does that shock you? I can see that it does." The smile fell away and her face became hard. "Don't pretend this isn't why you brought me here. You wanted me to find some nice friends and learn how to behave. Well, I found someone nice, and he's more than a friend. If you're thinking of going over and beating the shit out of him, and I can see that you are, you'd better forget it. If you lay one finger on Adam then we're both out of here and you'll never see me again. Not that the threat of that will disturb you much, I'm sure."

Guy's nostrils flared. "What about everything you said to me at the hospital? About being good and going to school and letting me hug you. Did you say all of that just to get out?"

Adele smiled again. "Most of it. But don't worry, I'm still going to school. Adam says I'll need a diploma. He thinks I should major in communications at college. I agree with him."

Guy stared. "You're going on to college?"

"Adam wants me to. He wants to pay for it and everything." She smirked at him. "Ooh, I knew that would light up your eyes. You're off the hook, aren't you?"

"What I am is confused," Guy told her. "Day before yesterday you tried to kill yourself. Today you want to go to college."

"Day before yesterday I didn't have what I wanted," Adele explained. "Today I do."

"What did you want?" Guy asked.

"Adam," Adele said with a shrug. "He was worried about the age thing and all that, but now he's not. He says he doesn't care about any of that anymore. He just wants me alive. Next to Baby, I'm all he cares about in the world."

Guy wondered if she came before or after the dog in Adam's affections. He shook his head and got slowly off the sofa to stand face to face with her. "Adele, I'm going to ask you not to go. I want you to give us a chance. You're only sixteen years old and—"

"I know what I want," Adele said coldly. "And I know what I don't want. What I don't want is any more forced time spent with you. You played a nice, guilty daddy role and did pretty good on getting us here and setting up this pseudo-rustic lifestyle. I gave it as long as I'm going to give it. I want to be with Adam."

"You don't know any—"

"I know all I need to know. He's not *you*."

Guy stepped back at the loathing in her voice. "I'm sorry," was all he could think of to say. "I'm sorry you hate me so much. I'm sorry I've failed you so miserably. I never meant to. I never meant to do anything but help you. I wanted to help get your life . . ." He couldn't finish. He turned away from her unforgiving features and walked dazedly out to the back porch. He sat down on a chaise lounge and looked at his hands. After a moment he heard the rustle of paper sacks and the clicking of suitcase latches. He felt like crying.

Everything for nothing. That's what he felt like. He felt like he had disrupted his life, given up all that made him feel secure and comfortable and confident as a man to come here and be made to feel like shit on a shoe. He felt like he was being humbled for no good reason, trod upon and crumpled and tossed away because it made someone or something feel good to do it. It angered Guy. He was trying to do good, dammit. Sure, there had been guilt involved in all his decisions, plenty of it, but guilt alone hadn't forced him to do what he had done. He loved his daughter and he wanted to do what was right for her.

He got off the chaise lounge and walked back into the house. He found Adele in her bedroom.

"Forget about me," Guy said. "Forget about us. I want you to think about you. What kind of future are you going to have with this man? Are you going to come home every night of your life and watch satellite television with a black poodle named Baby? Adam's got maybe twenty good years left, less if he continues his sedentary lifestyle."

"According to you and the surgeon general?" Adele continued her packing. "I happen to like watching TV."

"For now you do," Guy told her. "Two or three years from now you could be sick of it. What then?"

"Adam won't care if I go out. He said he won't."

"What if you meet someone else? Some young guy your own age? What if you fall in love, Adele?"

She slammed a suitcase shut. "Like you did? You don't even know what love is. You've never even been close to it."

Guy's mouth thinned. "That's not true. I was in love with someone when your mother and I got married, and it wasn't your mother."

Adele finally stopped and turned to look at him. "You were in love with another woman when you married my mother?"

"She was a journalism major, like me," Guy said. "We saw each other for about three months, until your mother called and told me she was pregnant. I had been planning to ask Carolyn to marry me. I changed my plans."

"Well, weren't we chivalrous and all that good shit. How dumb were you? Why didn't you marry the one you wanted to marry?"

Guy looked at her. "Because there was a baby coming and it was mine. Because I wanted to know my child."

Adele stared uncomfortably at him. Finally she said, "You must've been one stupid sonofabitch when you were younger."

Guy's fingers curled in anger. He turned abruptly away and walked down the hall to the living room and out to the back porch once more. Without thinking, he found himself looking toward the house he had seen Michael Bish come out of that morning. There was a glimpse of someone on the patio, then there was nothing. He wondered if she had been watching him.

She had certainly been surprised to see him jogging that morning. He had been surprised, too. He'd had no idea she lived where she did.

"I'm going now," Adele said from the living room. "If you need anything, please knock loudly on the door. We might not hear you the first time because of the television, and we wouldn't want anyone to be embarrassed, now would we?"

You little bitch, Guy thought before he could stop himself. If there had been something in his hand he would have thrown it at her. Instead he sat in mute anger as she slammed out of the house with her paper sacks and her suitcases.

What now? he wondered after he had begun to cool down. Did he leave or did he stay? What the hell did he do now?

You stay, a voice told him. This thing with Adam won't last. How could it? It won't last, and when it's over she'll need somewhere to stay. If you're still here for her it'll mean that much more, and maybe she'll be convinced that you're sincere about wanting to be her father.

What he wanted right now, more than anything in the world, was to go over and beat Adam Dupree senseless. The conniving con-artist. Putting on his eccentric ascetic act and molesting Guy's daughter the whole time. Guy felt sick at the thought of them together. He had known, hadn't he? He had known what was going on over there but he hadn't wanted to believe it.

He looked toward Michael Bish's house again before going back into the living room. He thought of running for a while, just to ease the tension in his shoulders, but he couldn't seem to make himself leave the room. He didn't want to go outside where he would see the house where Adam Dupree, and now Adele, lived. If he did he would be unable to keep himself from going over and dragging Adele out by the hair and bringing her back home. What he should have done in the first place. He should have acted like her father instead of trying to be her buddy.

He went into the kitchen for a beer and took it out to the back porch with him. Things certainly hadn't gone the way he'd planned. The story of his life. Nothing ever seemed to go the way he planned. When he heard the door in the living room open he remained seated. An absurd spark of hope leapt in his breast. She had been kidding. The whole thing had been a big joke, and now she was coming back to laugh at him and call him a fool for having believed her. Guy waited, his pulse pounding with the vignettes he created. Adele laughing at him, tears streaming down her face as she came to pat him on the back. Adele angry and indignant that he would have believed her capable of such a thing. Adele—

"I forgot my retainer in the bathroom," she said, sticking her head onto the porch.

Guy kept his back to her so she couldn't see the way his chest deflated. He lifted the can and tipped it back as he drained the beer. Adele was still watching him; he could feel her. Finally she came to poke him gently in the back. He turned and looked at her, his features purposely blank. One side of her mouth curled up. Her dark eyes were solemn. "It'll be all right," she told him. "All of it. You'll just have to trust me on this one."

Guy opened his mouth, but the words he was about to speak became drowned in a splatter of blood. The sight of the blood stunned him; it was bright red and it was all over him, even in his mouth. The sight of his daughter shocked him senseless. She was standing and teetering on her two legs while a huge hole in her chest poured forth with all the blood in her young body. The look in her eyes was one of amazement. Her mouth opened and closed, and finally brought forth more of the blood. Guy's arms reached instinctively for her, and his ears picked up the sound of another shot. At the same instant his left hip exploded in sudden, searing pain. With his good side he caught Adele as she fell. "Get down," he said automatically. Then he began to shout for help and an ambulance.

Adele's mouth was still open, as if she were trying to breathe through the hole in her chest. Her gaze locked onto Guy, never leaving his face. Guy's voice broke as he sank down to the ground with her.

"Adele, hang on," he told her. "Hang on for me. You're my daughter and I love you. I've always wanted you to be with me. Do you hear me? You can't leave me now. Please, God, don't leave me now. I'm sorry for everything I—" He paused in shock as he saw her eyes roll slowly back into her head.

"*No!*" he screamed when he felt her limbs begin to twitch. "No, God no!"

As the life drained out of her body he held her to his chest and began to sob into her blood-matted hair. He no longer thought of who might be shooting at them, or why. He no longer noticed the pain in his left hip, or the blood pooling on the concrete beneath them. He thought only of Adele, and of the waste of precious, precious life that had slipped away before his very eyes.

CHAPTER
EIGHT

MICHAEL ARRIVED HOME at eight o'clock that night to find her house and yard swarming with police. As she left her car she heard a shout, and two uniformed officers, her former peers, came to escort her inside. Michael stared in disbelief at their hard faces as they practically shoved her inside the door. "What . . . ?" she began, but she just as quickly shut her mouth. She would find out what was going on soon enough. There was no need to panic.

At least she hoped there wasn't.

When she saw her former commander she rushed forward. "What's going on, Captain Mawby? Why are you here?"

His usually friendly face was taut with tension. "Hello, Mike. Have you been at the hospital?"

"Yes," Michael said slowly. "And then I went out for dinner. Why?"

"What time did you eat?"

She shrugged. "Just now. I just finished. Why? What's going on?"

"Exactly where were you between six-thirty and a quarter to seven tonight?"

Michael lifted a hand. "I'm not sure. I was probably in the

car and on my way to the restaurant. I ate at Delberto's. Will you please tell me what's happened?"

Stan Mawby walked into her kitchen and gestured for her to follow. He pointed to the window above the sink. "Look over there, three houses to the south. The one with the apricot tree. You know who lives there?"

Michael nodded. "Yes, I do. What about him?"

"Sometime between six-thirty and a quarter to seven this evening, Mr. Driscoll and his daughter were both shot. The shots came from this direction. These casings were found in the cracks on your patio." Mawby opened his hand and Michael stared in slowly dawning horror at the contents of his palm.

"You think I did it."

Mawby said nothing.

"Why would I shoot someone from my own patio, Captain?"

"Why would you shoot an unarmed motorist on a routine stop?"

Michael's eyes rounded. "I *told* you. You mean you don't believe me now? You did before. You all did. You all said you believed me before that damned column in the paper came out and—"

She paused, realizing how incriminating the statement sounded. She had just spoken aloud a motive for shooting Guy Driscoll.

Guy Driscoll.

Michael swallowed and touched her throat. "Is he alive? Are they all right?"

"He's alive. His daughter is dead."

Michael's shoulders sagged. "Oh, God. Is he going to make it? How bad is he?"

Mawby ignored the question. "You arrived at Delberto's when?"

"I think it was around twenty to seven. Call the restaurant, they'll tell you."

"I will."

Michael stared at the uncompromising set of his jaw. "You can't possibly believe I did this, Captain."

He finally looked at her. "I don't know what I believe anymore, Michael." He hefted the casings in his palm. "We've taken all your weapons into police custody, all those we found in the house, anyway. My warrant includes your car." He said that and turned to order two men outside to search her car. Michael sat down on the sofa and put her hands to her cheeks in disbelief. She couldn't believe this was happening to her. This was crazy. Why would she shoot two people from her patio when the location was so obvious?

"This is crazy," she said aloud.

Mawby turned his attention away and picked up the phone. He called first Delberto's, and then the hospital, putting his back to Michael so she couldn't hear what was said. When he hung up she nearly jumped from the sofa. "What?" she demanded. "What did they say?"

"Delberto's said you showed up between six-thirty and seven, they couldn't be more specific. The nurses at the hospital say you left there around six-thirty. It proves nothing. You still had time to drive home, shoot the Driscolls, and then go on to the restaurant."

"Captain, I didn't shoot anyone."

"You visited Adele Driscoll's hospital room."

"Did the nurse tell you that?"

"She said you peeked in again today before you left, but Adele was already gone."

"I went to see if she had gotten her book back. She was upset the day before because the nurse had taken back her book, and Adele wasn't finished reading it."

"You spoke to her?"

"Yes. She thought I was a counselor, and she told me to get out of her room."

"Was she angry with you?"

"I . . . yes, I suppose she was. But that doesn't mean anything."

"I'm sorry, Michael. I'm going to have to arrest you on suspicion of murder."

"No," Michael said. "This is insane. Captain, you have to believe me. Someone has gone to a lot of trouble to set up this frame. Did you know David Eulert is back in town?"

Mawby and another officer exchanged a look. Mawby turned back to Michael. "You have the right to remain silent. If you give up that right—"

Michael's cry drowned out the rest. She couldn't believe what was happening to her. She couldn't believe what had happened to Guy Driscoll and his daughter. She couldn't believe someone hated her enough to do this to her. As the cuffs were placed on her wrists, she looked around the room and asked for someone to please call her sister. One of the officers present, a friend who had gone through the academy with Michael, inclined his head. He would call Sean. Michael thanked him and allowed herself to be led out of the house.

In the back of Mawby's car she began to calm down and think logically. She would need a lawyer. A good one. She would ask Sean to take care of that. Gordon knew a few people in town through his printing business. There went the rest of her savings, naturally. She would have to ask her father for help with attorney's fees.

And Oliver. Oh, God, she thought suddenly. Who's going to take care of Oliver?

Her eyes filled with tears as she thought of what his fate would be without her. He would go unturned in his bed. His sheets would go unchanged. His catheter would go untended. His baths would be skimpy, if the nurses took the time at all. Michael pressed a fist to her mouth to hold back a sob. Oh, Oliver, she thought. He was going to think she had abandoned him. Who would read to him? Who would talk to him? Who would treat him as if he were still a human being and not some brain-dead lump of organs and tissue and flesh?

Why is this happening? she asked herself over and over. Why am I being taken away from my husband?

In the front seat, Mawby adjusted his rearview mirror to look at Michael. When he saw her wet cheeks and reddened nose, he said, "Michael, have you ever considered getting some help?"

Michael looked up at the seriousness of his tone. His expression in the rearview mirror was grave.

"Help?" she echoed.

He gently cleared his throat. "I was talking about psychiatric help."

Michael's mouth went into a grim line. "You're a jerk, Captain."

Mawby's brows met. "It was only a suggestion."

"How would you like it if somebody suggested that *you* get psychiatric help?"

The captain's mouth twitched. "Okay. I'd probably call 'em a jerk. Right now, Michael, all the evidence points to you. Until it points to someone else, you're it. You know that, and I know you know that, so let's just try to get along with each other, all right?"

"Besides," said the other officer in front, "you gotta admit you did get pretty spooky after Oliver's shooting, Mike. Telling everybody Dave done it on—"

"Button it, Birzer," Mawby said sharply.

"Sorry," Birzer muttered.

"Spooky?" Michael said with a hoarse laugh. "You think I got spooky after my husband's shooting? Because I told everyone the truth? Because I told everyone that David Eulert was in love with Oliver?"

"Yeah," Birzer said frankly. "Because of that. Too many of us knew Dave. Hell, he was a war hero."

"You didn't know him like Oliver. Oliver knew David was gay, but he kept it from everyone because he didn't want to see David hurt. What hurt David was when Oliver married me. And he didn't count on Oliver telling me his secret. That's why David left, because he knew I would tell everyone and he knew I would blame him, and I do. He shot Oliver on purpose."

Stan Mawby and Birzer exchanged another look.

"This might come as a shock to you," Mawby began, "but Dave Eulert got married in January and is already expecting his first child—by a woman, of course."

"That means nothing," Michael snapped. "Gay men sleep with women all the time. It's how they get along in a society that won't tolerate anything else."

"You know all about gay men, do you?" Birzer asked.

"I know about David Eulert," Michael said.

"And you think he's the one who set you up and shot the Driscolls, is that it?"

"He certainly hates me enough. Before he left town he said it wasn't over. He said he wasn't finished with me yet."

"So you say," said Mawby.

Michael opened her mouth to tell him she had witnesses, but she decided it was best to say nothing more. Mawby was prepared to disbelieve anything she said, as was Birzer and apparently every other member of the Colson Police Department. Michael had never felt so alone and helpless in her life. It was as if they wanted her to be insane and guilty of having shot those people. Because if it was Michael, then of course they had nothing else to worry about. But if it wasn't . . .

Michael swallowed as a horrible thought entered her mind. For a fleeting instant, she had almost wished the gunman would strike again, if only to clear her name.

Don't do that, she silently told the person responsible. Don't kill anyone else. I'll be okay.

She thought she would, anyway. She hoped she would.

CHAPTER
NINE

VERNON WAS DELIGHTED with the news in the morning paper. He hadn't been aiming at the girl, of course, but he was happy to have the results waiting for him on his table in the embalming room. Michael Bish had been arrested as expected and was now in police custody. Guy Driscoll was in stable condition at the hospital, according to the paper. A quick phone call to his hospital informant told Vernon that Driscoll was seriously depressed. He hadn't slept a wink the night before, hadn't eaten anything, and he responded only in monosyllables when attempts at conversation were made. The one time he had spoken a complete sentence was to ask—and this came as a rude shock to Vernon—that his daughter be taken to any funeral home but Vernon Diest's.

Of course there *was* no other funeral home in town but Vernon's, so the girl had to come to him. It was state law that she be embalmed within twenty-four hours, so Guy had no choice but to use Vernon. At one time there had been two funeral homes in Colson, but with skill and manipulation, Vernon's mother had run the other home out of business. A bit of necrophilic activity caught on film had done the trick. Everyone in the business engaged in harmless touchy-feely at one time or another, Vernon knew, especially with a beautiful young corpse like the one on his table now. But Vernon didn't go in for anything more serious. It wasn't in him.

Why Guy Driscoll should ask that his daughter be taken elsewhere was a complete mystery to Vernon. He hadn't spoken to the man but for a moment or two. What could Driscoll possibly have against him? Vernon was affronted, and he asked his informant to keep that particular piece of information to herself. It wouldn't do for the public to start questioning Vernon's practices, not with his finances in the shape they were.

He could only thank God for teenage girls. One of the soft pink or dove gray caskets would doubtlessly be chosen, the ones with all the roses on the lid and on the handles. Those ran a couple thousand. Then there was the preparation charge. Vernon would instruct Elma to take special care with the little one's hair, to make it look like a dark cloud floating around her elfin face. She was such a pretty thing, after all. Vernon was almost sorry he had shot her.

But not quite. Her father's money would keep him afloat for another month anyway, and that was all Vernon asked.

When he finished reading the paper he tossed it onto his desk and rose from his chair to begin his work in the embalming room. He was amazed at how easy it had been, this killing business. And to think how many months he had wasted agonizing over it. He walked down the hall and reached inside the room to flick on the light. His pulse jumped when Elma suddenly rose up before him. Her face was mottled in color and streaked with tears. She pointed behind her to the corpse on the table, and then she pointed to Vernon. The accusation in her expression made Vernon snort.

"What? What's wrong with you?"

She thumped him on the arm and made her fingers into a pretend pistol that she mimed shooting.

"You think I did this?"

Elma nodded. She pointed to herself, made the pistol with

her fingers again, and then pointed to Vernon. He moved to the table and picked up one of the corpse's arms. When he felt Elma move up behind him he turned on her. "Yes, you gave me the pistol yesterday. It proves nothing. You should be glad this has occurred, Elma. We desperately need the money. What would happen to you if I go bankrupt and lose this place? Have you thought about that? Where will you go?"

Elma's gaze lowered to the face of the dead girl. Her eyes welled up again. Vernon grew impatient. "Go on now and leave us alone. I'll come for you when I'm ready for your services."

Elma didn't move. Vernon poked her in the side and forced her to look at him. "I said go on now. I'll come and find you when it's time to do her hair."

Something cold and alien flashed in Elma's eyes before she turned away from him. Vernon sucked in his chest and waited for her to turn for one last look at him before he said, "The attitude you've developed has not gone unnoticed, Elma. It is not appreciated."

Elma's lip curled slightly. Then she was gone.

Vernon shook his head in disbelief. Was she turning on him, too? His one loyal doglike ally? What did she and Driscoll know about him?

He was tempted to drop everything and go and find Elma, demand to know what she would have had him do instead. But the body needed his attention. Adele Joy Driscoll required his services, and Vernon had always loved his work.

More than five hours later, Vernon sat down on a stool in the embalming room. He was exhausted. To make up for shooting the girl, he had made her into a princess out of a fairy tale. Her lips were a perfect pink, just waiting for a kiss to bring her out of her sleep. Her eyes were lightly dusted with a pale pink powder, her cheeks had a rosy hue. He had filled out her face just a little around the jawline. In life she had obviously been on the thin side.

A reporter friend of the father had brought by a dress that morning. Pink, naturally. The friend had claimed she would be back later in the day with instructions for a casket. She took a brochure with her to the hospital so Driscoll could make a choice. Vernon had met the woman the year before, when her aged father had died. She was an older, authoritative type. Obviously, she had appointed herself in charge, since Driscoll was hospitalized. Vernon didn't think the two were very good friends, since she frequently referred to the man as "Mr. Driscoll," but having no friends himself, Vernon really couldn't say.

As for the service, Vernon was still waiting to hear a decision on whether there would actually be one in Colson. His informant at the hospital had suggested that perhaps the girl would be sent back to Chicago for burial. This was disappointing to Vernon, but it wasn't entirely unexpected. Relatives could hardly be expected to fly in to Colson, since the nearest airport was over ninety miles away. A Chicago service made more sense, now that Vernon thought about it, particularly since they hadn't lived here any longer than they had. Still, young people had a way of bringing out mourners, no matter what the circumstances. He could only hope Driscoll wanted to keep her in Colson. The charges for the service and the burial would bring in another thousand or two; Vernon hadn't decided yet. It was possible that he could pad the bill at will this time, if Guy Driscoll was as seriously depressed as his informant had claimed.

When he was ready for Elma he left the room and went down the hall in search of her. He found her in his office, of all places. She was sitting in a chair by the door with her head in her hands. When he touched her on the shoulder she flinched away from him and stood up. Without looking at him she brushed past and went into the hall. Vernon followed her to the embalming room to see her reaction to the dead girl. First reactions were important.

Elma didn't disappoint him. Her face screwed up as she

stood over the girl. Tears began to flow freely from her liquid brown eyes.

"Well," said Vernon, "how does she look?"

Elma didn't respond.

Vernon stamped his foot on the floor and Elma quickly looked at him.

"I asked how you thought she looked?"

Elma gave him the finger.

Vernon blinked. He couldn't believe what he had just seen. He stood speechless while Elma turned her back on him and picked up a strand of the dead girl's thick brown hair.

"Elma," he said sharply. "Did you just do what I thought you did?"

She didn't look at him and he angrily remembered to stamp his foot. He stamped, but she refused to look at him. She removed a brush from her pocket and went about her business.

"You look at me!" Vernon shouted, and he stamped the floor hard, twice.

Elma merely glanced at him over her shoulder. There was a bobby pin in her mouth. Her gaze was full of contempt.

"How dare you look at me like that," Vernon said, his back rigid. "You want to stay here? You'll show some respect if you do. I can hire anyone to take your place, Elma. Anyone. Don't think—"

Elma threw up her arms and backed away from the corpse as if to say, *Fine. Do it.*

Vernon felt his face grow hot. "Don't do that. Get back over there and finish what you started." He reached for her as she neared him to pass through the door. Elma ducked away from his touch. Vernon shouted angrily at her back as she walked down the hall. "Damn you, Elma, don't do this! If you walk away now I want you out of this house. Do you hear me? I want you out!"

She disappeared up the stairs without a backward glance. There was a sinking feeling in his chest as Vernon watched her go. It would probably be two weeks before he saw her again. What was he going to do in the meantime? He couldn't fix hair.

What the hell was wrong with her, anyway? When he had gone to her for the pistol last night, she couldn't have been happier to see him. She had been more than willing, almost anxious, to give the pistol to him. Now she acted as though she couldn't stand the sight of him. What had she supposed he was going to do with the damn thing? Bury it?

She couldn't have been in the van with him yesterday, he told himself. He had checked. There was no way she could have slipped in and seen what he did at Michael Bish's house.

Elma was guessing, and that was all. Since someone happened to get shot the same day she gave him the pistol, she was assuming Vernon was the shooter. She would get over it, he told himself. She would stop sniveling eventually and realize how much she depended on him.

He turned back into the embalming room and walked over to touch Adele Joy Driscoll's heavy brown hair. It was pretty the way it was, actually. Maybe he'd heat up the curling iron and curl the ends a bit. Just a cute little flip, something like Mary Tyler Moore had always worn. Her father surely wasn't expecting anything more.

After he plugged in the curling iron he heard someone at the front entrance. Vernon went to look and saw the woman from the paper, Driscoll's friend, outside. He let her in and greeted her with all the warmth and courtesy his mother had taught him to use when dealing with the bereaved, or their surrogates. She produced the brochure Vernon had given her earlier and opened it to show him the casket Driscoll had chosen. The gray one, naturally, with all the beautiful roses on the lid and on the handles.

"And the service?" Vernon inquired. "Will we be shipping her to Chicago for Mr. Driscoll?"

"Yes, she's going home. A cousin on her mother's side will be in charge there. The name of the funeral home that will receive her is written on the back of the brochure. Arrangements have been made for her to be picked up this evening and taken to the airport for a late flight out of Kansas City. Mr. Driscoll would like to see her before she goes, of course. He plans to leave the hospital this afternoon."

Vernon blinked. "You mean he's getting out? Already? I thought he was badly hurt?"

The woman's smile was understanding. "He is badly hurt. And of course he'll be returning to the hospital afterward, but he wants to see his daughter before she goes home. He's received a special pass from his doctor. Two male nurses will be along to help him. Mr. Driscoll is a very determined man when he's made up his mind."

"Obviously," Vernon said under his breath.

"When will she be ready for viewing?" the woman asked. "I know several people at the paper who want to come by, and a few young people from the school have called the hospital today to ask about her."

Any excuse to get out of work or school, Vernon thought, and he looked at his watch. "Now that the casket selection has been made, she should be ready for viewing by one o'clock. Please feel free to tell everyone concerned." He lowered his voice then. "No flowers have arrived yet. I didn't expect many, because they haven't lived in Colson long, but absolutely none have arrived, and the viewing room will look rather bare without them. I've ordered a spray, but . . ."

"I see," the woman said. "All right, then. I'll take care of it. I assume a few pots of mums will do?"

Vernon inclined his head. A moment later he showed the woman out. It was time to get to work. He had to call the man who lived next door to come and help with the casket. It was embarrassing, but Vernon couldn't afford any help, and his neighbor was an easygoing sort. His wife had suffered nightmares living next door to a mortuary, but she was dead now; Vernon had buried her six months ago. Her husband had helped with the casket then, too.

After the call was made, Vernon went back to the embalming room to check on the curling iron. He found Elma in the
room, gently twisting a dark strand of the girl's hair onto the
curling wand. Vernon smirked and approached her. "So glad
you decided to help."

Elma looked at him only after he stood beside her. The
expression in her eyes froze him before he could repeat the
words. Vernon inhaled unevenly and stood back. He wasn't
going to say anything to her. Not now. He needed her.

CHAPTER
TEN

GUY LAY ON HIS right side in the hospital bed and stared at the calendar on the wall. He looked at the large black, blocked numbers and thought of how truly meaningless they were. The tenth day of June had no special significance, it was just a day like any other. Just a black, blocked number on a calendar on the hospital wall.

Why do we give those numbers such significance? he wondered. The date someone is born. The date someone dies. What could it possibly matter? They were here and then they weren't—dates couldn't define their existence. Why were dates considered necessary?

He heard someone enter his room, and from the shuffling sounds on the floor he knew it wasn't a nurse. He craned his head over his shoulder and saw Adam Dupree standing just inside the door. Adam's dark eyes were swollen and red-rimmed. The beard on his face was heavy. His clothes were lined and wrinkled, as if they'd been slept in.

"Can I come in?" he mumbled.

Guy said nothing. The entry hole in his hip and the exit hole in his buttock began to ache.

Adam Dupree shuffled into the room and stood where Guy

could see him. "I won't stay long," he said. "I know you're hurting and not happy to see me right now. I know you're probably in a blaming mood, and you have every right to be, I'm not saying you don't. But I just wanted to tell you how precious your daughter Del was to me. She came on like a feisty little gust of wind, and she made my old head start working again, you know? She made me start asking questions and wondering about things. And Baby just loved her, bless her heart. Lord, that dog was crazy about the girl. She already knows something is wrong, Baby does. She's a smart little dog."

He paused as if waiting for Guy to say something. When Guy made no response, Adam shook his head and lifted his shoulders. "I'm sorry, Mr. Driscoll. I still can't believe this has happened. Colson's such a quiet place to live, you know? But here you and Del get shot, and they're saying Michael Bish did it. That doesn't sound right to me, but I guess I don't know much a—"

"What?" Guy said. "What did you say?"

Adam's heavy brows raised. "Which part?"

"About Michael Bish. What about her?"

"Uh, well, it was on the front page this morning. They arrested her for shooting you and Del. They found the casings on her patio."

"Get me a paper," Guy ordered.

"Huh?"

"Get me a *paper*, you idiotic pervert. Are you deaf?"

Adam stood and stared at him. "I'll get you a paper," he said slowly. "First tell me why you called me that."

Guy snatched at his TV control. "You know exactly why I called you that." He held up the control and punched the nurse button. "Any grown man who has intercourse with a skinny sixteen-year-old girl has definitely crossed the line into perversion."

Adam blinked rapidly. His chin began to quiver. "I don't

know where you got that idea, Mr. Driscoll. I really don't. I never laid a hand on that sweet child."

"Bullshit," Guy said, and he punched the button again. "She told me you did."

Adam wrung his hands together. "Del told you that? Why would she go and tell you such a thing, Mr. Driscoll? It's not true. I never touched her. She knows I didn't."

"May I help you?" a voice asked over the speaker in the handheld control. Guy asked for a newspaper. The nurse seemed surprised to hear from him.

"Mr. Driscoll, I swear to you. I never touched your daughter. She came over and we played Scrabble and watched *Jeopardy* and a bunch of other shows. We talked a lot and watched Baby play in the yard, but we didn't do anything else. The day I came to see her in the hospital she told me you didn't want her anymore. I said she could come and stay with me and Baby. She could sleep on the bed in Baby's room. She was all ready to move in when . . . well, you know."

Guy attempted to shift himself in the bed. The pain in his left leg made him shudder. Through his teeth he said, "You expect me to believe you?"

"I don't expect you to, no, but you should believe me, Mr. Driscoll."

"Why?"

"Because . . ." Adam paused before going on. "Because I can't do anything like that anymore. I haven't done anything like that for a long time now. Del knew and she was the only one in the world I ever told that to, so why she would go and lie to you about me I just don't know."

Guy stared at the other man. "You're telling me you're impotent?"

Adam looked at everything but Guy. "I am."

Guy believed him. He had no choice. Adam obviously was telling the truth. Adele had lied about the relationship, probably to hurt him, her pretend father. To grind his nose in the dream of simple small town life he had created for the two of them. After several moments of silence, Guy held out a hand. "I owe you an apology. Will you accept it?"

"Sure." Adam took the hand and gave it a firm shake. When he released it he said, "I can't tell you how shocked I am to hear what she told you. I'm real shaken, Mr. Driscoll. I thought I knew Del."

"Nobody knew her," said Guy. "Least of all me."

He had thought he could move her around like a playing piece on a board and she would stick to the rules. Not Adele. She played her own game the whole time.

"Can I . . . would it be all right if I went to the funeral home to see her?" Adam asked. "I just want to say goodbye to her."

Guy nodded. "I'm going there myself. I was supposed to have some help, but it's been two hours and I'm still waiting for someone to show up."

"You gotta come back here, right?"

"Right," Guy said in a dry voice. He looked at Adam then. "You're a pretty big guy. What are you, six three?"

"Six two and a half," Adam said.

"Think you could help me out of this bed?" Guy asked him. "If I have a cane and some support I'll be fine. The cane is over there in the corner. Can you get it for me?"

Adam retrieved the cane and brought it over to Guy. Guy propped himself up on the wooden handle and swung his legs out of bed. He winced as he placed his weight on his left leg.

"You okay?" Adam asked, watching him.

"I'm okay. See if there's a shirt and some jeans in that closet over there, would you?"

Adam looked uncomfortable. "Uh, isn't the nurse supposed to come in and help you?"

"Why should she when I've got you? Bring me some underwear while you're at it. I might not be able to get it on over these bandages, but I'm sure as hell going to try."

Twenty minutes later Guy was dressed and leaning on

Adam to walk out of the room. He met a nurse with a newspaper in her hand in the hall.

"Where do you think you're going?" she asked.

"Talk to the doctor about it," Guy said. "He okayed it." He took the paper out of her hand and gestured for Adam to go on. The nurse came to stand in front of them.

"You're to have a hospital escort, Mr. Driscoll. How can we be sure your friend here will—"

"We'll be fine," Guy said shortly. "Please step aside. You're impeding our progress."

The nurse exhaled through her nose and moved away from them. "Don't you move. I'm going to call the doctor."

"Call him," said Guy. "Keep moving, Adam. Let's get out of here."

With much help, Guy was able to sit in the passenger seat of Adam's truck with no major mishaps. Guy opened the paper and held it on the dash in front of him while propping himself onto his right hip with his other hand. Adam drove as carefully as he could and winced himself when he saw Guy wince at the bumps they encountered. When they arrived at Diest Mortuary, Guy's face was white and beaded with drops of perspiration.

"How are you doing?" Adam asked. "You want to rest a minute?"

"No. Let's go in."

"Are you bleeding somewhere? You look awfully white."

"I'm fine, Adam. Let's get moving."

"Okay." Adam left the truck and came around to help Guy out. Guy felt suddenly weightless as the bigger man took him virtually in his arms and lifted him from the pickup. When Guy placed his left foot on the ground he felt gravity at work again. He leaned heavily on Adam and turned toward the entrance of the funeral home.

"After we leave here I want to go to the police station," he said through gritted teeth.

"Why?" asked Adam.

"To ask them to let Michael Bish go. She didn't shoot anyone. She couldn't have."

"How do you know that, Mr. Driscoll? The paper says people who know her claim she's been acting funny since her husband was shot."

"She didn't shoot anyone," Guy repeated, and he sucked in his breath at the odors that assailed them as Adam opened the mortuary door. Flowers. The masked smell of chemicals. Hairspray.

Vernon Diest appeared before them the moment they were inside. "Mr. Driscoll," he said in his flat mortician's voice. "I hope everything will be satisfactory. Let me give you my personal condolences and express my great sorrow over your loss."

Guy looked past him. "Where is she?"

Vernon straightened. "Right this way. Please follow me."

Adam and Guy hobbled after him to the viewing room. When Guy saw the casket he felt something tear at his chest. When he looked inside, he felt the cry that was building up inside of him hitch in his throat. He forced his gaze away and squeezed his eyes shut. Adam sobbed openly, almost losing Guy as he stepped automatically forward to touch the hand of the sleeping princess in the casket. Guy opened his eyes and made himself look at his daughter.

She didn't look dead. She looked beautiful. She looked as if she might awaken at any moment and lift her arms in a lazy stretch. She looked as if her lips would part in a smile any second.

Vernon Diest had done a wonderful job, Guy had to give him that.

He sensed a presence behind him and he turned, expecting to see Diest. He saw instead a woman in a blue dress standing just inside the doorway. Her large brown eyes were full of sorrow and sympathy as she gazed at Guy. Genuine sorrow. Genuine sympathy. Guy nodded to her and she backed quickly out of the room. He didn't see her again.

As they left the mortuary Adam was still sobbing, partly onto his hands, partly onto Guy. Guy's own cheeks were wet, and once in the truck he fished around in his pocket for a handkerchief. Vernon Diest came outside behind them and gestured to Guy. Guy struggled to roll down his window. "Yes?"

"Was everything satisfactory?" Diest asked.

"She looked fine," Guy told him.

Diest was crestfallen. "Fine? Yes, well, I understand arrangements have been made to pick her up this evening and take her to the airport, where she will be flown to Chicago."

"You understand correctly."

"I see, yes. Well, would you like for her to remain on view until the truck arrives? Several people in town have expressed a desire to come and show their sympathy."

"Fine," said Guy.

"Fine. Yes. All right. Um, Mr. Driscoll, if you don't mind my asking—it's gotten back to me that you wished your daughter to be taken elsewhere. May I ask the reason?"

Guy looked at him. "Do you have the bill ready?"

"Yes, as a matter of fact, I do."

Guy reached into his right hip pocket for his wallet. He handed Diest a credit card and said, "I assume you have an expense sheet and something for me to sign?"

Diest disappeared inside the building and was back in less than two minutes. "Sign here," he said.

Guy signed his name and took his card back from Diest.

"Let's go, Adam."

Before Diest could open his mouth again, the noisy rumble of Adam's engine filled the air. Guy looked straight ahead through the windshield and thought about the way his daughter had poked him in the back yesterday when she'd come onto the patio. *Trust me on this one*, she had said, and for a moment he would have sworn there was some tenderness in her eyes for him. Just for a moment, before she was shot.

His vision of the princess dissolved and was replaced by the one that would haunt him the rest of his life: Adele staring at him in round-eyed shock, her eyes never leaving his, blood pouring from her mouth.

Guy's throat thickened and his eyes welled up with tears again. Within minutes they were at the Colson Police Station, and Guy sat in the cab of the truck and blew his nose. At his nod, Adam came around and helped him out, and together they made their way into the building. The desk sergeant stood up when he saw them coming. "What's going on here?"

"This is Guy Driscoll," Adam told the man. "He wants to talk to someone about Michael Bish."

Guy wiped the sweat from his forehead and thanked Adam. Adam said no problem. The desk sergeant went through a door and left them alone. A minute later he returned with a man who introduced himself as Captain Mawby. He brought in another man and introduced him as Detective Chalk.

"We understand you want to talk about Michael Bish," said the man named Mawby.

"Yes," Guy said. "I'm asking you to release her. She didn't shoot anyone."

"How do you know she didn't?"

"She wouldn't. I want to see her."

"That's not a good idea. I don't think you'd make it, anyway. You ought to be in a hospital bed."

"I want to see her," Guy said firmly. "I'm not leaving until I do."

"Why? Is this an interview of some kind?"

"Just let me see her."

Mawby hesitated, then he lifted an arm to beckon them back. "All right. I don't know what this is supposed to prove, but I don't want you dying in my building."

"Thank you," said Guy.

They were taken to an isolation cell, where Guy saw Michael in an exhausted sprawl on the cot. He motioned for Adam to let him proceed on his own. "Please wait here," he said to the men behind him. Using the bars on the cell, he hobbled over to the nearest point by Michael's head and whispered for her to get up. Michael's lids opened. She sat up to look at him, and her expression was one of caution. As she gazed at his white, sweat-dampened face, her eyes slowly filled with tears. "Have you come to accuse me?" she asked, and when he didn't answer, she put her hands to her face. "I'm so sorry," she whispered to him. "I'm so sorry for what happened."

"You didn't kill my daughter," Guy said, a statement.

"No." She looked up in horror and left the cot to come and reach for his hand through the bars. "You have to believe me. I could never have done something like that. I know we haven't gotten along, but please, please know that I'd rather die than hurt you or your daughter. I swear to you. I can't tell you how sorry I am that she's gone."

Guy studied her streaked face. He said, "I'm going to help you, Michael. Put your face up to the bars and kiss me."

"What?" Michael tried to pull her hand away, but Guy held it firmly in his own. "I believe you didn't shoot me. I want the men watching us to believe it, too. Kiss me."

"I don't know what you mean. I can't kiss you."

"You can if you want out of here."

She shook her head. "This is crazy. What will a kiss prove? I—"

"It'll prove more than you know," said Guy. "Humor me. Put your face up to the bars."

Michael hesitated, her blue eyes full of doubt. Then she reached through the bars with both hands and brought his face to hers. Her lips were tentative at first, soft and light, and then they clung gently to his mouth. Guy forgot about the ache in his left hip as he kissed her back. For three short seconds he was completely free of pain, both mental and physical.

When she ended the kiss he heard himself groan. Her fingers left his face with a caress.

"Was anyone watching?" Michael asked.

"Yes," Guy said. "Captain Mawby and Detective Chalk." He moved his eyes to the door and she followed his gaze. When she saw the men gathered there she blinked and looked back to Guy. "Did you tell them to watch us?"

"No. I told them I had to see you. I knew they would watch us."

She smiled wearily at him. "Now they'll think I'm insane *and* unfaithful to my husband. According to the paper I've been mentally unstable since my husband was shot. Next they'll say it was a jealous rage that made me shoot your daughter." Her face paled then. "I'm sorry. I shouldn't have said that. I'm glad you came here, and I appreciate what you're trying to do for me."

"I'm here for another reason," he said. "I want to know who would try to frame you."

Michael nodded. "I know of one possibility. His name is David Eulert. He's the man who shot my husband, and he's back in town. David hates me. He believes I ruined his life."

"I thought your husband was shot by accident?"

"So did everyone else. David was in love with my husband. The police department called it accidental and said I was crazy for telling everyone that David the war hero was gay. Oliver was the only one who knew."

"Besides you."

"Besides me. Which reminds me, if you're out in the halls exercising, could you go down to Oliver's room and check on him? Make sure they're keeping him turned and bathed?"

"Sure," Guy told her. His hand slipped on the bars then and he banged his elbow hard while trying to catch himself. Michael reached through to help him, and when he was stable again, he found his face close enough to hers for another kiss. He touched his lips to hers and she backed slowly away from him. "You look awful," she said. "You'd better get back to the hospital."

"After they release you," he said.

"I'll be out soon. My sister's hired a lawyer. He's asked the judge to set bail."

"Will you come and see me?"

"Why?"

"Why not?" Guy squeezed her hand and called for Adam. "My personal chauffeur," he said to Michael.

"Formidable," she said.

Once outside with Mawby, Guy said, "She didn't shoot me, and she didn't shoot my daughter."

"Look," said Mawby, "I've had my doubts about this from the beginning. But Michael Bish has shown some erratic behavior in the past—"

"If your wife was shot and in a coma I'll wager you'd show a little erratic behavior yourself."

Mawby stared at him. "Michael does that same damn turn-the-tables bit on me. You two must be a lot alike."

Guy looked at him. "Will you tell the judge what you saw here today, Captain?"

"I will, Mr. Driscoll." Mawby turned to Adam. "Get this man back to his hospital room, would you? He's making me tired just looking at him."

Adam said he would and he half-carried Guy out to his truck. Once in the cab he turned to Guy and said, "Michael Bish went to see Del in the hospital. Did Del tell you?"

"No," said Guy. "She didn't."

"Oh. That was a nice thing you did back there."

Guy looked at him. "You mean you didn't buy it?"

"Huh-uh. Del told me you never have girlfriends. She said one night stands were more your thing. She said she ought to know, whatever that meant."

Guy fell silent and looked out the window. He didn't say anything else the rest of the trip, and he only mumbled his thanks to Adam after he was back in his hospital bed and being attended to by two nurses. When Adam and the nurses were gone, he turned his face toward the wall and remained that way for the rest of the day.

CHAPTER
ELEVEN

MICHAEL WALKED OUT into the sunlight and blinked at the brightness of the day. "Like being in a damp cave," she told her sister, "fluorescent light or not. I can't thank you enough, Sean."

Sean smiled. "You can thank Guy Driscoll. Barry said the judge had decided against releasing you when Mawby called and told him about you and Driscoll. The judge hasn't dropped the charges, but he's taking it under advisement."

Michael's smile faded and she walked briskly to her sister's car.

"What?" Sean said. "Are you upset about this? No one thinks anything of your kissing him, you know. My God, they think you're a normal woman with normal needs. It's better than everyone thinking you're a nut."

"The word is adulteress," Michael said as she sat down in the passenger seat. "I do still have a husband, you know."

"Oh, for crying out loud," Sean said in exasperation as she got in and started the engine. "What you have is a brain dead, bedridden memory of a husband."

Michael looked at her sister, shocked. "He's not brain dead. There's still brain activity."

"He might as well be brain dead, Michael. There's no communication between the two of you. You can't spend the rest of your youth on Oliver Bish. He's gone, and he's not coming back."

"I don't want to talk about this," said Michael.

"I'm sure you don't," Sean replied. "You never do. But it's time to face some facts. People thought you were capable of shooting a man and his daughter. Why? Because you're strangely and unnaturally devoted to a man in a coma who shows only the most minute amount of brain activity. If he showed any less brain activity he'd be dead."

"Sean . . ."

"I'm not finished. You made a few accusations when Oliver was shot, and people chose not to believe you. They still don't. Nothing you say will change their minds about David Eulert, Michael. Nothing. And unless the pistol Vernon Diest used is found, then nothing will change their minds about you and him, either. Accept it. Take your lumps and keep going. Guy Driscoll has given you a unique opportunity, take advantage of it. Let people think there's something normal about you for a change."

"You . . . he . . ." Michael couldn't find the words on her tongue. Finally she blurted, "He wants to sleep with me. I know it. I can tell he does by the way he looks at me. It's like he can never get enough of watching me and it makes me crazy the way he looks at me. No one has ever looked at me like that before. And then when I kissed him I felt so guilty because here I was kissing him and liking it and there Oliver was in that bed in the hospital, just lying—"

"Did you say you liked kissing Guy Driscoll?" Sean interrupted.

Michael's nod was guilty. "Very much."

"Maybe you *should* sleep with him," Sean suggested. "Once people hear about the kiss, they're going to think you did anyway."

"I can't," Michael said automatically. "I'm a married woman. I couldn't do that to Oliver."

"Oliver would never know, Michael. Believe me."

"I'm not that kind of person. And I'm not sure what kind of person Guy Driscoll is. I think he can turn it off and on at will. I don't want to be involved with someone like that. I don't want to be involved with him. I've got other things to worry a—where are we going? I thought I told you I wanted to go to the hospital first to check on Oliver."

"Yes, you did tell me that. I'm going to take you home so you can get cleaned up. Oliver's certainly not going anywhere."

"Sean, you're making me angry."

"Get angry, then. I'm taking you home."

"God, you're stubborn."

"No more than you. He *is* good-looking."

"Who?"

"Guy Driscoll. His picture was in the paper yesterday."

"He has freckles," Michael said.

"Really? He looked tanned to me."

"On his nose and his cheeks."

"Huh. He doesn't look like he would have freckles. How old is he?"

"I'm not sure."

"Don't you like freckles?"

"No," Michael said, and she refused to say another word until they reached her house.

When Sean opened her door to get out, Michael told her not to bother. "I'll be fine now," she said. "Thanks for the lawyer, and for coming to get me. Call Dad and ask him not to worry."

Sean smiled at her. "He won't. He'll know better than to believe gossip. Don't be mad at me, okay? I only want you to be happy."

"I know you do," Michael told her. "I'll call you later."

"All right." Sean leaned back in her seat and backed down the drive.

Michael checked her mailbox and took the bundle of mail inside to place it on the kitchen table. After sorting through and finding the bills, she put them to one side and tossed the rest of the mail in the wastebasket. Then she went to take a shower.

The warm spray felt so good she nearly cried. Her muscles ached from sleeping on the cot in the jail, and the bones in her neck snapped and popped as she lifted her head to feel the water on her face. Instinctively she remembered Guy Driscoll's mouth on hers, the taste of him, and the way his fingers had squeezed her hand.

Then she clamped down on the memory and squashed it between mental fingers as if it were a dreaded bug.

She had to get to the hospital. Oliver would be waiting for her.

She hurriedly finished her shower and dressed in olive slacks and a pale yellow blouse. Her hair went into a quick ponytail, and then she was out the door. She drove directly to the hospital and walked without interruption to her husband's room.

Oliver was exactly as she had left him. She snatched his chart from the door, all the while speaking to him and telling him where she had been. The nurses had turned and bathed him as scheduled, she saw, and that made her sigh with relief. She checked him just to be sure—nurses had been known to write things down without doing them—and found him free of bedsores and smelling clean. His catheter was in good shape, and he appeared to be resting peacefully, with an almost contented expression on his sallow features.

Michael sank down into a chair and began to read the sports page to him. After she finished, she read two chapters of a Robert Ludlum novel to him. When she completed those, she stared at her husband for a long time. Then she left her chair and walked out into the hall. The nurse behind the desk seemed stunned to see her.

"Mrs. Bish, what are—how are you today?"

"I'm fine. Can you tell me which room Mr. Driscoll is in?"

The nurse told her, then said, "He was in to see your husband earlier. He came thumping down here on his cane and—"

"Thank you." Michael left her and walked away in the direction of Guy Driscoll's room. She found him sleeping soundly. She entered the room and sat down in the chair by his bed to study him. His face was still slightly pale against his rich brown hair—his freckles were more prominent—but there was color in his cheeks that hadn't been there yesterday.

The phone on his table rang and Michael hurried to jerk it up before it could wake him. "Hello?" she said.

"Guy Driscoll, please," responded a female voice.

"I'm sorry, he's sleeping," Michael said. "Would you care to leave a message?"

"Who is this?"

"A . . . friend."

"All right. This is Gail Byers in Chicago. Tell Guy that his daughter's arrival was without incident. The service was an hour ago, everything went fine. Many of her friends came. I'm shipping all the burial information and the bill for the plot by Federal Express. He should receive it tomorrow."

"Uh, does he know where she's buried?" Michael asked.

"Of course he does. Right beside her mother. If he has any questions, ask him to call me. He has my number."

Michael hung up and turned to see Guy awake and watching her. His green eyes were calm, but curious.

"Who was that?" he asked.

"Gail Byers," Michael told him, and she relayed the information given to her. Guy's gaze drifted away to a spot beyond her as she spoke. When she fell silent he remained distant, and after a moment she edged toward the door. "I'll go and leave you alone. I wanted to thank you for looking in on Oliver. It was kind of you. If there's anything I can do for you in return, let me know."

Guy said nothing. Finally, Michael nodded and left the room. She went back to Oliver and made herself comfortable in a chair while she tried to imagine what was going on in Guy Driscoll's head. She often thought it would be nice to have a child. She was certain she wouldn't feel nearly so lonely, but she was also certain she would feel twice as afraid. It would be an awesome responsibility to try and raise a child alone, with no help.

At one time, immediately after the shooting, Michael had thought of having some of Oliver's sperm removed so she could try artificial insemination. Her father had convinced her of her foolishness.

"Half the women in the country are trying to raise kids alone, and a lot of 'em are doing a damn poor job of it. A boy needs a man around and a girl needs a daddy to show her love. You want a baby not because you're ready for parenthood, but because you want a living facsimile of Oliver. That's pretty damned selfish, if you ask me."

Michael saw reason, as she always did when it was her father doing the talking, and gave up the idea. Now, as she sat and wondered at Guy Driscoll's anguish, she realized she might never know what he was going through. She might never have a baby of her own.

Oliver's phone rang and she blinked in surprise as she reached over to pick it up. "Hello?"

"I'm sorry," said Guy. "I haven't been good company lately. Will you come back?"

"I shouldn't. You need to be alone."

"I need to be with you."

Michael grew flustered. "You don't even know me. Please, Guy, don't do this. You know my situation. You know I could never do . . . whatever it is you think you want me to do. I'm going to hang up now. Goodbye."

Her cheeks were aflame as she hung up the phone. It rang again almost immediately and she snatched it up. "I told you I can't, so please leave me alone."

Captain Mawby chuckled in her ear. "Are the bill collectors hounding you, Michael?"

Michael's cheeks grew even hotter. "Hello, Captain. Why are you calling?"

"To tell you about the casings we found on your patio. I guess you're clear. They didn't match up with any of your registered weapons. Unless you've got something unregistered hidden away somewhere."

"Why would I hide the gun and leave the casings behind for you to find? I told you, someone tried to frame me."

"Maybe so."

"What are you going to do about it?" she asked.

"Investigate," Mawby said.

"Uh-huh."

"We will. We're going through the records to find the names of all registered nine millimeter owners."

"Nine millimeter?" Michael echoed, and in a flash of sudden recollection, she thought of Vernon Diest, the mild-mannered mortician with the incredible disappearing pistol.

She opened her mouth to tell Mawby, then she slowly closed it again. He wouldn't believe anything she said. None of them would. Her eyes stung with anger at the knowledge.

"We'll be in touch with you, Michael. Take care of yourself." The captain hung up and left Michael breathing out her frustration into the receiver.

She couldn't go on this way. She knew she couldn't. Anytime something unreasonable or irrational happened, people would be looking at her. That crazy Ogilvie girl. They had called her crazy for wanting to be a cop, for wanting to carry a gun and patrol town in a car. And now, even though she had been cleared of shooting Guy and his daughter, most of the people in town would not trust her.

She had to do something.

Michael looked hard at her comatose husband, as if he could provide her with the answer. A moment later she collected her purse and left the hospital. She was going to visit a neglected grave.

CHAPTER
TWELVE

ELMA SAW THE WOMAN drive up in her gray car, and she thought to go and warn Vernon, but she decided against it. Instead she stood behind the heavy drapes at the second floor window and watched. Vernon didn't need any help. He could handle everything by himself. He certainly didn't need Elma to come and tell him that Michael Bish was out in the cemetery a hundred yards from the house. Elma saw her get out of the car and walk to a marker in the ground. Elma knew the marker; it was Michael's mother, Janie Ogilvie, born May 4, 1938, died on July 7, 1987. Elma knew almost all the markers, except for some of the really old ones that were hard to read. No one had been to see Janie for some time; the silk flowers placed at her grave last Memorial Day were all faded and torn by the Kansas wind.

Elma didn't think Janie's daughter had come to be with her mother now, either, since Michael seemed to be looking at nothing but the big stone house.

Again she started to look for Vernon, and again Elma changed her mind. Let Michael Bish come. Vernon deserved whatever they would do to him if he was found out. He truly did. He was a horrible pig, and he deserved to die for what he had done to that young, pretty girl. Elma couldn't believe she had once loved him. She couldn't believe she had once followed him around the house like an orphaned puppy, begging for him to turn and see her.

If only his mother were still alive and taking care of the place. Elma had loved Alissa Diest. She had been so smart and so kind to Elma. Elma had watched the things she did, she watched every movement, and she tried very hard to be like Alissa, but there was no one like Alissa. Vernon's mother had been one of a kind.

She had certainly known how to rule the men in her life. Even Elma's father, who had beaten Elma regularly and sexually abused her on occasion, had laid down under Alissa's law. If everyone did as she said, things went along fine. If anyone dissented, Alissa threw the house into such turmoil that the dissenter soon relented and begged her forgiveness.

Elma had assumed Alissa's son possessed the same strength of character. She was wrong. The night she saw Vernon pull the gun from his jacket when Michael Bish stopped his van, she knew she was wrong. When Vernon couldn't get the pistol to fire and was shot himself, Elma felt a prayer had been answered. She had taken the pistol then. She had taken it and hidden it, hoping to save Vernon from himself and make him finally realize that his place was with her. She would make him as strong as his mother. She would push him when he needed to be pushed and coddle him when he needed coddling. She would make up for the strength he lacked.

But Vernon didn't want her. He called her stupid and grew angry when she wore his dead mother's dresses. He shouted at her and waved his hands and made her afraid to be around him. He gave her black looks that left her in no doubt as to how he felt about her. And then he had come to her, all smiles and charm, and asked her for the pistol she had taken. He wanted to get rid of it, he told her. Or that's what Elma thought he had said. The next day she knew she had been mistaken.

And now that sweet girl was dead, her poor father was wounded, and Michael Bish was in the cemetery and looking hard at the place where Vernon Diest lived.

If Elma was brave she would search for the pistol and take it out there and give it to the suspended police officer. She would turn Vernon in and be done with it. But she wasn't brave. She was afraid.

She was afraid of being called an accomplice, since she had aided Vernon that night by running away with the pistol. She was afraid of losing Vernon, which meant losing the house. Elma had nowhere to go. She had no one to turn to. Her father had long ago disappeared—not that Elma would go with him again. But she simply had no one else.

Even though it meant lying and living with a murderer, Elma would do nothing. Her future, as well as Vernon's, was at stake. Her only solace was in knowing that her once beloved Vernon did in fact need her, no matter what he said to the contrary. He needed her as much as she needed him, and if she were a little more like Alissa, his dead mother, then she would prove it to him once and for all. In a situation like this, Alissa would have had the reins from the first night. She would have held the pistol in front of Vernon's nose and chided him for his stupidity. She would have kept the pistol, and her knowledge, and used it like a weapon against her son, to keep him in line.

Which is what she should have been doing all this time, Elma sternly told herself. But she simply wasn't capable, and she knew it. Especially when Vernon turned on the charm, as he had when he came for the pistol. When he smiled at her his mouth was so sweet and his eyes were so dark and lively that she found herself utterly swept away by his handsomeness. She knew he had the same effect on other women, because she had watched them in the chapel and in the viewing rooms. When Vernon spoke to them, they leaned attentively forward, and they went on watching him when he walked away from them. Vernon brought no one home, however, and he never made dates. Elma guessed his worries over the bills and the upkeep of the house had consumed him. He wasn't functioning normally.

If only Alissa could see him now, Elma thought. She wouldn't recognize her son for the murderer he had become. Alissa had done some underhanded things during her reign, but never had she physically hurt anyone. Never had she schemed and plotted and killed people when the business was hurting and no one was dying. Elma looked at her hands and knew in her heart that Vernon would not escape punishment. Eventually, someone would discover his crime.

And then what would happen to her? She lifted her head and looked out the window again. She didn't know. She couldn't say. Perhaps the county would assist her. Perhaps the kind man next door who gave her seeds for her vegetable garden would take her in. He had been a widower for some months now. He might—

A firm hand on her arm made her jump. She jerked her head around and saw Vernon grimace as he looked at the garden dirt on her hands.

"You get cleaned up," he said to her. "Today's our lucky day. Mrs. Glick, the one with the bald spots, just died at the hospital. I'm going to pick her up and I'll be back soon, so have everything ready and waiting for me."

Elma looked at him in surprise. He had never come to find her before bringing a corpse in. It was always after that he came to look for her, when he needed the hair done. And had he actually asked her to prepare his embalming room for him?

"You can do that, can't you?" he said to her frown.

Elma nodded. *Why now?* she asked with her eyes.

Vernon avoided her gaze and looked past her out the window. His eyes rounded slightly. "What the hell is she doing out of jail? Why is she here? Surely they can't have released her already." He looked at Elma then. "How long has she been out there?"

Elma shrugged. She couldn't know.

Strong hands came up to grip both her arms. Vernon put his face close to hers and shook her a little when she tried to squirm away. He stamped his foot hard and she looked at his face. "Watch her," he said. "When I leave, watch her and see what she does. She might try to come in here. Tell me if she does, Elma. Tell me if she tries to break in and snoop around in here. I'll get a restraining order. I'll say she's harassing me, and she won't be able to come anywhere near me. Have you got that?"

Elma would have given him the finger again, but her arms were pinned against her sides. She gritted her teeth and nodded to him. He released her and stepped back. His chest was heaving slightly. His palms were wet. Elma rubbed her arms and turned her back on him. He stamped his foot once and she felt the vibration in the floor. She turned her head to look at him.

His nostrils flared. He said, "I'm sorry I grabbed you. All right?"

Elma looked forward again. Let him be sorry. She felt a draft behind her then and she knew he had gone. She looked over her shoulder to make sure, and saw nothing but last night's blanket and pillow in the corner by the door. She slept in a different spot every night, a habit incurred from nights spent with her drunken, molesting father. If he couldn't find her, he couldn't molest her. She refused to sleep in the caskets, as Vernon was known to do. It wasn't right. Elma did fine on the carpeted floors with her pillow and her blanket. She ate from her garden and whatever she could find in the kitchen. Vernon didn't buy many groceries, so there was never much food. Elma could cook, but she had never gotten this across to Vernon. The pan of rolls she had prepared not long ago had been to show him she knew her way around an oven and a stove, but Vernon had taken no notice.

He was meticulous about his paperwork and his lists and his receipts, but he wasn't so meticulous about his diet. What he put into his body was mostly pre-made sandwiches and TV dinners. Elma grew vegetables for herself in a small plot between four cedar trees, where some of the oldest graves in the cemetery were located. No one came to look at those graves, so no one found Elma's garden. No one but the neighbor, anyway, and he didn't care.

Elma thought of him again, and of how he might need someone around the house. She wondered if he would consider her. She could clean, and she wasn't as stupid as Vernon made her out to be. Sometimes she just had trouble understanding people. What they meant. What they were trying to tell her. She wasn't stupid.

She thought of asking the neighbor the next time she saw him. She could, she knew. She could ask him anything, because he always brought a pen and paper out for her to write on when he saw her. He was the nicest man Elma had ever known.

She would, she decided. The very next time she saw him, she would ask Arnold Dupree if he needed a woman around his house.

For now, she was supposed to be looking at Michael Bish. Watching her.

The only problem was, she couldn't see her anymore. Her car was still there, but Michael Bish was gone. Elma left her post and went running down the stairs, hoping the sound of her footsteps would scare Michael away if she were trying to come in. She saw nothing as she dashed into one room after the next, but as she finally reached the entrance she saw that the front door was ajar. Elma sucked in her breath. Had she come in? Had she gained entrance to the house while Elma was in her reverie?

A hand snagged her by the arm and a terrified squeaking sound came from her throat as she whirled to meet her assailant. It was Vernon. He pulled her into his office and motioned for her to be quiet. Elma struck him angrily on the arm and attempted to get away. He snatched her back, grabbing at her with his hands and inadvertently groping at one of her breasts. Elma went rigid. Her breathing stopped. Vernon fell immediately away from her. When she turned to look at him, she saw that he was red-faced. And sexually aroused.

"I'm sorry," he was saying. "I didn't mean to do that. I wanted to try and catch Michael Bish coming into the house. I saw her looking. I know what she's after. She thinks she'll come in here and find the pistol, and that'll be the end of me. But it won't, because I got rid of it just like I told you I was going to. I buried it where it will never be found."

Elma lifted a hand and straightened her blouse. Vernon's eyes followed her hand and his face reddened all over again. He backed away and looked out the window. He said, "Damn, she's—", but that was all Elma caught because he turned away from her as he spoke.

She was confused. What was wrong with him? Why, when she hated him so, did he act civil to her? Why did his face redden and his body harden now, when it was so obvious she wanted nothing to do with him? Elma was utterly bemused by his behavior. She turned and was on her way out of the office when she felt him stamp the floor. She stopped and glanced over her shoulder, allowing her eyes to betray none of her emotions.

Vernon stood, mouth open, as if he had forgotten what he wanted to say. Finally, he said, "You still haven't washed your hands."

Elma frowned at her crusted fingernails. Then she turned her back on him and left the room.

CHAPTER
THIRTEEN

GUY MADE HIS WAY into Oliver Bish's room and was dismayed to find no one but Oliver present. He had been hoping to find Michael there. Yesterday she had been adamant about not coming to see him, but he was just as adamant about seeing her. Bad taste though it may be to visit her in the hospital room of her comatose husband, Guy told himself he had no choice. Thinking about her was infinitely preferable to thinking about certain other areas of his life, and while he was so focused on her, he thought it would be nice to talk to her.

But she wasn't there. Exhausted by the trip, Guy lowered himself into a chair and gazed at the man in the bed. Oliver Bish was the complete opposite of himself. Oliver was tall, blond, and angular—a good-looking jock. Guy stood five-eight and had thick, dark brown hair. He was muscular without being stocky, with no trace of fat on his runner's body. He knew women were often intrigued by his green eyes, but they were nothing special. There was nothing about him that he would call attractive, yet he considered himself a decent-looking man. Not as good-looking as Oliver Bish, maybe, but Michael hadn't turned up her nose at kissing him.

The thought of the kiss made him smile. He looked at the

unresponsive man in the bed and said, "I had to talk her into it. But it did get her out of jail."

He moved the chair closer and winced at the pain in his hip as he did it. "I don't know if you can hear me or not, but I have to tell you I can't get Michael out of my head. She won't have anything to do with me because she's devoted to you. She won't even talk to me. But I'll tell you something, Oliver . . . I'm not going anywhere."

"Neither is he," said a voice behind him, and Guy turned to see a man in a white coat addressing him. "Mr. Bish could linger on like this almost indefinitely."

"Doctor . . . ?" said Guy.

"Spantzer. And you are?"

"Guy Driscoll." Guy held out a hand and the doctor lightly shook it.

"I've read your work, Mr. Driscoll. You're a fine journalist."

"Thank you. Are you Mr. Bish's physician?"

"Yes, I am, and as I told you, he's not going anywhere for a while. So, your task will be doubly hard, I'm afraid."

"My task?"

"Wooing Mrs. Bish away. It's unlikely she'll divorce him in his present condition. It's even more unlikely that he'll die."

The elderly doctor was certainly frank. Guy smiled politely and leaned back in his chair. "Do you have any suggestions?"

"Not a one," said the doctor as he came to lift one of Oliver's arms to check his pulse. "But the whole town will be watching with interest after that business in the jail yesterday, of that I can assure you."

"It was a kiss," Guy said.

"It was the first page of what many are hoping will be a soap opera script. Michael has been infamous in Colson for a number of years now, beginning with her insistence on taking wood shop rather than cooking class in high school. That was only the first time Michael Ogilvie made the paper; it certainly wasn't the last. Michael's father raised both his girls with traditional male values, and those two are as intensely earnest and stubborn as they come, Michael more so than Sean, since Michael was Ogilvie's last chance for a boy. They are also perfectly delightful females and a joy to look at."

Guy smiled in silent agreement. Then he looked at the doctor. "Would some of this notoriety have to do with the shooting of Oliver, and the man she accused?"

"Oh yes, of course," the doctor said as he strapped a blood pressure cuff around Oliver's arm. "David Eulert was a town favorite. A local hero. Half the females in town were in love with him. You can imagine their outrage when Michael came forth with her allegations."

"I can imagine," said Guy. "What happened?"

"Beyond a heated shouting match, nothing. David left town in the middle of the night, and no one saw him for some time. I'm told he's in town now, visiting his people. When he left, Michael considered her allegations verified. Many argued with her. The embarrassment and humiliation were enough to make anyone leave, some said. No one blamed David Eulert. Everyone blamed Michael Ogilvie, the woman who stood up and told what she knew to be true. The woman who refused to back down under pressure from her fellow officers on the police force. If Michael had been a man, David would probably have been investigated. But Michael isn't a man. And since she isn't, she was branded a paranoid, loud-mouthed harridan who wanted only to cause trouble."

Off came the blood pressure cuff. Guy took a deep breath. "You believed her, obviously."

"I believe her because I delivered her. I've known her to lie only one time, about one thing. Her sister Sean once threw a broken pop bottle at Michael while they were arguing. The cut she received was very deep and bled profusely. Michael was very frightened, but she was more frightened by the thought of what her father would do to her sister if he knew the circumstances. She lied to her father, and to me, and said she had fallen down on the glass in the alley behind their house. I knew better, of course, because of the location of the cut, and the angle, among other things. When her father was out of hearing, I asked Michael the truth, and with great reluctance she told me. She also made me swear I wouldn't tell her father. I never have."

"You're saying she's honest to a fault," Guy stated.

"Yes, I am, and yes, she is. If she says David Eulert is a homosexual, then David Eulert is a homosexual."

Guy opened his mouth to ask another question, but he closed it when he saw Michael enter the room carrying a newspaper and a can of soda. She frowned deeply when she saw him. "Hello, Dr. Spantzer," she said. Then, in a lower voice, "Guy, what are you doing here?"

"Just visiting," he said. "You look nice."

Michael nervously touched her cream slacks. "Thank you. Uh, Dr. Spantzer, how are you?"

"Fine, Michael. Everything is the same. No change. I'll see you tomorrow. Goodbye, Mr. Driscoll. It was a pleasure meeting you."

Guy nodded to the old doctor. When Spantzer was gone, Michael looked at Guy and said, "Why are you here?"

"I told you. I was out for some exercise and thought I'd stop in for a visit. The doctor came in and we started to talk."

"What about?"

"You, mostly."

Michael's eyes darkened. "What about me?"

Guy smiled at her. "What you were like as a little girl."

The corner of her mouth twitched. "He probably said I was a mean little tomboy with endless cuts and scrapes."

"No."

"No?"

"He said you were hell on broken pop bottles in back alleys."

Michael's mouth twitched again. Finally she smiled. "He told you I lied."

"The one and only time he knew of."

"What else did he say?" she asked.

"Not much. Are you worried?"

"I'm annoyed."

"Don't be," Guy assured her. He looked around himself then. "I guess I'm in your chair. I notice you don't have any others in here."

She shrugged. "They need them in other places. One's all I need."

"If you come and help me up, I'll get out of yours," he suggested, and he noticed that she hesitated before stepping forward. "Don't worry," he said. "I won't touch you any more than I need to."

Michael exhaled through her nose and went to take him by the arm. He jumped at the cold touch of her hand and she apologized. "It's the can I was holding. I'm sorry." She helped him out of the chair and onto his cane and commented that he seemed to be recuperating very quickly. Guy gave a short laugh. "It's all the running I do. Makes me tough as gristle."

"Don't joke," said Michael. "You're probably right."

"I'm sure I am," he said, and he turned his head to look at her while she was so close to him. Michael kept her eyes averted, refusing to look at him. Guy sighed and contented himself with breathing in the scent of her while she was beside him. When he was away from the chair and steady on his cane, he looked up and saw another stranger standing in the doorway of the room. No doctor, this time. Michael looked up at almost the same moment and her intake of breath was audible. The hand on Guy's arm began to tremble slightly.

"You have no business here," she said in a tight voice. "Please leave."

The man shook his head. "I didn't believe it when I heard it. Anyone but Mike I said. Now I guess I have to believe it." He looked at Guy. "You must be Michael's boyfriend. I'm David Eulert."

"The name is Driscoll," Guy said, "and I believe the lady has asked you to leave."

"The lady?" Eulert lifted a brow. "If you mean Mike, then I'm sure she wants me to leave. And I will. I heard about Vernon Diest, Mike. I guess you're shooting men in the back with bullets rather than lies these days."

Michael's hand fell away from Guy's arm. Her lower lip quivered. "Get out of here, David. Get out now. Don't ever come back here again."

The dark-haired David Eulert smiled and half-turned in the doorway. "Did you hear I got married, Mike? We've got a baby due in the fall. I certainly hope my marriage is stronger than yours was. Or should I say is?"

"That's enough," Guy said. "Leave."

Eulert looked at him. "Strange. You really don't look like her type. I'll be going now. See you later, Mike."

When he was gone, Guy turned to Michael. "Is he always so charming?"

"No," said Michael.

"So that was David Eulert."

"That was him."

"He's got a problem, and it isn't his sexuality," Guy said. "Anyone can see I'm your type."

Michael's lips curved in a guilty grin. She relaxed and gazed at Guy in appreciation. "Thank you."

"For what?"

"For believing me about him. About everything. For making me smile."

"Anytime," Guy told her. "Come and see me, would you?"

Michael paused. "I'll think about it."

"Don't think about it. Just come and see me."

Guy was serious, and he could tell it made her uncomfortable, so he inclined his head and started out of the room. He felt her eyes on him as he departed, and he was tempted to turn for a last look, but it would have thrown him off balance to do so.

"Guy . . ." she said suddenly, and he stopped and took his time turning around so he wouldn't fall. He looked expectantly at her.

"Don't they have any crutches to give you? It looks painful moving around on that cane."

He smiled. "I couldn't use the crutches. Too awkward. I kept knocking things over. It's easier to get out and around this way."

"Shouldn't you be spending more time in bed?"

"I'm there twenty-two hours a day. That's plenty, isn't it?"

She looked skeptical. "What does your doctor say?"

"He says I can go home Friday if I'm determined to do it. I don't know if I am or not. It depends on you."

"Me?" Michael said in surprise.

"I have a better chance of seeing you here," Guy said. "At home you'll be three houses away."

"Guy, don't say—why is it so important for you to see me?"

"I'm not sure," he admitted. "All I know is that thinking about you makes me ache in a different way than thinking about my daughter. I'd rather think about you."

Michael was silent a moment. Then she said, "You're using me. You're using me to run away from your pain and guilt. You think you can deny the hurt if you pretend an interest in the first woman you see."

Guy met her look. "I'm sure you'd like to believe that. And maybe that's exactly what I'm doing. Then again, maybe I've been interested in you since the first time I saw you. Maybe I've been battling my conscience over your circumstances and finally said to hell with it. I want to know you anyway. Maybe you want to know me too, I don't know. All I can do is try."

Michael said nothing. She glanced behind herself to the man in the bed, and when she didn't look at Guy again, he turned to leave.

Once in the hall, he thought about what he had said to Oliver earlier, about not going anywhere. He might have to reconsider. One touch from Michael, a simple hand on his arm, and every nerve in his body had come instantly alive. Everything he learned about her only intensified his desire to know more. She had fire and wit and determination, she had confidence, intelligence, the prettiest blue eyes he had ever seen, and she was exceedingly loyal . . . to a man in a coma.

Guy gave his head a shake as he made his way down the hall. He hoped she was right. He hoped he was only grasping at her to keep from facing his guilt. He hated to think of the hell he was going to put himself through if she was wrong.

CHAPTER
FOURTEEN

DAVID EULERT DROVE his black Dodge pickup through town and went directly to the large stone mansion that belonged to Vernon Diest. He eyed the mortuary entrance for several moments while mentally preparing what he would say. He was going to have to make every statement count. He and Vernon Diest could possibly be of great help to one another. When he was ready, he left the cab of the truck and went to open the door. It was locked. He rang the bell beside the door and waited. He pounded on the glass and called for Diest. Finally he saw movement inside the house. Vernon came to the door with a quizzical expression. His sleeves were rolled up and his hands appeared damp. "May I help you?" he asked as he opened the door.

"I think so," David said. "My name is David Eulert. May I come in?"

"What is this about?" Vernon asked suspiciously.

"Michael Bish."

Vernon's right brow twitched. His nostrils flared. He stepped aside and held the door open. "Come into my office. It's down the hall to your right, the third door."

"Were you in the middle of something?" David inquired, and he looked pointedly at Vernon's rolled-up sleeves.

"As a matter of fact I was," Vernon answered. "But it's nothing that can't wait."

When they were both seated in his office, Vernon behind the desk, David in the chair in front, David looked around himself and cleared his throat. He had never been in the back rooms of a mortuary before. It was an office just like any other, but knowing what kind of office it was gave it an aura of creepiness that made the fine hairs stand up on David's arm. Vernon Diest was creepy, too, with his probing black eyes and emotionless face. As a cop, David had learned that many funeral homes around the country were actually mob-owned operations. It was more convenient for them to take care of their own. He had also learned that a few funeral homes had been involved in child pornography rings and the like. Vernon Diest could certainly fit that bill, David decided.

"Well?" Vernon said to him suddenly, his voice impatient. "You wanted to talk about Michael Bish?"

"I was her husband's partner," David said. "She told everyone I shot him. She told everyone I was gay."

"Oh," said Vernon. "You're that David Eulert."

"I live in Springfield now," David went on. "But my family sent me the newspaper articles about you and Michael. You said she shot you. You were unarmed and she shot you. Is that right?"

"No, I had a pistol," Vernon said with a leer. "I had a pistol, but a deaf mute girl was hiding in the back of my van and after I was shot she leapt out, snatched up the gun, and hightailed it off to parts unknown. What do you think, Mr. Eulert?"

David was smiling. "A deaf mute girl? That's a good one. Okay, so you weren't armed when she shot you. I know you've filed suit against the town, but what are you doing about Michael Bish?"

"What do you mean, what am I doing about Michael

Bish?" Vernon responded. "She's supposed to be in jail for shooting some poor man and his daughter, but today I saw her here of all places. She was watching me."

David nodded. "The man she allegedly shot showed up at the jail and put on a show for everyone by acting like her boyfriend. The judge let her go."

Vernon's lip curled, and more to himself than to David, he said, "So Driscoll went to the jail after leaving here yesterday."

"I thought the two of us might bring some kind of suit against her," David suggested. "Something that would prevent her from coming after you again."

Vernon looked at him. "What if she comes after *you* again, Mr. Eulert? Aren't you afraid she'll call you more names?"

David opened his hands. "No one believed her."

"Then why did you leave town?"

"It was best. Are you interested in a joint suit, Mr. Diest, or am I wasting my time here?"

Vernon eyed him. "What if I said yes? Just what are you proposing, Mr. Eulert?"

"Something more than a restraining order. You said she was here today. We might bring her up on charges of harassment."

"Yes, I thought of that. But why should you want to be in on the suit?"

"She slandered me. She shot you. Do we allow her to go on destroying lives at will? She needs to be put away."

"How would we do that, Mr. Eulert?"

David looked at him and shook his head. "We? We're powerless, Mr. Diest. We're victims."

Vernon eyed him. "We can't touch her."

"No," said David. "But the courts can. A judge can send her away for extensive psychiatric evaluation and possible confinement."

"I take it you'd like to come back to Colson and live," Vernon said, and David lifted his head in surprise.

"What makes you say that?"

"A hunch."

David shrugged again. "It would be nice to know I could stay. This is my hometown, after all, and I have a wife now and a baby on the way. I lost my job with the sheriff's patrol two weeks ago. No one but my wife knows yet."

"So you've been spending your time dreaming up ways to have Michael Bish committed. What do you want from me, Mr. Eulert? A job?"

"The Colson police would take me back in a minute if someone could prove Michael Bish's instability," David said. "For that matter, they would probably take me back now."

Vernon frowned at him. "But you haven't applied."

"No. I've been doing a lot of thinking. I asked myself who in town would want to shoot Guy Driscoll? He hasn't been here long enough to make any serious enemies, and if it wasn't Mike who shot him, then who was it? My next question was, who would stand to gain the most by framing Michael for a murder? Now, call it a long shot if you like, I'm sure Captain Mawby has thought of the same thing, but I'd say it was someone with a hefty lawsuit against Colson. A lawsuit that hinges upon Michael Bish's guilt or innocence."

Vernon snorted in anger. "How dare you come into my home and say such a thing to me? I'll tell you what I'll tell Captain Mawby: *prove it.*"

"Can't do that without a gun or an eyewitness, and something tells me you've thought of everything, Mr. Diest. Knowing and proving are always two different things. It looks like the two of us want to prove the same thing, that Michael Bish is unstable. So why not work together?"

Vernon turned cold. "What do you think you know?"

"That you shot the Driscolls and left the casings on Michael's patio. You even used a nine millimeter gun, same as police issue. But it wasn't Michael's gun, and they will have figured that out by now. And with Driscoll's little show yesterday, they won't be looking at Michael anymore. Which means they'll be looking elsewhere. And if I know Captain Mawby, he'll be looking at you."

"He can look all he likes. He'll find no evidence to connect me with any murder."

David nodded. "I thought you'd say that. And you're probably right, Mr. Diest. Still, it would certainly be nice not to have to worry, wouldn't it?"

Vernon's eyes narrowed. "What do you mean?"

"Just what I said. It would be nice not to have to worry."

"About what? Being arrested?"

"No, about Michael Bish."

Vernon stared at him, and David rose from his chair. "Shall we go forward with a suit?"

"No," Vernon said. "I don't want to be seen with you. And I want no part of your plans."

"Fine." David moved toward the door. "In that case, I'll go forward with a slander suit on my own. My lawyers, of course, will call you forth as a witness. I know you're going to cooperate and do everything you can to substantiate my claims about her mental instability. It will do wonders for your own case, won't it?"

Vernon only looked at him.

David nodded and left the mortician sitting in his chair. He didn't like Vernon Diest, but Diest would come through for him, David was certain. The tiny spark of fear in his black eyes said so.

On his way down the hall he peeked in a room and saw a woman leaning over something on a table. He stepped inside the doorway and then stopped. It was a body on the table. The woman was doing something to the dead person's hair.

"Excuse me—oh shit," David said as he backed into a jar on a shelf and knocked it off onto the floor. The resulting shatter brought the woman's head around, and her eyes rounded when she saw David. Her mouth opened, as if to cry out, but no sound came forth. David frowned at her.

"It's all right," he said quickly. "I was just leaving. I went through the wrong door."

The woman said nothing. Her eyes were still round with alarm and she backed slowly away, until she was on the other side of the table.

David advanced a step and saw her look quickly around herself, as if searching for a weapon. Why didn't she call out? he wondered.

And then he knew.

She was the deaf mute girl Diest had referred to when talking about the van and the pistol.

"I'll be damned," David said softly, and then he sensed a presence behind him. He turned and found Vernon Diest glaring at him.

"What do you think you're doing? Get out now."

"I took a wrong turn. I'm leaving."

David left the room, and as he went he heard Vernon ask the woman in a solicitous tone if she was all right.

"She's deaf!" David called behind him as he walked down the hall to the door. There was an angry, muffled response, but David only smiled to himself and kept going. He had Vernon Diest's number.

CHAPTER

FIFTEEN

MICHAEL THREW THE COVERS off on Friday morning and leapt out of bed like a person with a purpose. She did have a purpose, though it wasn't a conscious one. She showered, dressed, and went about picking up the house. When she found herself picking up Oliver's things and putting them away in a closet, she momentarily paused and asked herself what she was doing. No answer was forthcoming, and after a mental shrug she resumed the task. For the first time in months, she actually felt like vacuuming the carpet and mopping the kitchen floor. She wanted the sink in the kitchen to be spotless, and the toilets and bathtub to gleam white. She cleaned house with fierce concentration, and when she was done, a comfortable sense of satisfaction took her out to the patio to drink a soda and look at the sky.

While looking at the sky, she stole a glance at Guy Driscoll's house. He was coming home today. She had heard the nurses at the hospital talking about it last night. They were glad to be rid of him. He asked too many questions, and he refused to stay in bed. He complained about the meals and had sent Adam Dupree to get him some fresh fruit, which he asked the nurses to keep in the hospital refrigerator for him.

Adam Dupree would be picking him up that morning and driving him home, and the nurses had chuckled to each other that the two men reminded them of cartoon characters, with one smart little dog barking out orders and one big dog with brawn and little brains carrying them out. Spike and Butch, they had said, giggling all the while.

Michael smiled to herself and wondered how Guy would react if he had heard them talking.

He probably would have laughed.

She stole another glance at his house and thought about the last time she had seen him. The things he had said to her and the way he had looked at her frightened Michael. She hadn't gone to visit him, and he hadn't come back to Oliver's room to see her. She doubted if that was the end of it, but perhaps he was taking some time to consider what she'd said to him about using her. Perhaps he had agreed with her and decided to leave her alone. Perhaps he was working through his guilt and sorrow on his own. He would have plenty of time to do it, Michael knew. The nurses last night had said the paper told him to stay home another four weeks, until he was completely healed.

Guy wouldn't stand for that, Michael thought. He would be ready to return to work in another week or so. And the week after that, he would be running again. She felt she knew him in that respect. He didn't appear to be a man who enjoyed much idle time.

Adele Driscoll had probably known that. The daughter whose blood had pumped out all over her father on the same back porch Michael was looking at. She would have known. Adele had been shot from the location where Michael was now seated.

Michael quickly finished her soda and returned inside the house. Without questioning her actions, she took out a recipe book given to her as a wedding present and found a recipe for a broccoli and rice casserole. While preparing the casserole, she found a recipe for homemade bread. She had to leave and go to the store for the ingredients in that recipe. When she returned she made the bread and finished the casserole with the same fierceness of concentration with which she had cleaned her house. Without stopping and asking herself just what she was doing and why, Michael found herself able to accomplish quite a few things on that Friday.

As a matter of routine, Michael was not good in the kitchen. She ate her vegetables raw, and liked her oatmeal instant. She ate cold cereal and dark breads and turned on the stove only to heat soup or make pasta. But she could follow instructions as well as anyone, so the casserole and the bread both turned out well. She was proud of herself as she gazed at the finished products, and she wondered what her sister and father would say if they knew. Sean was forever teasing her about her tasteless taste buds, and her father had used threats many times to get Michael in the kitchen.

While wrapping up the bread, she was finally forced to acknowledge what she was doing. But she still didn't ask why, and on the way over to Guy's house, she told herself she was better off that way.

As she stood on his front porch and knocked on his door, she felt her knees weaken. Her heart began to beat faster. Moisture appeared in her palms.

I shouldn't be doing this, said a tiny voice. *He's going to be encouraged by this. He's going to think I'm just as attracted as he is.*

You are, said another voice, an honest one, and Michael swallowed.

Adam Dupree opened the door. Michael recognized him and smiled timidly in greeting. He lifted a hand in an awkward wave and stepped back. Michael had never actually met the man, but anytime someone in the neighborhood lost a dog, a cat, or a small child, the neighbors automatically suspected the shy bachelor who lived alone with his poodle.

"Can I help you?" Adam asked.

"Is Guy here?" she said, and immediately felt stupid. Of

course he was there. "I mean, I'd like to come in and see him. I've brought some food."

"Oh, well, I guess that's okay." Adam moved aside and opened the door wide for her to pass. "Did he know you were coming?"

"I . . . no." Michael stepped inside and came to a sudden halt. Guy was just coming out of the hall. He wore nothing but a pair of briefs. In one hand he carried scissors and tape. In the other hand was his cane. When he saw Michael he abruptly stopped, but his surprise was only momentary. He smiled at her. "You should see your face. Excuse my state of undress, but I've been practicing changing my bandages. My clothes kept getting in the way."

"Are you . . . did you change them all right?" Michael stammered. "I mean, are they secure?"

"As secure as I can get them. If you or Adam would care to come over and have a look, I'd appreciate it."

Adam looked at Michael. Michael looked at Adam. Then both of them started over. Michael eventually fell back and pretended to look for the kitchen. "I've brought you some food," she said over her shoulder.

He made a reply, but Michael didn't hear him. She put her food down on the table, then walked back into the living room in time to see Adam pull Guy's underwear down and inspect the bandage on his rear. Michael turned away and headed back to the kitchen.

"Looks okay to me," she heard Adam say. "A bit bunched in the middle, but okay. Try to keep the tape away from the red parts, see? Just like the nurses said."

"Thanks," Guy said, and then she heard Adam tell him he would see him later and to call if he needed anything.

"I will," Guy told him. Then he came in search of Michael. "It smells good," he said as he entered the kitchen. "What is it?"

Michael glanced at his naked chest and bare legs and then forced herself to look at the food as she spoke.

"A broccoli and rice casserole, and some homemade bread."

"That's very nice. Are you staying for dinner?"

"If you . . . go and put something on, I will."

He smiled and pulled up his cane to turn; then he paused. "It's good to see you again, Michael."

She looked up at the quiet sincerity in his voice. He was looking at her in that way again, the way no one had ever looked at her before, not even Oliver. Slowly, she moved toward him. "I think I missed you. I've been thinking about you a lot."

"I've been thinking about you," he said. "I never stop."

She was close to him now. So close her breath stirred the hairs in the center of his chest. She wanted him to reach out and take her in his arms, but she sensed that he was waiting for her to make some move, to give him permission. Michael took a deep breath and reached out for him. Her hands found warm flesh, and her lips found the firm skin of his neck. His arms came around her and she heard a long, trembling sigh come from him. Sweet pain raced across her chest and she held onto him even tighter. She lifted her head to search for his mouth, and after a brief exploratory kiss he pulled away from her. His breathing was uneven as he said, "I'm going to fall down any minute now. My leg is buckling beneath me."

Michael stepped away from him in surprise. She had completely forgotten about his hip. Shame and embarrassment colored her face and she lifted her palms to her cheeks. Guy reached out and caught one hand. He took her into the living room and sat down heavily on the sofa, dragging her with him. He pulled her against him and drew her face to him to kiss her long and deeply. When he released her his breathing was even sharper. He filled his lungs and pressed his forehead against hers. "I thought I'd never be able to kiss you," he told her. "I thought I'd never be able to touch you, or hold you."

Michael sighed and offered her lips again as they sank

down onto the sofa. She lost herself in him. She lost herself to the sensations brought on by his hands and his mouth. She had forgotten what it felt like to be touched. She had forgotten how wonderful the butterflies and the slippery warmth were, the delicious aching and the fiery need. As she kissed him she slowly slipped a hand down his stomach and past the band of his briefs. He stiffened and then gasped as she touched him. His hands tightened on her and he tipped her chin so he could look at her face. What he saw there reassured him, and he kissed her with a hunger that made Michael shiver. She held on to him, feeling the warmth and hardness of him and moving her hand instinctively. Moments later, when he tore his mouth away from hers and jerked slightly, Michael slowly withdrew her hand and placed her head against his chest to hear the thudding of his heart.

Guy's arms lifted her up, but when he would have rolled her over she resisted him. He looked at her, and she slowly shook her head. He sank back onto the sofa and she saw his adam's apple bob. His hands clutched at her shoulders and she heard him whisper something to her. "What?" she asked softly, and she lifted her head to look at him.

"Kiss me again."

Michael shifted and raised herself, and as she did so, the phone rang. She looked at Guy.

"Ignore it," he told her.

Michael couldn't. "I'll bring it to you." She left the sofa to retrieve the handset on the table in the corner of the room. She handed it to Guy, who never took his eyes off her for an instant, even as he said hello. Michael watched him as he spoke and listened. She looked at his chest and his muscular legs and his well-shaped feet. She stared at a tiny pulse that ticked in his throat. She looked at his mouth and his watchful green eyes.

Suddenly she was flooded with guilt. Suddenly she couldn't believe what she had done. Her throat became blocked and her eyes teared up. She saw herself kissing him, touching him, caressing him, and then she saw herself massaging Oliver and bathing his white motionless limbs.

Guy saw her expression and he dropped the phone midsentence to reach for her. "Michael, don't—"

It was too late. She was already up and running for the door. She could hear him calling after her, but she ran all the faster, fleeing from him as if he were some frightening creature from a bad dream. She ran and ran, and when she reached her house she locked and bolted the door behind her, as if he might try to come in. When she was safe inside her clean home she jerked open the closet door and yanked out Oliver's things. She put his shoes by the door and hung his jacket over a knob. Only then did she collapse onto her bed and bury her face while she sobbed. At that moment, Michael wanted to die.

CHAPTER
SIXTEEN

VERNON'S EXPRESSION WAS worried as he watched the service for the dead bald woman. He wondered how David Eulert had come up with everything he had. How had he reached such an obvious conclusion about Vernon's shooting of the Driscolls? Did anyone else suspect him, or was Eulert simply been blowing smoke about Captain Mawby? Perhaps Michael had not lied about David Eulert after all, which caused Eulert to suspect that she wasn't lying about Vernon. The entire business was driving Vernon insane. He would have liked nothing better than to throw up his hands and leave town the way David Eulert had. But Eulert, the silly fool, was eager to come back. He wanted to come home and be a hero again. Vernon was older, but he knew about David Eulert's accomplishments. Everyone in Colson did. David was a high school athlete who became a decorated police officer. He left the force for a time to go and fight Saddam Hussein in the Gulf War, and he came back with a medal for bravery. Once back in his old job on the police force, he was placed with a new partner, Oliver Bish. Oliver Bish was just like David, an athlete and a cop. They were partners for only four or five months, Vernon couldn't remember exactly, when a bullet from a dropped gun struck Oliver, or so the story went. After meeting Eulert and considering his behavior, Vernon formed an opinion that supported Michael Bish's statement concerning the matter. David Eulert was obviously volatile and very much capable of committing murder.

Vernon knew blackmail when he saw it, and blackmail had been the entire point of David Eulert's little visit. Eulert wanted Michael Bish, and he wanted to ensure that he got her. Vernon didn't like Michael, certainly, but his enmity had none of the hue and form of David Eulert's cold rage. Homosexuals in the denial stage were obviously dangerous people, Vernon concluded. He would watch Eulert closely, learn what he could and attempt to find a weak spot. The ex-jock-cop had no business trying to coerce Vernon Diest.

As the service concluded, Vernon went out to close the casket. His neighbor, Arnold Dupree, stood nearby, waiting for a signal from Vernon to come and help load the casket for the short trip into the cemetery. As Arnold helped him, Vernon saw the other man wink and smile at someone behind him. Vernon turned and saw a flash of blue in the corridor. Elma. She was wearing blue today. He had seen her on the staircase earlier. He looked back to Arnold Dupree again and frowned. Did he know Elma, or was he just being friendly?

Vernon shook himself then. Of course he didn't know Elma. She squeaked like a mouse and ran whenever any man was present. She was terrified of men, a perfect example being the way she had cowered from David Eulert. Vernon had never seen her stand still for any man but him and her father. And lately she wasn't standing still for Vernon. If he entered a room she occupied, she exited. If he went in search of her, she hid from him. Just last night he had attempted to sit her down and tell her what David Eulert had wanted, what he had said, but she refused to sit still and watch his mouth. The minute he touched her she flinched away from him. The urge to hit her had been almost as great as the urge to bruise her with his mouth. Vernon had been thoroughly disgusted by both urges and let her go.

But he still wanted to talk to her. He needed to tell her what David Eulert had said to him, if only to hear himself saying the words. He wanted to see understanding in those wet brown eyes of hers. He wanted to know that she knew what kind of trouble they were in, that she understood all he was doing and trying to do. She had to know what he was going through to keep the place . . . and her.

Vernon couldn't understand the sudden change in Elma. Why she spat rather than fawned, and why the merest touch from him made her look as if she wanted to gag. He couldn't take that. It made him want to touch her all the more, if only to prove that she wouldn't become sick if he touched her. He couldn't believe the lust that built up inside him just by thinking about her thin body. Last night he had found himself fantasizing about her while masturbating. He knew it was nothing to be worried about; after all, he hadn't had intercourse in some time. But it was disturbing, nonetheless, because the repugnance he had previously felt for her had subtly changed into something else. Something that filled his nostrils with the smell of sweat, damp earth, and other heavy, musky odors when he was around her. It was a smell not necessarily of sex, but of sexual intentions, with her glands secreting and his pheromones singing. He was becoming infatuated with her.

When he saw Arnold Dupree's smile and wink, there had been an actual spark of jealousy in Vernon. Arnold Dupree couldn't know his Elma. Not his girl. She knew Vernon and only Vernon. He was the only man she allowed close, the only one she communicated with. She belonged to Vernon, and right after the service he was going to find her and talk to her about David Eulert. He needed to see her expression. He thought it might guide him in some way.

Finding Elma after the service wasn't as easy as Vernon had anticipated. He searched every room of the huge house at

least once, and he was making a second check of the third
floor, his own living space, when he heard a rustling sound in
the kitchen. He crept into the room and saw her sitting on the
floor, a package of saltine crackers at her feet. Vernon closed
the door behind him and turned on the light. Elma jumped
up, and her brown eyes were round with alarm. Vernon
stepped forward. He looked at her, looked at the crackers,
then he moved slowly toward the refrigerator and took out
some cheese. "Have some cheddar with those," he suggested.

Elma blinked at him. He pushed the cheese to her, then he
took a knife from a drawer and moved to cut off a few chunks.
"Have some cheese. You're too thin, Elma. You really should
eat more. I always buy enough for both of us, you know."

Her throat hitched as she swallowed a dry cracker, and
Vernon moved to get her a glass of water. Elma went on staring at him. He placed the water on the counter beside her.
Then he went about taking out some food for himself. He sat
down and unwrapped two ham sandwiches. When Elma
looked at him, he gestured for her to sit down opposite him.
Elma turned to leave the room. Vernon jumped up, caught
her by the arm, and steered her back to the table. He forced
her down in a chair and shoved some food at her.

"Stay here," he said. "I want to talk to you."

She blinked.

"Eat," he said. "Then we'll talk."

Elma shook her head, and Vernon grew exasperated.

"Elma, please. Do you know what please means? I'm asking you to please sit here and eat with me. All right?"

Her liquid eyes were confused and suspicious. Finally she
nodded and sat watching him.

"Eat something," he urged. "I want you to eat. You look
like you're starving. What do you eat? I never see you eat
anything."

Elma picked up the ham sandwich in front of her and took
a big bite. She looked pointedly at him as she chewed.

Vernon nodded. "That's better. Close your mouth while

you're chewing. It looks awful when you chew with your mouth open."

Elma rolled her eyes and swallowed the bite of sandwich in her mouth.

Vernon watched her and felt he had won a round. She was sitting at the table with him and she was eating. He finished half of his own sandwich and sat back in his chair. Her eyes were on the window behind him and he thumped the table so she would look at him.

"That man who was here day before yesterday, the one who scared you? His name is David Eulert." Vernon went on to give her some background, recalling what he had read in the paper, and what he had heard through local gossip. Elma watched his lips intently, her brows drawing together as he spoke of Michael Bish and her husband Oliver. When Vernon came to Eulert's visit, and all the man had said to Vernon, Elma began to shake her head.

"He's trying to blackmail me," Vernon explained. "He didn't come right out and say it, but that's what it amounts to."

Elma pointed at Vernon and drew a question mark in the air.

"Me? What about me? You mean what am I supposed to do? I don't know."

Elma's head lowered. Her eyes slipped past his face to the window and her expression became dull. Vernon thumped the table in anger.

"What *am* I supposed to do? He threatened me. He can't prove anything, of course, but it's bad enough that he even showed up here. What if next time it's Captain Mawby who shows up to—Elma, where are you going?" He rose to catch her again, but she jerked her arm away. She went to a memo pad by the phone on the kitchen wall and jerked off a piece of paper. She made a writing motion with her hand and looked expectantly at Vernon.

He stared at her. "You can write? You're going to talk to me?"

Elma exhaled through her nose and waited patiently while he scrambled for a pen. When he handed her a ballpoint she stepped away from him and began to scribble.

Vernon watched in amazement. She knew how to talk to him. She had known all along, and she had never picked up a pen to do it. Why?

She handed him the piece of paper. It read: *Ignore all he said to you.*

Vernon wadded up the paper. "That's easy for you to say."

Elma bristled and snatched another sheet of paper. She scribbled furiously again, and this note read: *Gun is gone. No motive other than being poor. Everyone is poor. He has nothing on you.*

The last *nothing* was underscored three times.

Vernon placed the sheet of paper in his pocket. He looked at Elma and said, "Why haven't you ever communicated with me like this before?"

She shrugged.

"You mean you had nothing to say?"

She nodded.

"I don't believe you. Why let me believe you were a complete retard?"

Elma took another sheet of paper and scribbled for a moment. The note read: *What good would it have done? You despise me. Tell me again what this David person is planning for Michael Bish.*

Vernon lifted his shoulders in an imitation of Elma's earlier shrug. "I told you. He's going to sue her for slander and try to prove her mentally unstable."

He needs you to do it. Why else would he come?

"To intimidate me into doing what he asks. He thinks I'll lie for him, that or he wants us to lie together, to a judge. I was ready to go along with him until he threatened me." Vernon's palms came together and he clasped his hands together till his knuckles turned white. Then he relaxed. "I'm not in this alone, you realize. Like it or not, you're as much a part of this as I am. You became a part of it the night you ran off with my pistol."

Elma nodded. She knew that.

"And you say we should do nothing, because Eulert can prove nothing."

She nodded again.

Vernon stared at her in consternation. "This makes me angry, Elma. I have to tell you that. Knowing that all this time you could have communicated with me if you chose. As it so happens, you're right. He can't prove anything. The pistol wasn't registered. It came over in a coffin from France. A man whose brother had served in the Gendarmerie, the French national police force, wanted it buried with him. I took it. It was untraceable to begin with and now it's gone."

Elma lifted a brow at his admission, and Vernon felt stronger suddenly. Strong and invincible. He put his hands on his hips and strode across the kitchen. He stopped behind her and playfully put his hands on her waist to turn her around. "Is that one of my mother's dresses?" he asked her.

Her nod was long in coming.

"I thought I recognized it. Take it off, Elma. Right now. Just like you did before."

Her eyes lowered. She shook her head.

Vernon stamped his foot. "Why not?" he said when she looked at him. "You didn't hesitate before. You stripped naked right in front of me. Now I'm asking you to do it, and you say no. Shall I help you?"

He tore at one of her sleeves, and Elma grew suddenly furious. Her arms came up to flail and scratch at his face, and a choking noise came from her throat as she fought him. Vernon automatically pinned her arms to her sides and held her frail, birdlike body against his while she continued to struggle. A surge of excitement rose up in him that was nothing like he had ever experienced. He managed to keep both her arms down with one hand, and with the other he caught hold of her face and turned it to meet his. A keening noise began in her as he fastened his mouth to hers, and a second later he felt incredible pain as she bit down hard on his lower lip.

Vernon howled and released her to catch the blood that spurted from his torn flesh. Elma broke away, dodged his fist, and ran through the kitchen to the hall, and on to the stairs. Vernon started after her, his face purple with rage, but the blood on his shirt stopped him. He didn't have that many good shirts. He needed to stop the flow and take care of his lip. He would take care of Elma later.

As he sat down on the toilet in the bathroom he realized his hands were quivering. He stood to look at his face in the mirror again. His lip was bloody, and his eyes were burning. Vernon didn't recognize himself.

CHAPTER
SEVENTEEN

GUY FINISHED PACKING Adele's clothes and sat on her bed to rest a moment. He had been on his feet most of the day and his hip was aching. His gaze wandered to the pictures on the walls, and he found himself looking at a photograph of someone he would swear was a young William Holden. Reduce the amount of hair and it was *Golden Boy* all over again. But no, Guy saw as he squinted, this guy's name was Jon Bon Jovi. The name clicked and he remembered hearing several of Bon Jovi's songs blasting from the CD player in the corner of the room. Adele had liked all kinds of music, and was something of an aspiring musician herself. She had also written poems and liked to meditate on occasion. While going through the things Adam had brought to him, Guy found a book in which Adele had written random thoughts and long, rambling letters to her dead mother.

Many of the letters concerned her feelings toward Guy. On one page she couldn't stand him, he was the dumbest jerk in the world. The next page he was okay; he needed work, but he was trying. Her ambivalence was obvious to Guy, and though it hurt him to read some of the letters, overall he felt better for having seen them. He knew his daughter didn't hate him, and he suspected she might even have loved him. She just refused to admit it, to herself or anyone else. His absence after the divorce had hurt her deeply, he knew that. The divorce sent her into a downward spiral of alcohol, sex, and depression that became the reason Guy had to get her away from the city. He was responsible for the despair that had driven them here, and for having brought her here; he was responsible for her death.

"Shit," he muttered to himself as his eyes filled up. Michael was probably right. He had been obsessing over her to keep from thinking about Adele, and now that there was no Michael to obsess over, Adele was in his mind constantly. Over and over again he saw her in his arms as he lowered her to the ground out back. The startled expression in her eyes, and the heavy odor of the blood that left her in what seemed like waves. Each time he closed his eyes to sleep he saw her gaping mouth and heard the sound of her gasping for air. He drove himself mad with images of her death, and the imagined last words she had tried to speak to him.

He called Adam twice in the middle of the night to come over and keep him company, just to sit in the same room with him and talk about Adele. Adam didn't mind. He came and brought beer, and together they watched old movies and spoke whenever they felt the urge. Guy asked Adam to drive him by Michael's house once, but he couldn't make himself go up and knock. Not after remembering the expression on her face, the terrible self-loathing in her eyes, the last time she had looked at him. He tried to call her once, but the moment she heard his voice she had hung up, so that was out, too. Guy left her alone after that. He had to. He didn't want her to hate him.

Meanwhile, it was time to get on with his life, and that meant getting back to work. Living came easiest when it was wrapped up in dealing with facts, statements, and events. Guy had been working on some long-range projects at home and using the phone for interviews, but he was ready to return to the *Beacon*'s office and lose himself in the mainstream again. He could use the cane with no problems. He was a little slower, but slow for him was normal for most people.

He glanced at his watch and then picked up the phone by Adele's bed to call the managing editor of the paper.

"I'm ready to come back," Guy said when Bill Glasstock answered.

"Like hell you are," said Bill.

"I can obtain a doctor's release."

"Do it. What about driving? Can you do that yet?"

"I have." He had driven himself to the store on Sunday afternoon. It hurt like hell, but it was good to be behind the wheel again. Willing though his neighbor was, Guy didn't like depending so much on Adam Dupree. He didn't enjoy depending on anyone, and his reluctance was compounded by the guilt he felt over having misjudged the man.

Curious, he had asked Adam exactly how he came by his money, since he didn't appear to work. Adam explained that he lived on a settlement given to him by the electric company. Like a man Adam had once seen on a weekly news program, he too had been a victim of electro-magnetic fields. He had once lived in a house very near some power lines, and it turned out he had lived too close, for the stray electricity from those power lines gave him excruciating headaches and made him irreversibly impotent. The doctors had proved it in court. When he moved to a different house, the headaches went away, but that was all. The suit was settled out of court, and Adam was paid a considerable sum for the loss of his manhood. If he lived simply, he would be comfortable for the rest of his life.

Guy had never heard of the case, but he knew that wasn't unusual. The electric company would keep everything as quiet as possible. Adam didn't appear overly distressed about his impotence, but then Guy supposed he had come to terms with it by now. He was just a big, friendly guy with a poodle to keep him company. He had mentioned a widower uncle somewhere in town, but the man never came to visit and, as far as Guy knew, Adam rarely saw him. Adam stayed at home with Baby and read the paper and watched TV and went for walks.

The very fact of his inactivity led Guy to wonder if the EMF exposure had done more to Adam—he did seem incapable of maintaining attention to anything or anyone for very long—but Adam might have always been like that. Guy didn't know. Adam answered only the questions he wanted to answer, and skilled reporter that Guy was, he couldn't pry any further answers from his neighbor.

The attempts made him hungry to be back and prying at information on a regular basis. He missed the action. And at the office he would at least be able to escape his thoughts. He wouldn't think about Michael, and he would only occasionally think about Adele. His mind would be occupied with other things and other people.

He couldn't tell the managing editor of the Colson *Beacon* all of this, but he did manage to communicate his determination to return to the job. Glasstock sighed in his ear and said to see him when he had a release from his doctor. Guy hung up and phoned the doctor who had treated him in the hospital. The man agreed to see him the next day, but admitted reluctance at signing a release. "We'll see how you look tomorrow. How are you feeling?"

"I feel fine. I'm sore, but—"

"That's not what I meant. How are you emotionally?"

Guy grew irritated. "What kind of question is that? My daughter's dead and I'm alive. How do you expect me to feel?"

"I expect you to be anxious to go back to work so you can distract yourself."

"Isn't that healthy?" Guy said in a dry voice. "Isn't that the way most of us deal with our problems?"

The doctor chose to ignore him. "I'll see you in the morning, Mr. Driscoll."

"You will," Guy said to him.

Annoyed, he replaced the receiver and looked around himself. Most of Adele's things were packed and ready to be sent back to Chicago. Guy didn't know what to do with her clothes and shoes, so Jill's cousin Gail had offered to take them off his hands. She had two growing girls and the clothes would come in handy. A few things Guy had kept, like the book Adele had written in, and some other small treasures that had obviously been important to her: a pair of diamond earrings that had belonged to her mother, and a charm bracelet Guy bought for her eighth birthday. Everything else was going to the Salvation Army store.

"Sorry," Guy said to Jon Bon Jovi as he stood and removed the photographs from the wall and tossed them into a wastebasket.

When the room was clean, Guy dragged the boxes into the living room. Time to call Adam once more, for help in loading the things and getting them to the post office and the Salvation Army store.

Adam came over right away, and together they drove in Adam's truck to a nearby discount store, where Guy hobbled in to buy some strapping tape and a marker to address his boxes. While inside he saw a familiar face. David Eulert was on the stationery aisle, poring over different writing utensils. In his hand was a thin yellow legal pad. When he looked up and saw Guy on his cane, a flicker of recognition briefly lit his eyes. He casually replaced the yellow legal pad and smiled thinly at Guy.

"You're looking well, Mr. Driscoll."

Guy ignored the greeting and looked at the legal pad. "Change your mind?"

"Yes. I did." David Eulert smiled and turned on his heel, leaving Guy alone on the aisle. Guy picked up a marker and some tape and made his way to the registers at the front of the store. There was no sign of David Eulert.

Strange, Guy thought. Once in the truck outside, he asked Adam if he had seen David Eulert come out.

"Who?" Adam asked.

"Never mind." Guy looked around the parking lot and finally saw Eulert sitting in a black Dodge pickup. When Guy looked at him, he turned his face away.

What the hell was he up to? Guy wondered.

"The post office?" Adam asked.

"Yes," Guy said, then, "No. Just drive around the block. I want to see what this guy does."

"Who?"

"David Eulert."

Adam looked confused.

"Just drive," Guy told him, and Adam drove. When they came around the block again, Eulert's pickup was gone. Guy shook his head and directed Adam on.

In the post office, Guy saw yet another familiar face. He spoke the doctor's name, and the man turned. Dr. Spantzer's smile was tired. "Hello, Driscoll. How are you?"

"Better every day," Guy told him. "In fact I'd like to go back to work, but I don't think my doctor is willing to sign a release."

Spantzer winked at him. "Come by my office tomorrow. I'll examine you and see what we can do. Inactivity never did anyone any good, particularly a man in as good a shape as you appear to be in."

Guy smiled. "Thank you. I appreciate it."

"Don't mention it." The doctor's smile wilted a bit then. "You haven't seen Michael for a while, I guess."

"What makes you say that?" Guy asked.

Spantzer lifted a shoulder. "Oliver has taken an unexpected turn for the worse. I don't think Michael has left his side for longer than it takes to eat a sandwich and go to the bathroom."

"You said he wasn't going anywhere," Guy reminded him.

"I know. I don't know what's happened. I think the bullet has moved, but I can't say."

"Is she all right?"

"Michael? She doesn't look good. She needs to go home and get some sleep. Could you handle that?"

Guy shook his head. "She won't let me near her."

Spantzer sighed. "That figures. I suppose I should call her sister. There'll be a battle, but Michael is too exhausted to win. I'll see you tomorrow, Mr. Driscoll."

"Tomorrow." Guy waved and watched him go. He liked the doctor. And he thought Spantzer liked him. Neither had mentioned it, but Guy remembered a visit to a doctor a very long time ago, when he was six years old and had a broken arm. He thought that doctor might have been Spantzer. He thought of mentioning it tomorrow, to see what Spantzer said. He might not remember, but it would be interesting to see if he did.

When he reached the truck, he noticed Adam's face was all screwed up. Guy opened his mouth to ask what was wrong, but at that moment he heard a voice on the radio speak a name familiar to him. He listened and heard it again. It was a local disc jockey, reporting to the police department and the city of Colson that Oliver Bish, the police officer in a coma for nine months and twenty days, had just died at Colson Memorial Hospital.

Adam looked at Guy. "You want to go over there?"

"No," said Guy. "Take me home."

CHAPTER
EIGHTEEN

ELMA WATCHED FROM a second story window as Vernon and Arnold Dupree left to pick up another body. She didn't know exactly who had died, but Vernon's jubilant mood meant it was someone important. He couldn't be happier now that people were dying and money was in the bank. The only dark cloud on his horizon was the business with David Eulert and Michael Bish, and Elma thought she had convinced him the safest action was no action. She wasn't certain, however, because Vernon was so difficult for her to read. One minute pleading with her and behaving like an unsure child, the next pawing at her and asking her to strip.

In that moment, Elma had tried desperately to think what Alissa Diest would have done, but instinct took over and made her behave as only Elma could. She told herself if she could only lie still and be brave long enough to give him what he wanted, then maybe she would have some power over him. It was just so hard. Harder than when her father had pawed and molested her. Perhaps because she had once fancied herself in love with Vernon. And maybe a part of her remained in love with him, she didn't know. He was just so frightening when he behaved the way he had in the kitchen.

Panic had gripped her and all she could think of was to escape.

He was mad at her, she knew. She had seen the black fury in his eyes. But he couldn't stay mad at her for long, not if they had a body coming in. He would need Elma.

When she saw the arrival of the body, however, she had cause to change her mind about Vernon needing her. From her hiding place near the embalming room, she saw the contents of the unzipped mortuary bag. It was a man, and men didn't need their hair done. Elma had to wonder who this man was. He looked younger than the average dead person. She crept from her hiding place and slowly entered the room.

Vernon looked up and smiled broadly when he saw her. Elma relaxed. He would be all right for a while. He was still in a good mood.

"Guess who this is, Elma?"

Elma shook her head. She didn't know.

"Oliver Bish. Michael Bish's husband. He finally left us." He looked at Elma and winked. "I wonder if he had some help? I hear Michael and Guy Driscoll are sleeping together. Perhaps Michael grew tired of waiting."

His brow became furrowed then. "Michael didn't want him to come to me. She caused such a scene the doctor had to sedate her. Her and Driscoll. God only knows what these people think about. Would they rather ship the bodies to Kansas City to be embalmed? What do they think I'm going to do, crap on their loved one's faces? I'm an artist, for God's sake. I take moldered flesh and turn it to porcelain. Take this man, for example. He's been dying for a long time now, witness the atrophy of his muscles and the pallor of his skin. . . . What I will do, Elma, is restore him to the man he was . . . the man Michael fell in love with. I can do that, you know. Just watch, my precious love. Just you watch me."

Elma stared at him, not entirely sure if he was speaking to her or not. Precious love?

He smiled at her once again. "Shut the door and come over

here. You can sit on the stool behind me and watch me work. I won't have to tell you to be quiet so I can concentrate, will I? That's what I like about you, Elma. I never have to worry about noise with you."

Elma didn't trust his smile. She stayed right where she was. Vernon didn't notice; he went busily to work, throwing himself into the project with an absorption that Elma eventually found amazing and worthy of her admiration. He was truly gifted when it came to preparing corpses. His mother had known it. She had trained Vernon from the time he was a small boy.

Watching him, Elma began to doubt her own convictions. How could she be angry with him for wanting so desperately to hold on to his heritage? For doing anything to preserve the business he had grown up with and struggled to hold on to by all legitimate means. He had never done anything unlawful before, not that she knew of, anyway. Oh, she had seen him punch an occasional corpse when angry, but that was only frustration at being under his mother's thumb. That thumb was gone now, preserved and prepared by Vernon himself. He was his own man.

When he was finished, Vernon seemed suddenly drained of all energy. His face was lined and tired as he pulled the sheet over the naked body and walked across the room to turn off the light. Suddenly he remembered Elma. He turned the light on again and gestured for her to follow him out of the room. "Sorry," he said, "I forgot you were there."

Elma went out with him, and in the hall she stopped and touched his arm. She gestured back to the embalming room, then she made an OK sign with her fingers.

He looks good, she was trying to tell him.

"Yes," Vernon said, and he smiled wearily at her. Suddenly he frowned and looked down the hall to the entrance door. He looked at Elma again and said, "Would you get that? Someone is at the door."

Elma shook her head, but Vernon had already turned away

and was moving toward his office. Helplessly, Elma stamped her feet. Vernon kept moving. Elma had no choice but to go and see who was at the door.

The woman standing outside seemed just as surprised to see Elma. "Hello," she said. "I'm Sean Parkinson. Michael Bish is my sister. I've brought some clothes for Oliver to wear."

Elma bobbed her head and stood aside so the woman could come in. The woman was already speaking again, but Elma couldn't understand her because her head was turned away. Elma tapped her on the arm and the woman looked curiously at her. Elma pointed to her ears and shook her head. Next she pointed to her mouth and shook her head. The woman blinked in confusion. "You don't . . . speak?"

Elma passed a hand across her mouth.

"Or hear?"

She shook her head again.

"Oh, I'm sorry. I'm really very sorry. I . . . is Mr. Diest available? Do you understand me? Mr. Diest?"

Elma pointed to Sean Parkinson's lips and nodded.

"I see. You read lips, is that right?"

Elma smiled.

"All right, fine. Can you tell me where I might find Mr. Diest?"

Elma pointed toward his office, and led the way down the hall. She felt absurdly proud of herself for dealing with the woman. She had never dealt with any member of the public before. Never. Vernon would be proud of her, too. She showed Sean Parkinson into Vernon's office and stood just inside the door, waiting for Vernon to look at her.

He never looked at her. His eyes were for Sean Parkinson alone. His smile became warm and pleasant, all trace of tiredness gone. His hands reached across the desk to clasp Sean's, his touch excruciatingly tender. Elma felt her chest tighten as she watched him. The hurt she suffered was surprising. She hated him. She despised everything he did. But he could still hurt her.

Vernon was asking Sean how Michael was, and if she would feel up to the casket selection anytime soon. Elma couldn't see Sean's face, but she assumed she had asked for a brochure, because Vernon reached inside his desk to remove one and hand it to her. Evidently, Michael would make her decision from the brochure, the way Guy Driscoll had. She saw Sean hand the suit she carried over to Vernon, and then Elma left the room. She didn't want to watch him anymore.

Even Sean Parkinson, the sister of Vernon's mortal enemy, was swayed by his charm. She smiled and blushed and was completely fooled by the mortician. Elma went to sit on the stairs at the end of the hall. When Sean emerged from the office she passed Elma and waved goodbye. Elma waved back, glad to see her going so soon. Vernon followed the woman out a moment later, and when he saw Elma sitting there he patted her absently on the shoulder. Elma shrugged away his hand.

Vernon stomped the floor hard. "Don't do that," his lips said to her.

Elma gave him the finger.

Vernon's nostrils flared, and Elma would swear she saw red in the cavities when he reached for her. She dodged and ducked, thinking to run under his arms and head for the second floor, but this time he was too quick for her. He caught her by the back of the neck and slammed her hard against the wall in the hall. Elma's cheek throbbed with pain, and she knew there would be no escape this time. He remained clear of her sharp teeth and easily warded off her fists and kicking feet. She went rigid and stayed that way, hoping he would tire of the game and release her to return to the embalming room to dress the corpse of Oliver Bish.

He did not. Instead he pressed the length of himself against her backside and pushed her even harder against the wall. He kissed her cheeks, her ears, and her neck as she tried to turn her head away from his mouth. He groped at her breasts and between her legs, and she could feel him yank down on her underwear. Elma opened her mouth, but no audible sound came out as he unzipped his pants and held her up in front of him. When he entered her she squeezed her eyes shut and tried to imagine herself blending into and becoming part of the wall. It was impossible. He breathed hard behind her, and she could feel his lips moving against the skin of her neck, saying what, she would never know.

On and on he went, grinding her against the wall and touching her as if they were lovers. Elma felt the edges of her vision begin to darken, and she felt herself sliding away from the wall and against him. Vernon's limbs jerked spasmodically, followed by the rest of him. He thrust into her several more times, then he stopped and slowly withdrew. Elma was close to passing out when he turned her around to face him. When he kissed her on the mouth, she did pass out.

She awakened just moments later and found herself in Vernon's bed on the third floor. She was naked. She looked up with a start and saw Vernon sitting on the edge of the bed watching her. His expression was blank. When he saw her looking at him he said, "I don't know why I did that, Elma. It's hard to explain, but when you fight me, when you make me angry, I have to prove I can . . . *minimize* you, I guess is the word I'm looking for. Ever since you started hating me, controlling you is all I can think about. You were never attractive to me before. I never wanted you, though I know you wanted me. Now I do want you, and you don't want me. The strangest thing is, I feel bad about hurting you, but I liked the sex part and I want to do it again."

Elma covered her eyes and shook her head. Vernon touched her anyway. As his hands covered her breasts, she looked at him, her eyes pleading. He patted her hand and said, "I know you understand everything I've said to you. Just saying it made me understand it. It's going to happen again and you know it. You can fight me if you like, Elma, but please try not to faint again, all right?"

CHAPTER
NINETEEN

MICHAEL WAS GROGGY when she awakened, and she imagined for a moment she was still at the hospital and sitting beside Oliver's bed. When she saw her own wallpaper, her own bedroom, she frowned in confusion. Then everything came back to her. She groaned aloud and put her hands to her face. Her shoulders shook.

It had happened because of her. Because of her and Guy Driscoll. Oliver simply hadn't been the same after the night Michael had gone to Guy's house. It was as if he had sensed what was happening, as if he had known she was thinking about another man and decided to stop fighting and let go. Michael couldn't live with herself, the guilt was eating her up inside. Oliver had probably believed she didn't love him anymore. He probably thought she was slowly going to abandon him, so he had saved her the trouble and simply turned off his will to live.

Michael crammed her fists into her mouth and choked back a sob. She hadn't meant to do that to him. She hadn't meant to hurt him. She had no excuse other than loneliness, and that was no excuse at all. Not really. She had been lonely before. She had been lonely plenty of times in the last nine months.

But never as lonely as she felt right now.

Another long moan escaped her and she turned to bury her face in the pillow. A moment later a soft voice spoke to her, and she lifted her head to see Sean enter the room. Her sister sat down on the bed and reached for Michael's hand. "I've brought the brochure from Diest's Funeral Home. Would you like to look at it now, or will you eat something first?"

Michael sat up and wiped her cheeks. "I'm not hungry, Sean."

"Do you want to take a shower and change your clothes? I'll still be here when you're finished."

Michael smiled wearily at her sister before glancing down at herself. She had been wearing the same clothes for two days. She told Sean she would shower and change.

"I'll go and start some coffee," Sean said. "I took the suit you suggested to the funeral home."

"You did? While I was sleeping?"

"You've been asleep for twelve hours, Michael. You were exhausted."

Michael frowned. "What time is it?"

"Almost three-thirty."

The passage of time seemed unreal to Michael. Suddenly she looked at her sister. "Did you speak to Vernon Diest?"

"Yes, of course. I also spoke to his assistant, though she couldn't speak to me. I didn't know he had an assistant until today, though now that I think of it, I do recall a daughter being mentioned when Vernon's mother married the man from Tennessee. That must be her, which would make her Vernon's sister by marriage. She's a pretty little thing, really, or she would be if she weren't so thin. I don't care what they say, you *can* be too thin."

Michael was frowning again. A sister? "You say she doesn't speak?"

"Or hear, from what she was able to communicate to me. She does read lips, though."

Michael found that interesting, though she couldn't immediately say why. Something niggled at her, something that wanted to push through, but it didn't quite penetrate. She shoved it out of her mind and left the bed to go into the bathroom and shower.

She found herself wondering what she would do with herself that day, since there was no Oliver to go and sit with in the hospital. There was the casket to attend to (her lip curled as she thought of the man in possession of her dead husband at that moment), and there was the funeral to arrange. Afterward there would be thank you cards to write, but what after that? The police force obviously wasn't going to reinstate her; Michael would have heard something from them by now. Or perhaps they were waiting for her to get over this latest crisis before telling her they were officially releasing her from her position as a law enforcement officer.

She found she didn't care. The people she had worked with weren't the good friends she had imagined. She enjoyed being a police officer, but if the KBI investigation hadn't cleared her name, then she supposed nothing could. Vernon Diest had won that particular battle.

Michael had no idea where to look for another job. She thought briefly of leaving Colson and attempting to find work in another law enforcement department, but one inquiry into police records would be sufficient to send her on her way. Officers with records like hers weren't exactly sought after personnel. It didn't matter if none of it was true.

Thank God Oliver wasn't alive to see her come to this end. He would have been mad as hell at the department. He might even have quit in protest over her treatment. Oliver had been like that.

He had been many things. He had been kind and loving and often temperamental. He had been brash, and funny, and a prankster. He had been a little boy in a man's body, with a little boy's ideals and a little boy's heart. In the time they were together, Michael loved him madly.

"I'm sorry," she whispered into the spray of the shower. "I'm sorry I let you down, Oliver."

When she came out of the shower she thought for the first time of Guy Driscoll. Her mind instinctively cringed away, and she struggled to think of anything else. She didn't want to think about Guy. She never wanted to see him again. She couldn't. She would look at him and see her own guilt.

She wrapped herself in a robe and went out to the kitchen to pour a cup of coffee. Sean was poring over the casket brochure. She pointed to it and said, "This one looks beautiful. Appalachian oak."

Michael took her cup and looked over Sean's shoulder. "That is nice."

"It's the best of the line," Sean said, and Michael nodded.

"What do you think? I've looked all through this thing, and that one looks the best. Do you want to look at it?"

"No," Michael told her. "If you say it's the best, then it's the best. You can call Vernon Diest and tell him."

Sean looked at her. "Are you sure?"

"I'm sure. And sign everything for me. I don't want any contact with the man."

"All right," said Sean. "I'll have him make out everything in my name. You can pay me and I'll pay him. You won't even have to look at him. Are you all right, Michael?"

She nodded.

"You don't look all right. You haven't looked all right for several days now, even before Oliver died. You look depressed, Michael."

"My husband just died," Michael said. "I have a right to be depressed, don't I?"

Sean frowned at her sister. "You know exactly what I'm talking about. You won't even look at me when you talk to me, and that's not like you at all. You haven't had any thoughts of suicide, or anything like that, have you?"

Michael lifted her head and forced herself to meet her sister's eyes. "Yes, I have had thoughts of suicide, but I believe that's rather normal in a case like this one. Don't worry, all my guns have been confiscated, and I don't have any drugs or rope in the house. My garage has a hole in it, and I haven't seen a real razor blade in ten years." When she saw Sean's horrified expression, she tried to smile. "Relax, Sean. I'll be fine."

"Swear it," Sean said, her eyes worried.

"I swear."

"All right, then. I didn't want to tell you this because of your present emotional state, but I don't want you to hear it from anyone else. David Eulert talked to his lawyers yesterday about filing suit against you. He intends to sue you for slander."

Michael dropped her head and covered her face with her hands. "When is it going to stop, Sean?" she asked helplessly. "What have I done to deserve this?"

Sean had no answer. She picked up the phone to call Vernon Diest and left Michael at the table with her cup of coffee. Michael took her hands from her face and pushed the cup away. She had no energy to get dressed. She was too depressed.

CHAPTER
TWENTY

DAVID EULERT LOCKED himself in his parents' bathroom and wept inconsolably when he heard the news about Oliver Bish. Oliver was the only man he had ever truly loved, and the pain of his rejection and David's sorrow over having shot him would follow the ex-policeman to his grave. David never meant to shoot Oliver. He hadn't awakened one morning and decided to kill his partner and best friend. It was an accident of rage, a horrible fog of jealousy that had descended and sent David into exile and left Oliver lying in the police station parking lot in a lake of blood.

The two had been friends from the day they met. David laughed at everything Oliver said, and Oliver made David feel as if he were the bright and funny jock everyone said he was. He shone when he was around Oliver. He had never felt so proud and manly and masculine as when he was working and riding in a car with Oliver Bish. The two of them made a splendid pair, David always thought. Both were tall, muscular gods with perfectly formed physiques and glorious, gleaming smiles. People who saw them together always paused in admiration, and David loved the feeling of pride it gave him to be regarded in such a manner.

Naturally, there was a downside to these days of glory, and that downside was the time Oliver spent with Michael Ogilvie. David would ask his partner leading questions, trying to get him to joke about Michael the way he did about other women, but Oliver would never take the bait. When David realized Oliver was serious about Michael, he felt the first real envy of his life. He wasn't ready yet to admit that he himself had fallen *in love* with his partner, but everything Oliver did with Michael seemed a personal affront to him.

David began to verbally slam Michael whenever possible, constantly reminding Oliver of her penchant for causing problems because she had trouble remembering she was a woman. Oliver would only laugh at him and tell him he was stuck in another century. Michael could do anything she wanted to do. There were other women on the police force and he had nothing against them.

David had nothing against them because they weren't engaged to marry Oliver.

David was Oliver's best man. At their wedding he watched with gritted teeth as Oliver took Michael into his arms and kissed her. His heart was ready to burst at sight of the smile that spread across Oliver's face afterward, and when the bride and groom danced together at the reception, David felt slightly ill at the sight of them. For weeks afterward he was sullen and full of contempt for any remark the happy Oliver cared to make. Oliver shrugged him off most of the time, but he was curious about David's behavior and when he finally asked his friend just what the hell was wrong, David refused to tell him.

Until the day Oliver said the first unflattering thing about Michael that David had ever heard. It was in the morning, right after the sergeant had dismissed them and they were getting into their cars to start patrol. A fellow officer hailed Oliver in the parking lot and asked him if he had watched the middleweight bout on television the night before. Oliver said no. The wife had been in the mood to talk last night, *all* night, so there was no television.

The other officer laughed and went on to his car. David started the engine and looked at Oliver. "Talk about what?"

"Babies and stuff. You know."

"She wants to have kids?"

"Yeah."

"Do you?"

Oliver shrugged. It didn't matter to him. Whatever she wanted, he guessed. He couldn't exactly say no, now could he? She'd be upset if he did.

"So let her get upset," David had said. "If you don't want kids, there's no sense in having them until you do. I sure as hell don't want any for a while."

"Yeah, me either," Oliver said, his voice thoughtful. "But you know how Mike is. She's got to plan everything out and have it just so."

David had reached over and laid a hand on Oliver's thigh then. "I'm here if you need to talk to me, Big O. I want you to know that. If you ever have problems, or if you just want to go out for a beer, call me. I guess I'm trying to say I miss you."

Oliver thought nothing of the hand on his thigh, so David gave it a squeeze before he removed his hand. A few nights later Oliver called and wanted to go out for a beer. He needed to get away, he said. David met him in a bar and they drank and played shuffleboard and darts and had a good time with each other. In the parking lot, the drunken David had reached over and put his arms around Oliver. "I love you," he said to the other man. "I really love you."

Oliver had patted him on the back. "I love you too, Dave. You're like the brother I never had."

"No," David argued. "I don't wanna be your brother, Big O."

And then he had attempted to kiss Oliver.

For the next few days there was a tenseness between them as they patrolled and made their stops. Oliver didn't talk about the night at the bar. He told David as far as he was concerned, it never happened. "You're my friend and you're a good cop. I'd like to keep you as my partner, but I can only do that if we both forget and don't talk about it again, okay?"

It wasn't okay with David. The truth had been told. Oliver knew David loved him. How could he pretend not to care how David felt? Did he think David would be happy just to go on sitting beside him in a car day after day and never be able to touch or talk to him?

On a Friday about three months after Oliver's wedding, David stood at his locker and unabashedly watched as Oliver put on his uniform. Oliver felt David's admiring gaze and he turned to glare at him. The glare did it. After review David slowly followed his partner out to the car, deliberately lagging so the lot would empty before he made it outside.

Oliver was standing beside the car and waiting when David emerged. He looked at David's drawn gun and told him to stop fooling around and put it in its holster so they could go.

"And one more thing," Oliver had said. "Don't ever let me catch you looking at me like that again. Someone could see you." Oliver had turned his back then and opened the car door to slide behind the wheel.

David pointed his revolver and fired.

And now, almost ten months later, the act was finally complete. Oliver was dead.

A knock on the bathroom door brought David's head up.

"Dave? Are you in there?"

It was his wife . . . the woman David had married to shut everyone up after Michael Bish made her accusations. He still couldn't believe Oliver had actually told someone about him.

"I'm going to take a shower," he said loudly. "Use the back bathroom if you have to go."

"I don't have to go. I wondered where you were, and I thought I heard a funny noise, like crying."

"I was blowing my nose," David told her. "It's too damn dry in this house. I'll be out in a little while."

Lying to his wife came easily to David. His entire marriage was based on a lie. Sex with her was the biggest lie of all. Fantasizing about Oliver Bish was the only way David could come to orgasm. Most of the time he faked it. Thank God he had managed to make her pregnant right away. The pregnancy had stilled most of the wagging tongues in Colson and made a lot of people look askance at Michael Bish. He had slept with other girls in his life as well, three of them, anyway, and all lived in Colson. He couldn't exactly brag about his performances with them, since he hadn't gotten off with any of them. In fact, he had gone limp inside the second girl. But they weren't the sort to come forward and tell tales of comparison, so he was all right.

David had experienced sex with only one male in Colson, a counselor he met as a troubled teenager. Sex had occurred twice, both times at the man's mobile home on the outskirts of town. The counselor was retired now and living in Arizona. David never thought of him, and he had met no one else he was sexually interested in until he came to know Oliver Bish. Oliver was the only man David had ever actually wanted to have sex with, but upon his self-imposed exile he had discovered a different life and a different attitude in Springfield.

Finding young blond males who looked like Oliver was easy. After moving to the city, David found many who were eager to give him what he wanted. In nine months he had more sex than he had had in his entire life. But it was empty, and he hated being a nobody in a city the size of Springfield. He missed the popularity he had known in Colson. He missed being respected and looked up to by the townspeople. He missed being a hometown hero.

So he found himself a wife and made her pregnant so he could come back. The vacation bit had worked for a while, but now he had to figure out what to tell his parents about losing his job. He was fired because he had been caught having sex with a young boy in his patrol car. He told his wife he was laid off due to budget cuts. He guessed he could tell his parents the same thing. They would believe him. They always had. Timing was the thing.

His dad would be upset, of course, because it meant David and his wife would need somewhere to stay indefinitely, and good old Dad couldn't exactly boot out a pregnant woman. David's relationship with his father suffered greatly after Michael made her accusations. David's father, an ex-marine himself, had begun to look suspiciously at his son, and in the days before David departed for Springfield, there had been many loud arguments.

The pregnant wife had been meant to soothe his father as much as anyone, but David didn't know if it worked. His father still watched him.

David had so much to thank Michael Bish for. Really. She had destroyed his entire existence, and it was time to try and repay her.

Now would be the perfect time, he realized. Now, when her grief was fresh and stinging. No one would be surprised if the guilty widow did something crazy following the death of her husband.

With the possible exception of Guy Driscoll.

But David wasn't worried about him. Anything Guy Driscoll thought he knew about Michael would be irrelevant in the light of events to come. He might even be considered a contributor to the cause.

David hadn't been able to purchase the pen and pad he had wanted. Driscoll had seen him in the store, and if the man was as sharp as David thought he was, then he would remember seeing the paper before.

It was stupid to have put the things down. If David had been thinking right, he would have gone ahead and paid for them and simply used some other paper.

But he hadn't been thinking, and he had been so rattled to see Driscoll standing there and staring at him that he had followed instinct and left the store.

He would have to be careful. He couldn't rush in blindly in

his own grief and perhaps foul things up by forgetting one tiny element, something that, overlooked, would prove to be crucial. Like Vernon Diest, everything had to be prepared beforehand. Vernon at least he could count on.

David stood up and took off his clothes to get into the shower. He always thought better in the shower. The warm spray seemed to get his mind working.

He let the water pound directly onto his head for a moment while he thought.

Vernon Diest. He would have Oliver right now. And he would probably have someone digging Oliver's grave.

David closed his eyes as a picture formed in his mind. A picture of Oliver's casket being lowered into the hard, rocky earth.

He shivered and reached for the soap.

CHAPTER
TWENTY-ONE

VERNON WAS IN LOVE. Or, more to the point, he was deeply in lust. The colder and more resistant to him Elma was, the more he wanted her. He did things to her and made her do things to him that he had only dreamed of doing with other women. For the twelve hours he kept her in his bed, he was master, liege, and lord, and he threw himself into the role with an abandon that was both terrifying and exhilarating. He delighted in the sight of her naked body. He reveled in the smell of his hands and parts of his skin because they smelled like her and because they smelled like sex. He loved the way she closed her eyes and opened her mouth, the way her hands gripped the edges of the mattress, and his only regret was that he could not hear her moan and groan. He was certain he had brought her to orgasm at least twice. He had felt the contractions of her vaginal muscles. Quickly he looked at her face, but nothing in her eyes confirmed his suspicions.

Her brown orbs were empty, and they remained so throughout the hours he spent with her. When he finally allowed her to rest, she fell immediately into a deep, troubled sleep. He sat on the bed and looked at her, at the bruises that had arisen on her skin, and felt nothing like remorse. She was his to do with as he pleased. He would take care of her, she didn't have to worry about that. He would clothe her and feed her and see that her needs were met. And she would see that his needs were met.

Vernon was more relaxed and at peace with himself than he had been in months. He was back on track and in control again. All it took was twelve hours in bed with a deaf mute.

He chuckled to himself and got up. He felt fine. He wasn't tired in the least. He glanced back to Elma again and saw her lids flutter. Vernon went to place a tender kiss on her forehead.

"Mine," he whispered to her. "Like it or not."

Elma shifted in her sleep and turned her head.

Vernon left her and went down the long hall to his mother's room. He opened the closet doors and turned on the light. Time to get everything out. Elma could wear whatever she wanted. He knew she needed some underwear.

He took all his mother's dresses out and laid them on the bed. While doing so he found some garments he didn't like, had never liked, and he tossed these in the corner. He didn't want Elma wearing them. She could take her pick of what was left.

Next he examined the shoes in the bottom of the closet. He thought Elma's feet might be slightly smaller, but his mother had often encouraged the girl to wear her shoes, so he supposed it was possible for her to walk in them without falling down. Many of the shoes went with specific dresses, and if Elma was to wear the dresses she would need the shoes. Anything would be better than those black flats she wore with everything.

He turned his attention to his mother's dresser and found a brush and comb and other items for hair lying on top. Elma would need those. Her brown hair was really quite thick, Vernon had discovered. And such a nice color.

He gathered the things from the dresser and took them to his room. Then he went back for the dresses and the shoes, which he placed on one side of his own closet. Elma would be surprised when she awakened to find everything right there waiting for her.

After picking out an outfit for her to wear, he put some food on the table in the kitchen and then went downstairs to attend to Oliver Bish. Viewing was to begin in exactly thirty minutes, and Vernon didn't have the man dressed yet, much less in the Appalachian oak coffin Sean Parkinson had called him about. He placed a quick call to his neighbor, then he dressed the corpse as quickly as he could and added a few finishing touches with makeup. Arnold Dupree came over, and together they went to the second floor and brought down the heavy oak coffin. After they had placed Oliver in the coffin, Arnold wiped his forehead and said, "I haven't wanted to say anything to you before now, Mr. Diest, because I figured she was none of my business. But I've been thinking lately, and I—"

"Can we talk later?" Vernon said impatiently. "I've got to get him into the viewing room and arrange the flowers that have arrived."

"I'll be real quick," Arnold promised. "It's about Elma. If it's okay with you, I'd like to hire her to come and look after my place."

Vernon stopped and went very still as he stared at the other man. "Elma?" he said finally. "You want to hire Elma?"

"To clean and maybe even to cook," said Arnold. "She can sleep in my wife's old sewing room, or she can go on staying here. I just need some help around the house. I think she needs some help, too."

Vernon blinked. "How . . . do you know Elma?"

Arnold's face creased in a frown. "What do you mean, how do I know Elma? We're neighbors, ain't we? She got a garden on the other side of the fence from mine. Hell, I give her seeds."

"A garden?" Vernon echoed, his face a blank. He cleared his throat. "Has she ever . . . does she talk to you?"

"When I remember to bring a pen and paper." Arnold stood back. "You're looking kind of funny, Mr. Diest. If you think I'm suggesting something improper here, you can forget that right now. I like Elma and I always have, but I don't mean for her to do anything but keep my house. Now are we clear on that?"

"Yes," Vernon said calmly. "What did you mean when you said you thought she needs some help? What kind of help?"

Arnold shrugged. "I ain't saying nothing against you, Mr. Diest, but that girl looks like she's starving to death. I figure to feed her good and get her looking healthy again."

Vernon stiffened and straightened his back. He looked squarely at Arnold. "I'll call you when I'm ready to transport him to the cemetery. All right?"

"Fine. And Elma?"

"I'll talk to her and see what she says. I can't make you any promises. I do need her here, you know."

"I realize that. If she goes to work for me, she can come over at any time. Just like I do."

Vernon heard the hint in the last sentence. He smiled at the older man. "You can't know how much I appreciate your dropping everything to come over when I need you. It's very big of you, Mr. Dupree. I'm in your debt."

Arnold smiled back at him. "Let me know what she says."

"I will. Goodbye now."

When the man was gone, Vernon's hands clenched into fists. He lifted an arm to strike the corpse in the oak coffin, but he thought better of it. Instead, he made himself gather the flowers delivered to the vestibule by the local florists, and he placed them around the coffin. When he was finished, he unlocked the side exit of the chapel and viewing rooms and looked at his watch. One o'clock. Time for the first wave.

He wasn't disappointed. Family came first. Mother, sisters, and aunts. The remainder of the afternoon was filled with people who drifted in to see Oliver Bish. Police officers, distant relatives, high school buddies, teachers, old girlfriends, and sundry others, all of them wearing long faces for their fallen friend. Vernon refilled the tissue box twice before it was time to close the doors and go up to dinner.

Upstairs he found Elma in his bathroom, sitting in the tub. When he looked inquiringly at her she gestured for him to bring her a pad and pen. He did and she wrote two words: *I'm sore.*

"Sorry," Vernon said flatly. He sat down on the edge of the tub and touched her breast. She turned away from him and he smiled. He took her chin and forced her to look at him. "You talked to Arnold Dupree long before you talked to me. Why?"

Her brows met. She wrote: *He gives me seeds for my garden.*

Vernon snorted. "What garden?"

Behind graves in oldest section of cemetery.

Vernon crumpled the piece of paper. "Stay away from him. He's trouble, Elma. He's watching us. He watches everything we do. I think he'd like to separate us and get you to talk about me."

Elma rolled her eyes at him. Vernon instinctively lifted his hand, but he only smoothed her hair with it. His smile was bitter. "I can't even find the will to hit you. Not after what we've just experienced. Did you find the clothes I brought in for you?"

She nodded. Her eyes were uncertain.

"We can share a closet," he informed her. "I want you to sleep with me from now on. In my bed."

Elma closed her eyes and shook her head.

"Oh, yes," said Vernon. "You will. I'm going to feed and take care of you. Just what you've always wanted, Elma."

She opened her eyes and looked at the clear water in the tub. Vernon forced her to look at him. "We're together now, me and you."

Elma's lip curled just the tiniest bit, and Vernon leaned over to kiss it. He laughed when she splashed him.

"Come out of there now," he said. "Let's have some dinner together before I have to go back down."

Elma pointed to her pubic mound and made a face.

"Sore. Yes, I know. You told me. What can I do?"

She held up her thumb and forefinger and rubbed them together.

"Money? Is that what you want?"

She shook her head. No.

"Cream? Lotion?" Then he smiled. "Vaseline. You want some Vaseline?"

She dropped her shoulders and sighed. Then she nodded.

It obviously wasn't what she wanted, but the paper pad was empty and she was going to settle for Vaseline. Vernon stood and went through his medicine chest. He tossed her the Vaseline and stepped out of the bathroom just as his phone rang. He walked over to pick up the receiver. "Hello?"

"This is David Eulert," said a male voice.

"Mr. Eulert," Vernon repeated tonelessly.

"Has my attorney been in contact with you yet, Mr. Diest?"

"No."

"I'm sure he soon will be. Have you been thinking about your testimony?"

"You have nothing on me," Vernon blurted. "You have a lot of supposition, but that's all you have."

"That may be all I need, Mr. Diest. I hear you're going to bury a friend of mine soon. Which section of the cemetery will he be in?"

"He'll be with his own people. Will you be attending the service?"

"Afraid not. His wife won't allow it. I may come by this evening, though, if you're agreeable. I won't stay long. This is the best way I know to avoid a difficult confrontation with the woman. She can be extremely unreasonable, as I'm sure you know."

"What time shall I expect you?" Vernon asked.

"It depends."

"On what?"

"Many things. Goodbye, Mr. Diest."

Vernon hung up the phone. His stomach threatened to begin quivering. He turned and saw Elma looking curiously at him. She was wearing the dress he had picked out for her. She looked sweet and pretty.

He drew in a deep breath and relaxed. He went to put his arms around her and she immediately stiffened. Vernon ignored it and held her close to him, rocking her slightly.

"I won't let anything happen to us," he said against her hair. Then he looked at her. "That was David Eulert on the phone. He's up to something, I don't know what. I gave him nothing."

A look of relief entered Elma's eyes. Her mouth even curved a little.

Vernon smiled at her. "He'll do what he likes, of course, but he'll do it without me."

Elma's mouth tightened. She looked pleadingly at Vernon. He shook his head.

"I can't do anything about it. I don't know what he's planning, so I couldn't possibly stop him."

Elma picked up the phone receiver and pretended to dial. Then she handed the receiver to him. Vernon replaced it. "Are you insane? I'm not calling anyone. What would I tell them?"

Michael, Elma mouthed. *Call her.*

Vernon frowned and turned away. Elma whirled away from him to find something to write on. She found a grocery receipt on the counter and scribbled, *Tell Michael.*

"Tell her what? That I suspect David Eulert is up to something? I'm sure she's going to believe me."

Elma lifted her dress and went to the phone. She placed the fabric over the receiver and put a hand to her throat.

Vernon watched her. "You want me to disguise my voice, is that it? Forget it, Elma. Why should I help Michael Bish? Why should I do anything for her? I don't care what happens to the woman."

Elma's hands twitched. Her face reddened with anger. She opened drawers in the kitchen until she found a large piece of paper. On the paper she wrote: *I can't live here anymore. I can't stay here with you. You hurt me. You made me sore. You're not the man I thought you were. You kill and hurt for money and spite. Your mother would be ashamed of you, Vernon.*

She gave him the paper and waited, her lip quivering. Vernon read it and crushed it in his hand. He looked at her and said, "Where will you go? To Arnold Dupree?"

She nodded.

Vernon slapped her across the face. Elma shuddered and stood her ground, her eyes defiant. Vernon looked at the red imprint of his hand on her cheek and wondered suddenly how he had come to be in this position. He wondered why he couldn't find his old contempt for her, and why he was suddenly so certain he couldn't go on without her. He couldn't believe what she had come to mean to him. It wasn't true or real or anything like love was supposed to be. She had forced him into it, he was certain. He would never have come to want her naturally. He was above wanting someone so simple as her.

But the thought of her leaving him panicked him like nothing else could. And judging from the loathing in her eyes, she would be gone the first time he left the house.

He walked over to the phone and picked up the receiver. "If I call Michael Bish, will you stay?" he asked. "No more threats of leaving?"

After a moment of hesitation, Elma nodded.

CHAPTER
TWENTY-TWO

GUY LOWERED HIS binoculars and felt ashamed of himself for attempting to look at Michael in such a manner.

But it was the only way he could see her, and try as he would, he couldn't rid himself of the desire to do that. It made him feel better to see her, especially when he caught her looking in the direction of his house. It proved to him that she still thought of him, and he reassured himself that someday they would come together again, on terms that better suited both of them. In the meantime, he could only look at her through his binoculars and listen to himself sigh.

He lifted the glasses again and saw Michael walk through her living room to pick up the telephone. A deep frown creased her face as she listened, and then she dropped the receiver in what looked like shock. She fumbled to pick it up again and hang up, and then she reached for her purse and a sweater. She was going somewhere. He could see only part of the living room, and the part he saw was heavily shadowed, but he assumed she was leaving the house.

His curiosity piqued, Guy decided to follow her. He quickly hopped out to his own car and started the engine. He caught up with her where the main street intersected with his own and he saw her turn toward town. She didn't see his car behind hers, or if she did she pretended not to notice. Guy let himself fall back once they were on the busy main street. He cruised several cars behind and eventually saw her make a turn into the parking lot of the high school. She hurriedly parked her car and ran inside an entrance that looked like it might be a gymnasium. Guy rolled to a stop just inside the school drive and sat. Her sister worked at the high school. He wondered if something had happened to her.

He couldn't think of any other explanation for Michael to drop the phone the way she had and drive directly to the school.

After twenty minutes had passed, Guy started his car and steered away from the drive. There was no emergency, evidently, and he didn't want Michael to come out and find him sitting there. He drove slowly away from the school, keeping his eye on the rearview mirror. When he saw a familiar black Dodge pickup pull swiftly onto the main street in front of him, he frowned. The truck belonged to David Eulert, and the driving was more than a little erratic.

Guy watched, and after a moment he pushed the Volvo forward. He didn't have anything better to do. Might as well try to get a reaction quote from Eulert concerning Oliver Bish's death.

The black Dodge pickup went directly to Diest's Mortuary and Chapel. When Guy saw the truck go inside the gates, he fell back and stepped on the brakes. Eulert was going to pay his last respects to his dead partner. The way he was driving, he was probably drunk. Guy backed his car up and turned it around to go home.

Inside the black Dodge pickup, Michael slowly regained consciousness. Her mind automatically replayed the last images she remembered in an effort to figure out where she was now. She had been walking through the school, heading toward Sean's classroom, where the janitor who had called

Michael said he found her lying unconscious. As she moved frantically down the hall in search of her sister, someone grabbed Michael from behind and shoved her into a darkened classroom. There was a sharp, painful stick in her side, the point of a knife, and then a hoarse, slurred voice commanded her to do exactly as it said.

Fear had pierced Michael's depression as the blade pierced her skin. She didn't want to die. She did as the voice said and wrote what seemed like nonsensical words on a piece of paper. So frightened was she that none of it had made sense while she was writing it. Now it did. On a piece of paper she had written: *Forgive me for all the horrible lies. I'm sorry.* And then she signed her name.

She couldn't see where she was now because of the blindfold on her head. After she had written the words on the paper, two strong arms took her in what could only be described as a sleeper hold. Her air was cut off and she lost consciousness.

Now her neck ached. Her throat was dry and scratchy. She tried to move her hands and found she couldn't. She felt fabric on her wrists, and the thought of its purpose chilled her. The fabric under the restraints would leave no ligature marks on her wrists. This person had thought of everything.

"Am I . . ." she began, but she had to swallow some saliva to wet her parched throat and start over. "Am I supposed to be committing suicide?"

If she was, then she couldn't understand why the person hadn't killed her already. He'd had her unconscious and at his mercy once. Why not then?

There was no answer to her query. She held herself still to listen, and she finally reasoned that she was in the back of some vehicle, a van or a truck. There was a carpetlike material beneath her, and the faint odor of oil and what smelled like a tire. She squirmed around and tried to find something to rub her head against, to nudge up the blindfold. There was nothing immediately around her, but she finally came up against cold metal and what felt like a wheel well. Then the vehicle stopped.

Michael held her breath and pretended to still be unconscious as she felt a draft on her arms and legs. Her abductor had opened something and was looking at her. A camper door? Michael wondered. A truck topper?

Then there came a hand on her leg, pulling her off the carpet by her ankle. She kicked out with all her might and connected with a soft middle. She heard a loud humph of air. Michael bumped blindly into the sides of the vehicle as she attempted to get out and flee. She didn't know where she was going, but she had to try and get away.

Strong arms grabbed her around her hips in a tackle as she cleared the vehicle and tried to run. Michael went down hard, her chin and chest scraping against a hard rigid stone of some kind that was right in front of her. She kicked with her legs as hard as she could and even tried to bite, but her drunken abductor held her easily at bay. He threw her facedown on the ground and sat on top of her. Michael opened her mouth to scream and he shoved a handful of dirt in her face. She gagged and choked and tried to turn her head away. The blindfold was ripped away and her head was held down by a firm hand. A piece of heavy, opaque plastic came over her head and was held in place by what Michael knew to be a tie strap. She had heard the familiar zipping sound many times as the straps were used in place of handcuffs to hold a suspect. There was no escaping the strap. Not without something to cut it with.

She could feel the strap tighten around her neck, and then a booted foot struck her in the side. She rolled over with the blow, and then she was falling, falling down into a dirt-filled pit. Michael landed hard on her back and felt the air leave her lungs in a whoosh. Her hands were free, and she automatically lifted them to claw at the tough plastic around her face. She kicked out with her legs and connected with hard earth.

The even plane of the dirt wall made her momentarily pause. She felt the wall with a hand.

Suddenly she knew where they were. Where *she* was.

She was in a grave in Colson Cemetery.

Her mouth opened to scream, but intake of air was impossible. Desperately she clawed at the plastic in an effort to make even a tiny hole to breathe through. Above her she could hear someone talking, but the words made no sense to her. It was him, her abductor. He was saying something, but she was fighting to breathe and couldn't hear him. She tried stuffing the plastic into her mouth to tear it with her teeth, but the fit over her head was too tight. Michael was beginning to lose. The edges of her vision were darkening and her head felt somehow thick and far too heavy for her shoulders to hold up. She felt her knees buckling and she sank down onto the damp earth. Her hands went on clawing at the plastic, but her fingers felt as if they belonged to someone else and were no longer a part of her. Finally, her arms fell to her chest.

Her captor folded the piece of paper she had written on and tossed it down to rest on top of her. Then he turned and headed for the truck.

Guy saw him leave. He saw the driver walk away from the grave and get in the black Dodge pickup and drive out of the cemetery. He was glad he had come back. It had occurred to him that the mortuary closed at nine, and that was reason enough for him to come back and see what David Eulert was doing. He was glad he had, for after leaving his car at the gate, he had crept up just in time to see Eulert throw something into an open grave. Guy hadn't been able to see what it was, but he was going to find out. He ran back to his car and took a flashlight from his glove compartment, then he went to the grave and shone the light inside.

Guy's jaw dropped. Adrenaline surged into his blood. He leaped down into the grave and reached for an arm to find a pulse. The identity of the unmoving woman in the bottom of the grave was unknown to him until he took his penknife from his pocket and slit open the plastic. In the beam of the flashlight he saw her blue features. A wild cry of fear and fury came from his throat, then he jerked her up to hurriedly begin resuscitation.

Michael responded to his efforts almost immediately. A moan came from her chest and her limbs twitched as he breathed oxygen back into her body. Ten minutes later, Guy heard a siren in the distance. It was coming closer. When the siren stopped at the gates of the cemetery, Guy tried to climb out of the grave. When that failed, he began to shout.

Two police officers appeared at the edge of the grave and asked him what the hell he was doing. Guy told them to get an ambulance and a ladder.

Michael opened her eyes and looked at him as he addressed the officers. Her blue lips moved, as if she were trying to speak to him, but no words came out. She reached up to grip his hand and he looked at her. He said her name, but he was unable to say anything else. The policemen went in search of a ladder, and when they returned, the ambulance had arrived.

Guy picked up the folded piece of paper that had been on Michael's chest and placed it in his pocket. Once inside the ambulance with her, he opened it and read it. The contents made him reach for Michael's hand and squeeze it.

At the hospital Captain Mawby cornered him and began to ask questions.

"How did you know she was there?"

"I didn't. I saw David Eulert drive into the cemetery. I followed him in because it was after nine and I wanted to know what he was doing."

Mawby raised a brow. "You wanted to know what he was doing?"

"The mortuary was closed for the evening. I'm a curious person."

"So you followed Dave in and saw . . . what?"

"I saw him toss something into the grave." Guy put a hand in his pocket and took out the note. "It was this."

The captain opened the note. His eyes flickered as he read it. He looked at Guy. "Are you sure it was David Eulert you saw?"

"He drives a black Dodge pickup."

"That same black pickup was reported stolen from Corby's Bar at eight this evening. I took the report myself. I'll ask you again. Are you sure it was David Eulert that you saw?"

Guy stared at him. Finally, he said, "No. I can't be absolutely positive. It was dark in the cemetery."

"But you did see the man throw this note into the grave. Did you see him put Michael Bish in the grave?"

"No. I didn't. I told you, I only saw him throw the note in. I went to see what it was and I found Michael." He looked at Mawby then. "Who called the police?"

"Arnold Dupree. He heard a shout in the cemetery. He thought vandals were out there. It was you."

"Yes," said Guy. "It was me."

"Mr. City Reporter, following people around. I suppose you think you stumbled on an attempted murder."

"What do you call it?"

"I don't know," said the captain. "I don't have all the facts yet. Is there any particular reason you've chosen to follow David Eulert around?"

"No particular reason," Guy said. "Like it or not, Mr. Eulert is still news. Oliver Bish died from his bullet."

Mawby's lip curled. "And you wanted to know how he felt about that. Well, how do you think he felt about that, Mr. Driscoll? Maybe the same way you felt when your daughter died and you didn't."

Guy said nothing, only stared at the man, until the captain turned and walked away. When Mawby left the building, Guy went to the desk and asked the nurse if the doctors were finished with Michael. He wanted to see her.

"They don't recommend it this evening," the nurse responded. "Mrs. Bish needs to rest. She's had quite a shock."

"I know that," Guy said. "I'm the one who found her."

"You can't see her," said the nurse.

Guy walked away from her and went directly into the emergency ward. The nurse rushed after him, her voice hissing at him to get out before she called security.

"Call," he said, and he went in search of Michael.

He found her in a bed behind some curtains. She wore an oxygen mask and her eyes were closed. He went to her and picked up her hand. Her lids opened. She smiled weakly at him and removed the mask. "My hero," she croaked.

Guy smiled and bent down to kiss her forehead.

"Thank you," Michael told him. "Thank you for what you did. How did you know? How did you know where to find me?"

Guy thought of his binoculars and cleared his throat. "I'll tell you later. How do you feel? Are you going to be all right?"

"Yes, I'll be fine. Another few minutes and I might not have been so lucky. I owe you my life."

He squeezed her fingers. "Did you see who it was?"

Michael shook her head. "No. I never saw him. Did you see anything?"

"I saw David Eulert's truck, but Captain Mawby tells me it was reported stolen earlier this evening."

Michael's look grew hard. "David Eulert? You didn't see him?"

"No," Guy admitted. "I thought it was him, of course, because of the truck, but I can't honestly say it was him."

"David would be smart enough to report his truck stolen," Michael said. She drew a deep breath then. "The lawsuit he filed is nothing but a clever ruse on his part, something to draw suspicion away from himself. He called me tonight from the school and pretended to be a janitor. He told me Sean had passed out and was lying on the floor. I went running down to the school, just like he knew I would."

Suddenly Michael sat up in bed. "I can't stay here. If he finds out I'm alive he might do something desperate. I've got to get out of here. Help me, Guy. Find my clothes."

Guy didn't move. "Where will you go?"

She blinked as she thought. Then she said, "To my father's house. He'll be leaving town after Oliver's funeral and he's asked me to stay at his place this weekend. David won't think to look for me there. Will you help me?"

"Only if you agree to let me come and stay with you after your father leaves. Otherwise, you'll be fine right here."

Michael paused and looked at him. She swallowed. "Absolutely not. It's too soon. People will talk."

"They'll talk anyway."

"I don't have anything to give you," Michael said bluntly. "I'm empty. I could never love you."

Guy lifted a hand to touch her cheek. "I'm not asking you to love me. I'm just asking you to spend some time with me."

"We'd end up in bed," Michael said. "You know we would."

"Not if you don't want to."

"You'd make me want to, and you know it." Michael fiercely shook her head. "My husband isn't even in the ground yet. I can't. Don't ask me to. I was wrong to come to you before. I knew when I did it that it was wrong. It's even more wrong now."

Guy raised his head as he heard sounds in the hall. The nurse was coming with the security guard.

"All right," he said to Michael. "I won't bother you again. Take care of yourself."

He started away and Michael grabbed at his arm. "Guy, you don't understand."

Guy removed her hand from his arm. "I don't want to. Goodbye, Michael." In the hall he met the security guard. Wordlessly, the man led him to the exit. Outside the hospital Guy looked around for someone to take him to his car. There was no one. He started back inside the hospital to call for a cab, until he remembered there was no cab service in Colson. He sighed and shoved his hands in his pockets. It was going to be a long walk to Diest's Mortuary and Chapel.

CHAPTER
TWENTY-THREE

ELMA CHOSE HER DRESS carefully the morning of Oliver Bish's funeral. Vernon was nervous, picking at her as if she were a small child, asking if she had brushed her hair and made the bed. She knew it was merely a way to distract himself from what was really bothering him, so she took only minor offense. The police had come that morning and shaken Vernon with their questions. He told them he heard nothing in the graveyard the night before, but their looks were skeptical. Arnold Dupree had heard, and his place was even farther than Vernon's. Vernon claimed he went to bed early and was asleep at the time. He swore he heard nothing.

The night before he had sworn to Elma there was no answer to the phone at Michael Bish's house. There was no way he could prove it to her, but he had been so earnest and disturbed that finally she believed him. Vernon returned to the chapel then, to open the doors for evening viewing.

When he came upstairs later he took Elma to bed and proceeded to work out his frustrations and punish her for threatening to leave him. He hurt her at first, but Elma detached in the way she had learned with her father and closed herself off from the pain. Soon Vernon exhausted himself and fell asleep on top of her. Elma rolled him off and went into the kitchen for something to eat. She wasn't afraid of him anymore. He was just a man, after all.

That morning she picked out a navy dress with a white collar and found blue and white pumps to match. When she stood before Vernon a tiny light appeared in his black eyes. "You look good," he said with some surprise.

Elma pointed to her wrist, where a watch would go, and Vernon said, "We have a while. The funeral is at eleven." Then he smiled at her. "Let's do it again. Right now."

No. Elma shook her head.

"Yes," he said, and he reached for her.

She ducked and stepped swiftly away from him. She pointed angrily at her dress and shook her finger at him.

He laughed. "I won't mess up your dress, Elma."

She shook her head again, as if to say, *That's right, you won't.*

Vernon turned petulantly away from her and went downstairs. Elma waited a few moments to let him cool off before she followed. When she went down she saw him at the mortuary entrance with Arnold Dupree. Arnold smiled and waved when he saw her. Vernon turned, and his look was worried. Almost panicked.

Elma had never seen him this way.

Slowly she moved toward them. She smiled in return at Arnold and saw him reach in his pocket for a pad and pen. He handed them to her and said, "Mr. Diest here says you're not interested in coming to work for me. I'd like to hear it from you, Elma. My house ain't big like this one, but it needs a woman's hand. I'll feed you proper and take care of living expenses. I'll give you spending money, too. What do you say, Elma?"

She looked at Vernon. He stared back at her, his black eyes nearly frantic with anxiety.

So this is what it's like, she thought to herself. This is the kind of power Alissa Diest had enjoyed for most of her life.

She smiled at Vernon. His nostrils flared and he looked quickly away from her, suddenly too proud to beg.

Her smile widened. She glanced at Arnold Dupree and shook her head. Then she wrote: *I'm sorry, but Vernon needs me here at the mortuary. As of this morning, we're engaged to be married.*

Arnold read the paper and ran a hand over his head. "The two of you are engaged?"

Vernon stared at Elma. His nostrils quivered. She smiled again and nodded.

"You proposed to her this morning?" Arnold asked Vernon.

For a long moment Vernon didn't speak. Finally he muttered a yes.

"When's the big day?"

"We haven't decided yet," Vernon said. Then he looked beyond Arnold. "If you don't mind, Mr. Dupree, I've got things to do before the service. You're welcome to come in, of course, but I really must get busy."

"No problem," Arnold said, a bemused look on his face. "I guess I just can't see you two as a couple. No offense, of course, but I never thought of her as your type."

"That makes two of us," Vernon said tightly. "But fate's a funny thing, isn't it?"

"Sure is. What time are you gonna be needing me today?"

Vernon looked at his watch. "At approximately noon. Can you manage it?"

"Can do. Say, I meant to ask if you heard the ruckus in the graveyard last night. I guess you heard about Michael Bish on the news today."

"I heard about her from the police," Vernon told him. "They were here this morning. They wanted to know what I heard."

"You probably heard it real good. Scared the hell out of me, a yell like that coming from a graveyard."

"I heard nothing," Vernon said, and he looked at his watch again.

"Nothing? Damn, son, you must've heard that. Sounded like a wounded bear."

Vernon politely shook his head. "Nothing. I'm a very heavy sleeper. Now, if you'll excuse me."

"Sure." Arnold stepped away from the door, but his brow was crinkled as he went. He inclined his head to Elma and sauntered off across the grass.

Vernon's look was furious as he turned on Elma. "How dare you tell that man we're engaged?"

She took out the pen and pad Arnold had left with her and wrote: *If I'm good enough to sleep with you, then I'm good enough to marry. What happens if I become pregnant?*

Vernon read the note and blinked. "Could you? I mean, are you capable? I never thought of it." He frowned when she nodded. "Were you . . . you weren't a virgin, were you? I wasn't the first man to ever . . . was I?"

Elma made a quick decision. She nodded.

"I was?" Vernon said, not at all displeased with the notion. "I was your first? You're joking, aren't you. You're well into your thirties, Elma. Surely there was someone before me."

Elma changed her mind and wrote two words on the pad. She showed it to Vernon.

"Your father?" he said. "What do you mean? You mean I'm the only man in your life besides your father, right?"

Her liquid brown eyes looked at him.

Vernon chose to believe his own interpretation. His smile was huge. "I've never had a virgin before. That must be why it feels so good with you, Elma. You've never had anyone but me."

She turned away from him to go into the chapel, but he grabbed her by the arm and made her look at him.

"Do you think you could be pregnant? I mean, when will you know? We'll have to do something about it if you are. Wait—no, we won't. I wouldn't mind having a son. But not if he's like you. Is your affliction hereditary?"

Elma slowly shook her head.

"Now don't look like that. You know what I meant." Vernon squeezed her arms suddenly and pulled her close to him. "I said you were mine, didn't I? I must have sensed that I was your first." He tipped her chin up to kiss her on the mouth. "I'm more than fond of you, Elma. It's just that I never saw myself marrying someone like you. I've always thought I would marry one of the girls from Corona Hill, or Eastport. A woman with breeding and charm. A hostess, of sorts, for the mortuary. You can't be that, Elma. You can't speak to comfort the bereaved. You can't even listen to them cry."

Elma removed his hands from her arms so she could write a response on her pad. She wrote: *I can clean Arnold Dupree's house. Go find your woman from the hill.*

Vernon wadded the piece of paper in his hand. "Don't do this, Elma. Don't threaten to leave every time I say something you don't like."

No threat, Elma wrote. *If I stay here, you marry me. Otherwise I leave and go to work for Arnold. I've never had spending money of my own before. I think it would be nice to have some.*

After reading the note, Vernon's jaw clenched. He reached in his pocket for his wallet. "You want money? I'll give you money." He threw two fifties at her. Elma caught one and scooped the other off the floor. As Vernon stalked away from her she smiled and slipped the bills into the front of her bra. He would marry her. She was sure of it.

During the service for Oliver Bish, Elma made up her mind to show Vernon just what kind of hostess she could be. She positioned herself in the hall outside the chapel and prepared to act as usher. She had seen Alissa and Vernon greet mourners and put on funerals a hundred times. She knew what to do. Elma had always been timid and shy around strangers before, but now things were different. She had a point to prove. She had the clothes and the shoes, all she lacked were ears and a voice. And what mourner needed those? she rationalized. It was only the appearance of listening that was required. Vernon was proof of that.

After the service she felt Vernon's startled gaze on her as she stepped forward and began to direct mourners to the exits. Most of the mourners didn't notice Elma. They cried into their hands and hid their faces behind damp handkerchiefs. Elma guided them to the side exits of the chapel, and when the room was mostly clear, she helped line them up into a semiformal line outside, where they waited to offer condolences to the family. Her lack of hearing or voice never came into play.

Vernon's expression was reserved as he attended to the family. Michael Bish, the widow, was closely guarded by her sister and brother-in-law. Elma was surprised to see her there, considering her ordeal of the night before. She had been even more surprised to learn the funeral was going on as scheduled. She had thought they would postpone it for a day, at least, in view of what had happened to Michael.

She guessed it had been Michael's decision to go ahead. She looked like a brave, fearless young woman, thought Elma. If only Vernon had been able to warn her last night.

But she had survived, and today, though slightly pale, she looked none the worse for having been attacked. She owed her thanks and her life to Guy Driscoll, according to the paper. Driscoll was the man Vernon had shot. The man whose daughter Vernon killed. Elma had been surprised to see Driscoll's name as the man who saved Michael Bish. It was as if fate were constantly trying to link the two. She didn't see him here today, though, and that surprised Elma. She would have expected Guy Driscoll to come.

The paper also mentioned that Driscoll had seen a truck familiar to him, but it was a truck reported stolen several hours earlier. Conveniently so, Elma thought, and she wondered if there was some way to implicate David Eulert without Vernon becoming involved.

With a prick of guilt, she realized that she herself was more involved than ever. She had knowledge of all these crimes and she did nothing to inform the authorities. This made her an accessory of sorts, she realized, and for a painful moment she saw the pale dead face of Guy Driscoll's young daughter, Adele.

The girl's blood was on Elma's hands as much as it was on Vernon's.

She blinked her eyes and saw Vernon usher Oliver Bish's mother away from the open coffin. Next came his sisters, and then Michael. There was no mistaking the animosity in the look Michael had for Vernon. Elma saw it and stepped quickly forward. Better for Michael to have her to look at, rather than Vernon. Elma moved to the head of the casket and gave Vernon a nudge with her hand. He fell immediately back and away and allowed her to take his place. Michael looked at Elma, and then she looked at Oliver. Her last good-bye to him was long and silent.

She nodded to Elma finally, and Elma moved to close the casket. Then she felt a hand on her arm. She turned to see Michael Bish addressing her.

"Can you read my lips?" she asked.

Elma nodded.

"I'd like to talk to you," Michael said. "Can you drive?"

Elma shook her head.

"Have you ever ridden the bus?"

No. Elma looked and saw Vernon staring at them. His black eyes were unreadable.

"You can catch it at the corner," Michael told her. "It comes by the mortuary at nine-fifteen every morning and passes my corner at nine-twenty-five. I live at—"

"If you're ready," Vernon said behind her, "it's time to go to the cemetery, Mrs. Bish. I understand you've already been to the grave."

Michael turned and glared at Vernon. Elma chose that moment to back from the room and disappear. She'd never be able to lie to the woman face to face. Elma hoped she never saw Michael Bish face to face again.

CHAPTER
TWENTY-FOUR

DAVID EULERT LOOKED hard at Stan Mawby. "I just filed a lawsuit against the woman, Captain. Why would I try to kill Michael Bish?"

"Where did you go after you reported your truck stolen?" Mawby repeated. "You didn't go home. I already asked your wife and your folks. They didn't know where you were. They didn't know your truck had been stolen. We recovered it, by the way. It was in the parking lot at the school."

"Great. Thanks, Captain."

"So?"

"So what?"

"Don't get cute with me, Dave. Where the hell were you?"

"I told you. I stayed at Corby's and drank beer."

"Yeah, I know that's what you told me. But you left, because I talked to Corby on the phone just a few minutes ago and he said you weren't there long. It's time to stop playing around and talk to me. If you don't, you could be in a lot of trouble."

David laid his hands on his mother's table and spread his fingers apart. He and the captain were alone in the house. His father was working, and his mother had taken his wife out shopping for baby clothes. He lowered his head in a pose of concentration, then he looked up at the captain. "All right. I'll tell you where I was. After I left the bar I walked to Diest's Mortuary. I wanted to say goodbye to my partner, and I wanted to tell him I was sorry one last time. Mike goes into fits every time she sees me, so I had to go when no one else was around. Diest kept the place open an extra half hour so I could come in."

"You know Vernon Diest?" Mawby asked in surprise.

"Let's just say he empathizes with my situation. We've talked about filing a joint suit against Michael Bish."

"And he let you sit in his mortuary after hours. How long were you there?"

David shrugged. "Until just after nine-thirty. About fifteen minutes before Michael was found in the graveyard, according to the paper. Call Diest, he'll tell you. He drove me home."

"I will. He's already told me that he went to bed early last night."

"Depends on what he meant by early. Give him a call."

"Why don't you and I go see him?"

"Right now?"

"Yes. He's not busy. The funeral is over. Unless you have something else to do?"

"Not a thing. Let's go."

David's movements were confident as he rose from his chair and pushed it under the table. Suddenly he asked, "Did you ever figure out why Driscoll was following my truck?"

"He said you were still news around Colson. The man is a reporter, Dave. He used to work for a paper much bigger than the *Beacon*. He wanted your reaction to Oliver's death."

"What does he think?" David growled. "What kind of reaction would he expect? Oliver was my partner and the best friend I ever had."

Mawby only looked at him. He opened his car door and gestured for David to get in the other side. David got in and said, "What did he expect to gain by following me? Was he going to jump out of his car at a stoplight and come up to my window?"

"I don't know," Mawby said. "Maybe someday you can ask him. He's a nice enough sort. He'll probably tell you."

"Is he still sleeping with Mike?"

Mawby started his engine and backed out of the drive. "I don't know, and I don't care. That's none of my concern, and it's sure as hell none of yours."

David closed his mouth and looked straight ahead. He wasn't going to get anywhere with Mawby.

When they arrived at Diest Mortuary, David was out of the car and approaching the door before Mawby could unbuckle his seatbelt. Vernon came to the door on the first ring, and David smiled at him. Through the smile he said, "I was here last night until just after nine-thirty."

Vernon frowned and started to open his mouth, but Mawby approached and he closed it again. Still frowning, he said, "Captain, I thought we took care of everything earlier."

"Not quite," Mawby said. "Was Mr. Eulert here to see you at any time yesterday?"

Vernon blinked and looked at David. David's eyes bored into his. Vernon hesitated, his nostrils flared, then he said, "Yesterday? No, he wasn't here yesterday."

David made a noise through his teeth. The captain put a hand on his shoulder.

"He wasn't here last night?"

"No," Vernon said, his black eyes shining. "Not at all."

"You lying sonofabitch," David spat at him. "I was here and you know it. You let me in."

Vernon raised both brows. "I let you in? I've never seen you before this moment, Mr. Eulert, though I confess I have heard of you."

Mawby's hand was tightening on David's shoulder. David twisted and tried to knock it off, but it stayed firm.

"Captain, he's lying. He knows I was here. Tell him I was here, you bastard. Say it, or I'll tell him what I know."

Vernon looked unconcerned. "I don't know what you're talking about."

"I'm talking about the night you shot Guy Driscoll and killed his daughter, that's what I'm talking about. You were trying to frame Michael Bish to hurry your court case along and bring in some money."

"That's the most insane thing I've ever heard," Vernon said with a scowl. "How dare you suggest I could be capable of so reprehensible an act?"

"He is and he did," David swore to Mawby. "But he was smart enough to get rid of the gun. You don't believe me, you check it out. He's been in trouble for months now. A friend at the bank told me—"

"That's enough," Mawby said. "You're not a cop here anymore, Dave. You leave the investigation of crimes up to us. Mr. Diest could sue you for invasion of privacy. Let's go down to the station and talk about this some more. You've lied to me twice now, and I'm going to give you one more chance to tell me where you were last night, and to prove it. If you can't do that, then we'll have to talk a little more seriously about making a charge against you."

"No," David said, and he tore himself away to back up from the captain. "There's no way I'm going with you. Not to *my* jail in *my* town. Half the people in Colson will think you're crazy, Mawby. You know that, don't you? You know they'll laugh at the notion that I could have done something like that to Michael Bish. Everyone knows what she tried to do to me. Everyone knows how she lied and forced me to leave. Find me three people who actually believe her and I'll go with you."

Mawby's frown was deep. "You're looking at one, Dave. I believe she told the truth. Now, are you going to come with me, or am I—"

He didn't get a chance to finish. David rushed him and

punched him hard in the gut. Mawby doubled over and David snatched the pistol from inside his coat and held it on the captain. "Don't you move," he told him. "I swear to God I'll shoot you. You're going to stand here and listen to me, because I'm going to tell you the truth, Captain Mawby."

"You're making a big mistake," Mawby wheezed. "No way out of this one, Dave."

"Shut up!" David screamed at him. "I told you she lied, and now I'm telling you he's lying." He waved the pistol at Vernon. "I'm a war hero and a decorated police officer. I was the best damned marine you ever saw, and I am *not* gay. Mike lied. She lied to hurt me, because I shot Oliver. Diest is lying, too. I was here last night. I came to see Oliver, and Diest let me in. Tell him, Diest, tell him or I'll blow your goddamned head off."

Vernon's black eyes were on the pistol. His gaze never moved from the barrel. That's why he didn't see Elma slip noiselessly behind David and hit him over the head with a shovel from Vernon's shed. David fell face forward to the ground before Vernon looked up and saw Elma. Mawby shot forward and kicked David's wrist; the pistol did a spin as it flew from his hand. David swept both legs around and caught Mawby's feet, toppling him to the ground. Elma dropped the shovel and ran to pick up the pistol. David crawled on his hands and knees to race her to it. Elma got there first. She picked up the pistol and held it in front of her as David grabbed her by the ankle. He jerked on her leg and sent her spilling to the ground. Reflex made her squeeze the trigger, and the pistol went off as she fell.

The round hit David squarely in the mouth, shattering all his teeth and giving him a grotesque red grin. The bullet went on to plow through his spinal column, sending him into a frenzied, kinetic dance, arms and legs going all directions. Elma, Vernon, and Captain Mawby watched in horrified awe as he jerked and twisted and flopped for what seemed an eternity. Finally he was still.

Elma's eyes filled. A loud squawking sound came from her throat. She dropped the pistol and ran from the sight of the dead David Eulert.

"Wait!" Captain Mawby shouted, and he repeated himself until Vernon reminded him Elma couldn't hear.

Mawby wiped his face with a hand that was shaking. "You think she'll be all right? Maybe you should go after her."

"She'll be fine," Vernon said. He looked at Eulert's unmoving form. "Shall I keep him here?"

The captain stared at Vernon. "Jesus, I can't think. Give me a minute, all right?" Was he the only one shaken up? What the hell was wrong with Diest? He was cool and unbelievably unperturbed.

"Okay," Mawby said finally. "I need to call some people first. We'll need to take pictures and notes to document everything."

"That's fine," Vernon said.

"Be right with you." Mawby walked back to his car. "I need to let dispatch know what's happened. What's Elma's last name?"

Vernon had to think for a moment. "Voycheck," he called to the captain.

The captain nodded. "That's right, I remember. Have you seen him lately? Her father, I mean."

"He was here a few months ago," Vernon told him. "Inebriated, as usual. He stayed the night and left the next day, same as last time."

Mawby nodded again and picked up his radio to call dispatch. The shocked silence on the other end was a reflection of his own feelings about what had just happened. Everything had occurred so quickly that there had been no time to move, no time to act on anything but instinct. Elma had done just that. She was in no way to blame for David Eulert's death. Stan Mawby would see to it she knew that.

As he requested assistance, Mawby found himself watching the silent Vernon Diest and thinking of Eulert's earlier statements. Dave had lied, though. He had lied about nearly everything.

Mawby still couldn't believe David Eulert was gone. The high school athlete. The beloved town hero, lying there not twenty yards from where Mawby sat in his car. The smell of cordite hung in the air, mixed with the heavy, coppery smell of blood.

The events and everyone's participation ran in his mind over and over again. Mawby couldn't stop thinking about the blast, or Dave's gruesome smile. The jerky nerve dance.

It had been a bloody spring in tiny Colson, and it was becoming a bloody summer.

Let it stop now, he thought. Let it stop with Dave.

All of it.

Mawby was tired of not knowing who or what to believe.

CHAPTER
TWENTY-FIVE

THE NEWS OF David Eulert's death spread rapidly through the town. Most people had to be told who Elma Voycheck was, but Michael knew immediately, and though her heart told her it was a sin to rejoice at the death of another, she couldn't help the feeling that justice had somehow been done. David for Oliver.

After Oliver's funeral she went directly to her father's house and departed for Springfield immediately upon hearing the news of David Eulert's death. There was no reason to stay behind for his daughter's sake now. The enemy had fallen. Sean and her husband had left only moments ago, leaving Michael alone in the house to gloat over her emotional victory, while at the same time mourning the loss of Oliver. Or the loss of Guy—she wasn't sure which one pained her the most that day. After he saved her, after he had revived her and given life back to her, she had hurt him yet again.

There was something symbolic in what he had done, in the idea of him breathing air into her lungs and restoring her to the realm of the living.

After her brush with death, her awareness of life was sensitive beyond all reason. She could feel her wings itching to break free and spread themselves in the sunlight. Even now, just hours after the funeral for her husband, she felt the first stirrings of restlessness and a yearning for something new, a different way of life.

She thought of leaving Colson, breaking away from her father and sister and the people in town once and for all. She could go wherever she wanted to go, do whatever she wanted to do. The bottle of wine she found in her father's refrigerator said it was more than possible. She poured herself glass after glass in dark celebration of her freedom from hospital rooms and doctors and nurses. She never wanted to look at another IV needle or catheter tube as long as she lived.

What she wanted to do more than anything was call Guy Driscoll and ask if he heard the news about David Eulert.

No, she thought. I can't call him. Not after what I said at the hospital. Not after what he said.

But she picked up the phone anyway and began to punch in his number. When there was no answer at his home, she dialed the *Colson Beacon*. They put her through to his desk.

"Guy Driscoll," he answered.

"Did you hear about David Eulert?" Michael asked.

There was silence, then, "Yes, I heard about it. You don't have to worry about him anymore."

"No. But it would have been nice to know why he tried to kill me. What his motive was."

"He hated you. You can understand that, I'm sure."

Michael held her breath. "Meaning what? That you know how he felt?"

"You know better than that. What do you want, Michael?"

"To talk."

"I thought you wanted me to stay out of your life?"

Michael put a hand to her head. "I'm sure you think I'm the biggest flake in the world. I'm hardly consistent, I know, but I can't seem to stop thinking and wondering about you. I feel like some terrible heavy cloak has been lifted off my shoulders now that both David and Oliver are gone. I feel like he,

David, was preventing me from living again. He watched every move I made and judged every action. I felt like I had to be the perfect wife for him and the public, not Oliver, though Oliver counted, too. Do you know what I'm trying to say?"

"I'm not sure," said Guy. "Tell me what this means in relation to me."

"Would you like to come over and talk tonight? I'm at my father's house."

"What are we going to talk about?"

"Whatever we think of. I want to see if we *can* talk. I want to know if we like the same movies and books and music. I want to hear about when you were younger, and I'll show you my father's scrapbook of Sean and me. Can we have just a sweet old-fashioned date together?"

There was silence for a long moment. Then Guy said, "What time?"

"When you leave the paper. I'll fix dinner."

"All right. Give me the address."

Michael gave it to him, and they hung up. Only after she went to the bathroom did she realize how hot her face was. She looked in the mirror and saw that her cheeks were flushed. She ignored all the guilty questions that had become a habit in the last year. There was no more Oliver. In truth, there had been no Oliver for nearly ten months. Scarier yet, even if there had been an Oliver, a healthy, normal Oliver, Michael thought she would still be drawn to Guy Driscoll. She knew she would be, and it was a huge relief to finally acknowledge the fact.

A tremor ran through her at the thought of his coming over in just a few hours. She went into the kitchen and put together a quick salad, and cheese sandwiches on squaw bread. She put the salad and sandwiches back in the refrigerator and went into the spare bedroom to put on shorts and sandals out of her overnight bag. On impulse she drove to the liquor store in the tiny shopping center on the corner and bought another bottle of wine. She wasn't a wine drinker, but she picked out a red wine that looked good to her. When she was all set, she sat on the sofa in her father's living room with her scrapbook of pictures and waited.

When she heard a car pull up outside she nearly tripped over herself trying to get to the door. She was suddenly bursting with anxiety and nerves. She calmed down when she saw the reserve in his features. He was being cautious, wary of her new warmth and openness toward him. She saw that he was getting along on his cane much better, and she commented on it. He smiled. "Next week I won't need it at all . . . I hope."

"Are you hungry?" Michael asked. "I made a salad and some sandwiches."

"Not right now, thanks. I could use a beer if you have one."

"I have one beer, and some wine. Shall I open the wine?"

"Let's split the beer and have the wine later."

Michael grinned at him. "Okay. Sit down on the sofa. I'll be right back."

Guy sat down and picked up the scrapbook. He flipped to the first page, and while he was looking at the second, Michael returned with two glasses of beer. She sat down beside him and pointed. "That was my great-aunt's horse. His name was Pepper. Sean and I used to ride him all the time. He was wonderful with kids."

"Big horse," Guy commented. "Who were the other two on his back behind you and Sean?"

"My cousins from Baltimore. City kids. Brats. We couldn't stand them."

Guy pointed to a picture. "Is that your mother?"

"Yes. How did you know?"

"You look like her. What happened to her?"

"She died of a heart attack about six years ago."

"How old was she?"

"Forty-five."

They found themselves face to face, looking at each other.

Guy was first to look away. He returned to the scrapbook. "These are nice school pictures. Were you a good student?"

"I was okay. Sean was the honor roll student. She was a hard act to follow."

"Did you try?"

"You bet I did. We competed all our lives, until adulthood, anyway. My father encouraged it."

Guy smiled and went on through the scrapbook, commenting on this picture and that one, until he reached the end. Michael took it from him when he was finished and put it away on a nearby shelf. Then she turned to him and said, "It's your turn. Tell me who you are."

He sat back. "I was born in Kansas, right here in Colson. My father worked for a parts manufacturer, and my mother worked in a music store. I had a baby brother, but he died of leukemia at the age of five. When I was twelve my parents were killed in an accident, and an aunt from Chicago took me home with her. I was educated in Chicago, and I worked there all my life until four months ago. I dated two girls in college and married early. My wife divorced me when she decided she couldn't stand me, and then she died of breast cancer. My daughter took it hard, so I brought her here. You know the rest."

Michael stared at him. "I guess . . . I really didn't want to know all that. All your pain. Have you, uh, had many girlfriends since your divorce?"

Guy smiled. "Two. They're both married now. I like all music but rap and country & western, and I like any movie that doesn't show the mindless slaughter of teenagers. In books I lean toward nonfiction and biographies. As for religion, well, I'm not a big fan of any organized religion, but I do believe there's a plan for us all." He paused then. "That's all I can think of right now. Your turn again."

Michael went to him and took his hands. "I don't like all country & western, but I love Jim Reeves and Patsy Cline. I read romances and westerns and mystery and suspense, and

I've been known to sit with my popcorn and enjoy a good gorefest on the midnight movie. I was raised a Baptist, but I haven't been to church in years."

Guy smiled and looked at the hands holding his. "Glad we got that straight. I'm ready for that sandwich now."

Michael blinked at his unresponsiveness to her and released him. She got up and headed for the kitchen. "Okay," she said lightly, or what she hoped was light. She took out the salad and sandwiches and removed the wine from the refrigerator. "Do you want to open the wine?" she called into the living room.

"Sure," he said, and he came into the kitchen. "Your father has a pleasant house. Very comfortable."

"If he knew you were here he would die," Michael said teasingly. "We were never, under any circumstances, allowed to bring boys to our home."

Guy opened the wine and poured it into two glasses. "Are we eating at the table?"

"Yes." She gestured behind herself, and Guy placed the glasses on the table. Michael found herself growing nervous again at his closeness. Her hands ached to touch him. She kept getting flashes of what his body looked like beneath his clothes, his hard chest and taut stomach, and his lean muscular legs. She was almost dizzy with the need to feel him against her. Calmly, she picked up her wine glass and took a sip as she sat down across from him.

He raised up his own glass and tasted the wine. Then he picked up his fork and took a bite of salad.

Michael swallowed as she watched him. She said, "I don't know how you can eat. I can't think of anything but kissing you."

Guy lifted his gaze. "You've had a few drinks. I'm just here to talk and have a sweet old-fashioned date."

Michael looked at her plate. "I haven't had that much to drink. You enjoy calling me on my contradictions, don't you?"

"Not half as much as you enjoy contradicting. Don't play

with me, Michael. If we started anything, you'd have an attack of conscience halfway through the evening and throw me out the door."

Michael got up and pushed her chair away. "Oh, you know me so well."

"Well enough. Sit down and eat your sandwich. Let's talk some more."

"About what?"

"Anything. How are you feeling today? Any ill effects from last night?"

Michael turned to look at him. Without thinking, she pulled her blouse off over her head and reached behind herself to unhook her bra. "What I'm feeling is desperation," she said as she approached him. She took off her bra and draped it over a chair. "I know I buried my husband today. I know I'll feel guilty tomorrow. Right now all I can think about is how good I'll feel once you're inside me."

Guy sucked in his breath and forced himself to look away from her breasts. "Michael, if I touch you tonight you'll hate me tomorrow. Put your blouse on and sit down. I'm not coming near you. I'll leave first."

Michael went to him and pushed his hands away to sit on his lap. He tried to force her off, but she held tight to him. His hands on her ribcage made her shudder. She began to kiss his face, tasting every inch of his skin. He held himself stiff and closed his eyes, but her lips were insistent. "Kiss me," she said against his mouth. "Kiss me, Guy."

His hands came up to imprison her face. He kissed her hard on the mouth, and then he forced her to look at him. "Michael, don't do this. I want us to get it right this time. Please, let's do it right."

She freed her head and kissed him again. "I don't know what you mean. This feels right to me."

"Now it does. But what about later? What about when the wine wears off? Will you still want me around? You ran away last time and nearly made me crazy."

"I'm not going anywhere." Her hand undid a button and slipped inside his shirt. Guy's flesh hardened at the coolness of her touch. He put his head down and closed his eyes again. "Michael, you know I want you. You know what this is doing to me."

She smiled and kissed the back of his neck. "Then give in."

"I can't," he said against her bare skin. "I love you."

Michael paused and leaned back to stare at him. He lifted his head to look at her. The green of his eyes was dark in the shadowed light of her father's kitchen. His look echoed the last words from his mouth.

Michael's lips trembled. Her eyes filled and she let her arms fall to her sides. Guy reached around her and held her. They sat together on the chair, her naked flesh goosepimpling against the fabric of his shirt. Finally she murmured, "I don't know what to say."

"Say you'll give us a chance. I don't want to risk losing you in favor of one night of sex. I can't trust your emotions right now and neither can you. Do you understand?"

Michael nodded. After a moment, she said, "You've always frightened me, you know. The way you look at me. Now . . . I . . . well, I feel differently."

Guy tightened his arms around her. "I'm not asking you to do anything but be with me. Don't worry about what you do or don't feel. Not yet."

Michael raised her hands to frame his face and kiss him on the mouth. When she lifted her head she said, "I've never met anyone like you, Guy Driscoll."

"Tell me that when you're sober."

She kissed him again. "Fair enough." She looked around then and shifted on his lap. "You want to play some Scrabble?"

He leaned his head back and smiled. "I'm a journalist and a former editor. You know I'll kick your tail."

Michael scoffed and climbed off him to scoop up her blouse. "Put your pencil where your mouth is, buster."

Guy took one last lingering look at her breasts as she put on her blouse. Michael saw him looking, saw the naked hunger in his eyes, and she felt a thrill course through her body. He loved her. He *loved* her.

A part of her had known all along, the same part of her that trembled at the intensity of his stare. Now she knew with every nerve and cell in her body that he spoke the truth, and nothing had ever felt so comfortable to her. Nothing had ever seemed so purely innocent and wildly sweet.

"Guy," she said suddenly as she placed the game on the table. "I've been thinking of leaving Colson. If I do, would you consider coming with me?"

He looked at her. "Where?"

"I don't know. Chicago, maybe?"

"Are you serious?"

She nodded. "I think so. But let's talk about it later. I have to concentrate when I play this game."

"Concentrate all you like," he said. "You'll lose."

Michael laughed. "Says you."

CHAPTER
TWENTY-SIX

MICHAEL LOST THE SCRABBLE GAME. She called for a rematch and Guy beat her again. Afterward they played a game with cards called "Knock Poker," at which Michael beat him seven games in a row. Since she was feeling better, Guy decided to leave. If he didn't go then, he knew he'd still be there in the morning, and he had already made up both their minds about that. He was selfish enough to want her to have genuine feeling for him when they made love. He wanted her to know she was in love with him, so there would be no guilt, no recriminations, no spectre of a dead husband in bed with them. And no running away.

He kissed her goodnight at her father's door and saw her smile sadly. "What?" he said, and touched her cheek.

"It's just . . . I haven't felt this good in a long, long time."

"I haven't either. I'm glad I came over. I'll call you tomorrow."

"Guy," she said, "about Chicago. I want you to take me everywhere. I want to see everything."

"We can do that," he said, and he kissed her again. "Goodnight, Michael."

"Goodnight."

He walked to his car and got in. He waved as he started the engine, and he saw her wave back at him and then step inside and close the door. Guy drove home and fell asleep on his sofa, his head full of dreams of dark blue eyes, wide, smiling lips, and round, full breasts with dusky nipples.

When he awakened the next morning his first impulse was to call her, to see if she had spent the night thinking of him. He looked at his watch and saw that it was a quarter to six. He would have to wait. She wouldn't be up.

While he was in the bathroom, his phone rang.

"Did I get you up?" Michael asked.

"No. I was in the bathroom."

"Have you already showered and shaved?"

"I was getting there. You're up early."

"It's a habit of mine. Want to or not, I wake up between five-thirty and six o'clock every morning. I thought you might like to come over for breakfast before you go to work."

Guy smiled. "I'd like that. What time will it be ready?"

"Whenever you are. I like fruit for breakfast."

"Any bagels?" Guy teased. "We eat bagels in Chicago."

"Only the frozen kind. I saw them in Dad's freezer."

"I'll be there in half an hour."

Michael laughed and said goodbye. Guy hung up and returned to the bathroom to shower and shave. He was happy she had called him. The sound of her voice gave him a warm feeling that was unmatched in Guy's experience. He couldn't wait to see her again.

On the way out of his house he saw Adam putting some boxes into the back of his truck. Guy spoke his name and waved. Adam smiled and waved back.

The sweet old fool, Guy thought. He had to like Adam, strange though he was.

He drove to Michael's father's house and saw her come to the door to meet him. When he left the car and walked up to the porch, her face lit up in a smile that made her look beautiful. He had to stop himself from grabbing her and crushing her to him. Instead he leaned toward her and dropped a light kiss on her lips. "Good morning."

"Good morning," she said shyly. "Come in."

Guy went past her and walked through the living room into the kitchen, where a feast of fruit lay on the table. He smiled at her over his shoulder and plucked a grape from a bunch in a bowl. She smiled back at him as he popped it into his mouth. "Did you sleep well?"

He shook his head. "No. Did you?"

"No."

They smiled at each other.

"Sit down," Michael said. "I'll get you some coffee, if you like. Or some juice?"

"Juice," Guy said, and he sat down. He picked up a fork and speared a piece of cantaloupe. Michael brought him the juice and sat down across from him. Her face colored as she looked at him, and Guy knew instinctively she was thinking about the previous night. She proved it in the next moment when she said, "Thank you for being such a gentleman. I was pretty wild, wasn't I?"

"I wasn't just being a gentleman."

"I know," she said.

"Have you changed your mind about us again?"

"No . . . I . . . you were right. We should take our time and let things progress slowly."

Guy looked at her. "Not that slowly."

"You know what I mean."

"I'm not sure. Do you still want to go to Chicago?"

"Well, um, right after I talked to you, Stan Mawby called. He went to his office early and found some papers on his desk. They were my reinstatement papers. I've been cleared by the Kansas Bureau of Investigation. I'm going back to work today. There'll be no grand jury."

Guy nodded. "That's good . . . isn't it?"

"Yes," she said, "it is. But people will be watching me now.

Again. And it really is too soon for me to become involved in another—"

Guy moved his chair back and stood up. "I can see where this is heading. You don't even have to finish. I left myself wide open for that one, didn't I?"

He turned and left the kitchen. Michael went after him. "Guy, don't go. I want to talk to you. I'm just saying it would be better if we hold off—"

He wheeled around. "Stay away from me. Don't ever call me or come around me again. I might forget I'm a gentleman and knock the shit out of you."

Michael stopped and closed her mouth. He glared at her then turned his back and walked out to his car. In that moment he hated her. Almost as much as he hated himself. He couldn't believe what a fool he had been. He couldn't believe how easily she had twisted him again. For a few hours he had actually believed they could make it. She had convinced him they could.

He drove away from the house and didn't look back. In his mind he was already calling the airline reservations counter. When he arrived at the paper he did just that. He reserved a seat on a flight leaving Kansas City for Chicago in exactly three weeks, the length of notice he would give to the managing editor. He didn't know what he would do once back in Chicago, or even if he would stay there. He knew only that he had to get away from Colson . . . and her.

Bill Glasstock, the managing editor, was sorry to hear Guy's news. "Maybe you should give it more time," he suggested.

"It was a mistake to come," Guy told him. "I thought I could change things. All I did was get Adele killed."

Bill shook his gray head. "I can understand your feeling that way, but you had nothing to do with what happened to your daughter."

Guy was silent.

"I'll leave the door open in case you change your mind. I sure hate to lose you."

"Thanks."

Bill extended his hand. "It's been a pleasure and a privilege working with you, Guy. You've got to be one of the best in the business."

Guy shook his hand. "Thank you."

"Any projects you feel you can't complete, hand them over to me now and I'll get them reassigned."

"Everything I have will be completed," Guy assured him. He left the office and walked out to his terminal to begin work. At ten o'clock he received a call from Springfield, Missouri. He was on the phone for an hour, and six hours after that he turned off his equipment, handed two finished articles to the copy editors, and left the building.

At home he found Adam Dupree waiting for him on his front porch. Guy left his car and frowned when he saw Adam's worried expression. "What is it?" he asked. "What's wrong, Adam?"

Adam's face twisted. "I hate to bother you, but I wondered if you could help me. I think something's wrong with my uncle."

"Your uncle?"

"My Uncle Arnold. The one who lives by the graveyard."

Guy raised his brows. "What's wrong with him?"

"I think he might be hurt. See, I take him fruit off my trees to trade for vegetables out of his garden. I don't see him much, we don't talk often, but there wasn't anyone over there when I went last night. And there wasn't any answer this morning, or this evening. I've tried to see him three times now, and he's just not coming to the door. His truck is there, though, so I don't know what to think. And I'm not sure what to do."

"Maybe he went out of town for a few days," Guy suggested.

"He's been out of town twice in two years, and he called me both times."

Guy tried to think. "Did you go in the house?"

"No. I just told you, there was no answer to my knock."

"Do you have a key? Is there a way to get in that you know of? Your uncle could be injured and unable to get to the door."

Adam's brow furrowed. "When I was a kid he used to keep a spare key on the underside of the old tractor sitting by his shed." He looked at Guy then. "Will you come over with me?"

Guy started to say no, but he changed his mind at the look on Adam's face. "Sure. Let's go."

On the way to his uncle's house, Guy told Adam he was leaving Colson. Adam looked at him in surprise. "Why? I thought you liked it here?"

"I did. I do."

When he didn't say anything else, Adam said, "Is it because of Michael Bish?"

Guy's look was dark, and Adam smiled sheepishly at him. "I could see the way you felt about her when she came to your house that day. What happened? What did she do?"

"Nothing."

"Did I ever tell you about my sister? I have a sister who went to school with Michael. Her name is Melanie, and she lives in Canada now. She and Michael used to get in squabbles all the time. Melanie liked to beat Michael up. She always used to talk about how tough Michael tried to be to please her daddy. She was never quite as smart or pretty as her sister Sean, but Michael tried hard to be everything else. She tried to be a good officer and a good wife, and she's still trying to be her daddy's number one girl, when Sean's got that spot sewed up. Melanie used to say Michael needed to get away from both of them. That's when she'd stop competing and find out who she was meant to be."

"She wants to be a cop," Guy said flatly. "She wants to be

around her husband's old buddies and show them how loyal she's been. She wants everyone to know that the almighty KBI has spoken and declared her innocent of all wrongdoing. She wants to live the illusion she's created about herself."

"Without you."

"Without any man who threatens to pull her off the martyr wagon."

Adam shrugged. "You're being a little rough on her. You're mad and probably stung. She's a woman who's been through a lot in the last year. More than most women could handle. I wouldn't blame her for being a bit confused and unsure of things."

Guy turned angrily in his seat. "Who asked you?"

Adam smiled. "No one."

"Just what do you know about women anyway? I was under the—"

"You don't need an erection to be able to think, Guy."

Guy fell silent. He turned and looked out the passenger window. "I'm sorry. I didn't mean anything."

"I know. Like I said, you're probably stung."

There was silence between them for a while. Guy glanced at the man sitting beside him and thought how incredibly wise Adam could be at times. Other times he seemed simple as a child.

"See?" Adam said as they reached his uncle's place. "His truck is there, right where it's been the last three times I was here. It hasn't moved." He pulled up into the drive behind the truck and parked. Guy got out of the cab and walked up to the door, while Adam went to look for the spare key.

"Hello?" Guy called, and he pounded on the door and waited. The house sounded empty to him.

"Here," Adam said, and he stepped up behind Guy and handed him a key. "Try it and see if it's the right one."

Guy put the key in the lock and twisted. The knob turned in his hand. He slowly pushed open the door. "Hello? Anybody home?"

There was no answer. He found himself looking into a dark, shadowed living room. There were papers and cups and other clutter everywhere, but there was no Uncle Arnold. He stepped into the room and felt Adam come in behind him.

"Arnold?" Adam called out. "It's me, Adam. Are you here?"

The heavy gloom of the dark room seemed to swallow his voice. Guy pointed to the kitchen. "You go look in there. I'll check the bedrooms and bathroom."

Adam left him and Guy went on through the living room and into the hall. The bathroom and main bedroom were as messy as the kitchen, but it was a normal mess, with no signs of either burglary or any kind of struggle. He met Adam in the kitchen and the other man looked perplexed.

"Everything looks like he just walked out the door. Where could he have gone?"

Guy thought for a moment. "Is there a basement or a cellar?"

"It's outside," Adam told him. "Off to the side of the house."

"Let's go have a look."

"I don't think he used it for anything anymore."

"Let's look anyway."

They went outside and opened the creaking, rusted hinges of the cellar door. The pitch-black interior released a damp, earthy smell and Guy hesitated before going down. He looked at Adam and Adam said, "I got shut down there once when I was a kid. Melanie did it."

"Did they run her out of the U.S.?" Guy asked, and he started down the concrete steps. Seconds later he was up again, brushing cobwebs and insects from his clothes.

Adam said, "Guess he's not down there."

Guy fought back a shudder of disgust and looked around himself. There were a couple of small sheds behind the house to check out. He methodically looked through all the buildings, Adam striding along behind him. Then he came back to the truck and looked inside. The keys were in the ignition.

"Did he always leave the keys in his truck?" he asked Adam.

Adam shook his head. "No, I don't think he would. Arnold wasn't a fool."

Guy leaned against the driver's door. "I don't know what to tell you, Adam. I'd say it's time to call the police and file a missing person's report."

"What will that do?"

"Probably not much, other than to let people know he's missing, so they can be on the lookout for him."

"Yeah," said Adam. "I guess it's time."

"How old was your uncle?" Guy asked.

Adam lifted a shoulder. "Fifty-six or seven. He was my father's youngest brother."

"How many were there?"

"Seven. Three girls. All the boys dead now but Arnold."

And maybe him, too, thought Guy. He couldn't think of any other reason for the man to leave his home and his truck unattended. "Come on," he said, and he went in the house to pick up the phone. He dialed the number of the police, then he handed the phone to Adam.

When the patrol car arrived at the farm, Guy stepped outside with Adam to inform the officers of all the areas already searched. He saw Michael emerge from the passenger side of the car and he stopped. He had never seen her in uniform before. She saw him at the same moment. Her eyes flickered and she said, "What are you doing here, Guy?"

"Helping Adam," he said.

The other officer looked strangely at Guy, and Michael tried to smile at him. "Guy is Adam's neighbor. Let's get this on paper and have a look around."

"We've looked," said Adam. "He's not here."

"We may find some clue as to where he went," Michael told him, and she took out a clipboard and began to ask Adam questions. Guy listened and looked coldly at her while she wrote down Adam's answers. She looked up at Guy once, and the expression on his face made her look quickly back down again. When her partner disappeared to begin a search, Michael approached Guy and whispered, "All I ask is that you let me explain."

"All I ask is that you leave me alone . . . officer."

"Guy, please. You know how stressful my situation has been. You know I want us to—"

"I'll be leaving soon. That should ease your stress considerably."

Michael's mouth hung open. She stared at him.

"Are you finished with Adam?" Guy asked, his voice still icy. She nodded.

"Good. Let's go," he said to his friend, and he went to open the passenger door of Adam's truck. Adam looked helplessly at Michael and followed. Michael put her clipboard in the car and walked over to Guy's window as Adam started the truck. "Are you going because of me?"

Guy gave her a withering glance and signaled to Adam. They left her standing in the drive, staring after them.

CHAPTER
TWENTY-SEVEN

FROM HIS THIRD STORY WINDOW, Vernon watched the police cars around Arnold Dupree's house. He hadn't thought they would discover Arnold missing so soon, but the evening before he had seen a pair of men snooping around the place. He saw a truck behind Arnold's, and someone he would swear was Guy Driscoll. The man limped, anyway. There was another man, and then two police officers had joined them. One of the officers was a woman, and Vernon had drawn a sharp breath when he recognized her as Michael Bish.

He didn't know what her presence meant, but his mind raced as he went over the possible conclusions. She had been reinstated, that much was certain. Which meant no one thought she was guilty. Which meant they thought he was a liar. Which meant they would probably be watching him from that point on.

"Dammit," he muttered to himself that morning as he watched them at Dupree's house.

Then he smiled. What did he have to worry about? He had taken care of Arnold, and he was the last problem Vernon would have to worry about for a while. No more threats from

Elma to go and live with the old widower. She didn't know yet, of course. She had no idea her wrinkled old friend was now lying at the bottom of an abandoned well thirty miles away in the next county. Arnold wouldn't be found for some time, Vernon knew. He had camouflaged every part of the well so that all the wood was hidden. Not many people even knew it existed. Vernon knew of it because his mother had once taken him there as a boy.

She had playfully hooked the back of his shirt with the bucket hook and lowered him into the well. Just for fun, she had said. Then she left him there for four hours, telling him it was his punishment for disobeying her. When she told him to use Blushing Rose powder on someone's face, she didn't mean Antique Rose. He would learn the difference or be out of the business. She had no use for retards or insolent boys who thought they knew better than their mother. He would have to decide which one he was.

"I'm a retard!" he had screamed at her.

"Are you sure? Are you sure you're not the other?"

"No, I'm a retard! I don't listen! I don't know better than you, Mother, I swear it!"

"That's better," she said, and when the four hours were up she took him out of the well and kissed him and hugged him and cried because she had to do these things to him.

A few years later, as a teenager, Vernon had gone back and blown up the well with some homemade explosives. The blasts had been small but effective, and the well was destroyed and later covered. To put Arnold Dupree inside, Vernon had been forced to tear apart the concrete cover with a sledgehammer. The work had been hard and it had given him blisters, but getting rid of Arnold had made it all worthwhile. Elma had nowhere to go now. Nowhere but home. Vernon's home.

At the moment she was enjoying a small amount of notoriety as the woman who had gunned down David Eulert. The people of Colson still had a hard time believing their beloved David had tried to kill Michael Bish, but it was right there in the paper for everyone to read. When Captain Mawby attempted to take him in for questioning, Eulert grabbed his gun. Not many could deny the guilt behind that action, but plenty tried. According to Vernon's hospital source, some said the whole thing had been staged by the police as a way to kill the gay David Eulert for shooting Oliver. Vernon had to chuckle at the bizarre inferences people read into a simple shooting, but a story in that day's paper, written by Guy Driscoll, had uncovered the true reason for Eulert's dismissal from the Springfield Sheriff's Department. Through a phone interview with an inside source, he had learned of Eulert's backseat sex with a young male prostitute.

The town would be buzzing by now, Vernon guessed. And the mortuary would be crowded that day, everyone wanting a glimpse of the dead gay jock. The funeral would be tomorrow at one o'clock, with burial in the cemetery immediately following the service. Vernon had considered putting Arnold Dupree in the bottom of David Eulert's grave and simply burying David on top of him. But that was too risky. He might have been seen in the cemetery. The way it was, he had gone over to Arnold's house, talked to him a minute, hit him on the head with a large brick, and stuck him in his trunk for the drive to the well. Simple and clean, for the most part, anyway. There had been a little blood in the trunk, but Vernon cleaned it up.

Elma was still in a funk over having shot a man. She hadn't looked at or responded to Vernon all the previous day. That morning he asked her to help with the embalming of Eulert, and she looked at him like he was crazy. *I killed him and you want me to help embalm him?*

Vernon had smiled at the expression on her face.

"You'll get over it, Elma. Trust me. I know what I'm talking about."

She sneered at him. Vernon didn't like it when she did that. She reminded him of his mother when she sneered at him like that, but he was powerless to do anything about it. Even if he hit her she'd just go on sneering. And he didn't want her to disappear on him.

She came into the bedroom behind him while he was looking out the window and tried to peer over his shoulder. He moved aside to let her see. She looked out for a moment, saw what he was looking at, then she turned to him, a question in her eyes.

"I don't know," Vernon responded. "The police were there last night, too. Arnold must have done something."

Elma rolled her eyes. *Sure.*

"Well?" said Vernon. "What else could it mean?"

She shook her head. Then she made a walking motion with her fingers and pointed at Vernon.

"No. I've got things to do. You can go over and find out what's happening if you want to."

Elma shook her head again. She lowered her eyes.

Vernon lifted her chin. "No one's going to say anything to you, Elma. They're not going to call you a murderer and throw rocks at you. The whole story is in the paper today. Have you read it? There's also a piece by Guy Driscoll about the reason David Eulert was let go by the sheriff's patrol in Springfield. He was having sex with a male prostitute in his patrol car and he was caught."

Brown eyes blinked as Elma took this in. Vernon saw the anxiety in her lessen. "See?" he said, and he gave her a swift kiss. "Anything more comes out and people will be patting you on the back for a job well done."

Elma looked out the window again and Vernon gave her a small pat on the bottom. When she looked at him, he said, "Go on over if you want to. If Arnold's there, tell him I'll need his help with a coffin, if he can make it."

Her look was still uncertain, and Vernon stepped away

from the window. "It's up to you. I've got to get back to work. Viewing begins at one today."

He went out of the room and left her standing by the window looking pensively at the goings-on at Arnold Dupree's house. Vernon had to smile at his own cleverness. *If Arnold's there . . .* He almost wished he could be there to see the look on her face when she found out Arnold was missing.

Missing was better than dead. If Arnold had turned up dead, Elma would waste no time in blaming Vernon. But *missing.* She wouldn't blame him for that. She'd think he was so greedy for money that he would have wanted to handle Arnold's funeral as well. Vernon was greedy, but he wasn't stupid. Besides, things had been going fairly well lately. Four people had died in only the last few weeks, leaving his bank account in good shape. The bills were paid, and there was no evidence of the financial woes David Eulert had hinted at to the police captain.

But he would be watched from that point on. He was certain of it. Suspicion would be high, so his profile would be low. He could handle it. He could handle the model citizen business and make jerks out of the cops sent to watch him. They would wonder what they were being paid for. They would wonder why they were watching poor innocent Vernon Diest, rather than a *real* criminal.

Vernon chuckled to himself as he went down to work on David Eulert. He walked over to the still white corpse on the prep table and smirked as he tore away the sheet. As he began to spray Eulert's orifices with disinfectant, Vernon briefly considered cutting off the man's privates and sewing them into his mouth—something he heard the Mafia did—but the thought of touching his severed penis and testicles made Vernon think of AIDS.

His lip curled as he began the embalming procedure. He placed one tube in Eulert's femoral artery and removed the blood; then he fixed another tube in the carotid artery to pump the pinkish fluid that would provide natural coloring for the body. Then he thought of something.

If Elma went to see what was happening at Arnold's, she might run into Michael Bish. Vernon didn't want that to happen. He had seen the way Michael tried to talk to Elma at her husband's funeral. Michael was going to prod Elma, and Vernon was certain his deaf little lovely couldn't take much of that. He dropped what he was doing and ran back upstairs. Elma was gone from the window.

Vernon searched the third floor and part of the second before he remembered the pressure gauge. He raced downstairs and found a bloated, pink corpse awaiting him. Eulert looked hideously huge, like a floater found in the water. Vernon tore out the tubing and turned off the machine, disgusted with himself for forgetting. He quickly stabbed Eulert in the belly with a trocar and watched the excess fluid spurt. Vernon still followed the method of embalming taught to him by his mother. There were any number of new chemicals and methods available, but Vernon had no use for them. Like his mother, he had no formal training, but he was an artist, specializing in one medium. His tools were spatulas and palette knives and powder atomizers. His paints were wax and the claylike, flesh-colored base coat.

When Eulert looked only slightly puffy, Vernon pulled up the sheet again and left the room. He had to find Elma. It was frustrating not being able to shout for her, and he found himself shouting for her anyway as he moved through each level. Finally he was forced to concede that she was not in the house. She had gone next door to see about Arnold, and Michael Bish had doubtlessly corralled her and was busy pumping her for information at that very moment. The picture was not a pleasant one. Vernon felt his nostrils flare as he left the house and walked across the drive and into the cemetery. He didn't know what he would say when he found her, but he would think of something. And he had to be careful, because those damned police officers would be watching him.

Vernon heaved a sigh. There were so many things he had to remember, so many things to keep on top of. It was a wonder he could function at all.

As he passed his mother's grave, Vernon kicked at the silk flowers by her marker. The arrangement fell over and lay on the grass, its silk petals quivering in the wind.

CHAPTER
TWENTY-EIGHT

ELMA HID IN THE HEDGEROW on one side of her garden and cried.
It was obvious something had happened to Arnold Dupree.
The police and other men were scouring the ground for signs
of anything unusual. They looked in Arnold's house and sheds
a dozen times and rendezvoused near the truck twice in the
thirty minutes she watched them. Arnold was evidently gone.
One man's mouth was saying something about the keys in the
truck. The man he was speaking to had a wad of chewing
tobacco in his mouth and Elma couldn't make out his reply.

Instinctively, she thought of Vernon and knew. He had
probably done something to Arnold. And it was all Elma's
fault, for taunting him with the possibility of her leaving him
to go and live with the old man. Elma couldn't believe the
things she had done in the last few weeks. She couldn't believe the person she had become. She was as bad as Vernon.
She had shot David Eulert as surely as Vernon shot Adele
Driscoll. She knew Vernon was on some level intimidated by
Eulert and his subtle threats. That frightened Elma, and it
was fear that had made her want to see Eulert die and had
propelled her to pick up Mawby's pistol.

And last night, though she'd wanted nothing to do with

Vernon and his advances, she had never felt more sexually alive and aware. When he mounted her wooden body and pushed himself inside her, she felt a sudden surge of pleasure that made her want to gasp aloud. Instead she had clenched her teeth and kept the sensations she was feeling to herself. It was like nothing she had ever known, and a part of her didn't want him to stop. When he did stop, she rolled away from him as quickly as she could, unwilling to let him see how her body trembled with the pleasure she had experienced.

Elma loathed herself for enjoying the act of sex after having killed a man. It was pagan. It was animalistic.

And now Arnold Dupree was gone.

She wiped her nose with a tissue from her pocket and backed out of the hedge. She went to her row of beans and began to pick some of the green pods. As she reached the end of the first row she saw a pair of shoes. She looked up and saw Michael Bish smiling at her. "Hello," Michael said.

Slowly, Elma nodded. Her impulse was to run, but she knew she could not. Guilty people ran.

"I'd like to talk to you," Michael said, and she withdrew a pen and handed Elma her police pad. "You can write, can't you?"

Another nod.

"Good. I have one question for you, Elma, and it's a very important one. I know you work for Vernon Diest, and I know you live with him. I hope you'll be truthful with me. The night he was shot, the night I shot him, did you at any time see him with a gun?"

Elma thought for a minute, then she wrote: *What does it matter now? Your name has been cleared.*

"It matters," Michael said after reading the note. "I still want people to know he pulled a gun on me. I want people to know he's a dangerous man."

Elma agreed. Vernon was a dangerous man. She had realized just how dangerous only a short time ago. What she had believed to be desperation on his part was actually a long sublimated desire to do harm to others. He had broken free of the restraints of morality and was acting upon his darker impulses with no qualms. What he had done to her was proof. Adele Driscoll had been only the beginning for him. He was changing every day, emerging from his chrysalis as a great black moth, testing his wet wings, flicking his antennae and tainting everything with his sticky, viscous bitterness. Elma shuddered to think that she had actually enjoyed sex with him.

But she had. And she would again, she knew. Despite what he was and what he was becoming, Vernon was hers, and Elma knew she could influence him. Arnold Dupree's absence told her that much. She could manipulate Vernon, and hopefully change him before the blackness in his eyes colored his heart. She could do it. She was as strong as Alissa had been, and she had sex on her side. For a man whose sexual appetite had been decidedly small for so many years, Vernon couldn't get enough of Elma. She would use his need of her to her advantage. To everyone's advantage.

She looked at Michael again and wrote: *I can't help you.*

Michael read it and sighed. "I know what you're worried about, Elma. If something happened to Vernon, what would become of you? Believe me, you would be helped. We wouldn't simply abandon you. The people in Colson are kinder than you know."

Elma nodded and wrote: *Yes, I've seen their kindnesses. What they did to you. The overwhelming sympathy they showed for Guy Driscoll when his daughter was shot. No flowers, no nothing. Instead they idolize men like David Eulert and gather like vultures at his death to pick at the bones of his character. Thank you, but no thank you. I'll do all right where I am.*

Michael read the note and looked at Elma for a long moment. Finally, she said, "You're much different than I imagined. Tougher. You don't look very tough, you know."

Neither do you . . . for a policewoman, Elma wrote.

"Thanks, I think," Michael said with a laugh as she read

the line. Then she looked seriously at Elma. "If you ever need anything, get in touch with me. I'll give you my address." She took the pen and pad and scribbled her address, then tore off the page and handed it to Elma. "Anything, Elma. This isn't a vendetta against Vernon Diest, and I don't want you to think I'm trying to trick you into betraying him. If you ever need me, I will help you. Remember what I said about the bus."

Elma clutched the note and for a moment she was tempted to grab the pad from Michael and tell her everything. Her conscience begged her to do just that. She held out her hand for the pen and pad and saw Michael's gaze turn suddenly cold. Elma turned and saw Vernon approaching them. His black eyes burned with hostility.

All thoughts of betrayal evaporated under his black glare. Elma backed hastily away from Michael and stooped to collect the beans she had picked. She looked up as Vernon entered the garden and saw him address Michael: "May I assume you have some official reason for being here?"

"Yes," Michael said. "I was about to ask Elma if she saw Mr. Dupree at any time yesterday."

Elma straightened and shook her head no.

"What's happened to Mr. Dupree?" Vernon asked.

"He's missing," Michael said. "What about you, Mr. Diest? Did you see Mr. Dupree at any time yesterday?"

"No, I did not. How long has he been gone?"

"No one is sure. The last time anyone remembers seeing him was at my husband's funeral. Did you see him after that?"

"I'm sure I did, though I can't say just when. He didn't come over to help me with anything, if that's what you're asking. Which reminds me, it looks like I'm going to have to seek elsewhere for help now that Arnold is missing. Come on, Elma. Let's go back to the house. I need to make some calls."

Elma held her beans in her skirt and looked at Michael. In her hand she held the address given her, and she did her best to conceal it from Vernon. For some reason, Elma trusted the other woman. Michael Bish had no quarrel with Elma. She wished her no harm. She wanted only to help. The address would remain in a secret place, a safeguard against whatever might happen, should Elma's plans for Vernon's reform fail.

Michael's look for Vernon was full of contempt as they walked away. Vernon put his arm across Elma's shoulders and gave her a gentle squeeze, making certain Michael saw the caress. To Elma he said, "What did she say to you, and more important, what did you say to her?"

Elma lifted her hands in a dismissing gesture. Vernon stared at her. "Don't lie to me, Elma. I mean it. What did she say? Did she ask questions about me?"

Yes. Elma nodded.

"What did you tell her?"

Elma held up her fingers and made a zero. She felt Vernon relax beside her. "That's good. That's wonderful. I don't know why I was so worried. You wouldn't betray me, would you? Not my own bride-to-be."

Briefly she had the urge to give him the finger again. It passed. She wasn't sure now whether she wanted to marry him or not. Not if he had done something to Arnold Dupree. But if he had, he had done it because of her. Her big mouth that made no words but nevertheless managed to get her and others into trouble.

She didn't think Vernon was serious about marrying her anyway. He just said that to keep her hoping and to stay on her good side. Elma shrugged off his arm and he put it right back across her shoulders, as if it had fallen off by accident. She walked on with him to the house, the beans still in her skirt, and he held open the door for her. It was the first time he had ever done so. Elma took the beans up to the kitchen and he followed her and picked up the phone. Over his shoulder she saw him dial the number of his friend at the hospital, the head nurse. He turned as he finished dialing and told Elma what had happened with David Eulert.

"The poor bastard looks awful. I really screwed him up."

Elma's brows knitted and Vernon laughed.

"God, I'm glad you can't speak to me. My mother would have taken one look at him and started screaming her head off. She would have turned blue and picked up that long stick she used to carry around and come after me with it."

Elma stared at him as he shook his head. She had never seen Alissa abuse him. She had never seen Alissa lift a hand to him. The woman had screamed plenty, but she had never harmed anyone. Not that Elma had seen, anyway. But of course by the time Elma arrived Vernon was grown and far too big to strike effectively. She turned away as he started speaking into the phone and slipped the piece of paper in her hand into her shoe. Later, when the beans were in a pot on the stove and Vernon was off the phone, she opened her hands to ask what he had come up with.

"One of the nurses' sons is coming over tomorrow to help me. I'll pay him ten dollars to help with the casket. Ten dollars. One thing about Arnold, he didn't expect payment for doing a man a favor." He lifted his nose then. "Are you cooking something besides those beans?"

Elma shook her head and lifted her brows. Why?

He grinned at her. "Good. Turn off that stove and come over here. I have to go down and rescue what's left of David Eulert, but first I need a moment of your time."

A spark leapt in Elma's belly. She couldn't believe it, but the way he was looking at her actually excited her. She went over to stand before him. He sat down on a kitchen chair and undid his pants. Then he reached up beneath her skirt and pulled down her underwear. He waited while she lifted up her legs to step out of the panties, then he instructed her to sit on his lap. She looked at him and cocked an eyebrow.

"Come on," he urged her. "We haven't got all day. Just sit down facing me and I'll take care of the rest. I feel like kissing you this time."

Elma carefully lowered herself onto his lap. He pulled her legs around him and lifted her hips until he could guide himself into her. Elma shuddered when she was sitting on top of him and he was all the way inside her. God help me, she thought. I love this monster. I must. I can't believe someone I hate could make me feel this way.

He brought her mouth to his and then he placed his hands on her hips to move her up and down. Elma came to orgasm almost immediately and he groaned with pleasure into her mouth. Moments later he peaked and tightened his arms around her. Elma expected him to stop kissing her, but he went on and on, until he grew hard inside her again and brought her to orgasm a second time. She relaxed until she was almost collapsed onto him, and she felt him pat the back of her head. She looked at him and he said, "I don't know what you've done to me. I don't know who I am or what I want anymore. I used to think I had it all figured out. I had a place to fill and I filled it. Now I'm starting to have other ideas."

Her eyes mirrored her confusion. He smiled at her and said, "I'm starting to think marrying you and having children is a good idea. I just don't want anyone to get in our way. Do you know what I mean? I don't want anyone to try to come between us."

She blinked and he said, "You're not committed to me yet. Not fully. I can feel that you aren't. You threaten to leave and you push me away when I want to touch you. That hurts me, Elma. You'll never know how much. Here I've fallen completely in love with you, and you act like you can't stand the sight of me. Don't you know you're all I can think about? If anyone a year ago had told me I would feel this way about you today, I would've called them crazy. You were nothing to me, a ghostlike little nobody who drifted around the second floor. Now it's different. Now I'm consumed with you. I want you to be my wife, Elma. I want us to be married and have a normal life, with no more hurting. When times get hard, we'll get through it together. We'll have each other and that's all we'll ever need. What do you say, Elma? Will you marry me?"

Moisture filled Elma's eyes. She searched his black orbs and found nothing but sincerity. He quivered with intensity as he waited for her answer. Slowly she lowered her mouth to his and kissed him. It was the first time she had ever done so of her own volition. He groaned into her mouth again; she could feel the vibration. Then she lifted her head and looked at him. His eyes danced with joy. "May I take that as a yes?"

Elma nodded.

CHAPTER
TWENTY-NINE

MICHAEL RETURNED TO her father's house after a day of searching for Arnold Dupree and found Ben Ogilvie's Buick in the driveway. She went inside and discovered him in his bedroom unpacking his small travel bag. "How was your trip?" she asked.

Her father turned to look at her. His eyes roved over her police uniform. "My trip was good, thanks. I see you've been reinstated. Congratulations." He came to give her a brief hug. Then he said, "Who was here?"

Michael frowned. "What?"

"Two glasses in the sink. Who was here?"

"Oh, that. Guy Driscoll came by this morning."

"What was he doing here?"

"He came to see me." Michael paused and smiled. "I'm a big girl now. You don't have to interrogate me."

"Don't you think it's a little soon to be seeing someone? Oliver's been dead only a few days."

Michael's smile faded. "Daddy, weren't you the one encouraging me to go out just a month ago? Find a life, you said."

"I didn't mean with another man." Her father gave her one

of his stern, don't-argue-with-me looks. "Michael, you've suffered a lot of bad press this year. Don't bring any more attention to yourself. Now that you've been reinstated you'd be well-advised to lay low and stay out of trouble. Soon people will learn to respect you again. That's what you want."

His daughter stared at him. She backed up until her knees were against her father's bed, then she sat down. "I thought that's what I wanted," Michael said. "I thought the same things you just said to me. But hearing it spoken aloud makes me realize how ludicrous the whole thing sounds. No wonder Guy is so disgusted. Why did I ever think hurting him was the right thing to do?"

"Because it is," her father said firmly. "Leave him alone for now. In six months, call him again. He'll still be around."

"No, he won't. He's leaving."

Her father exhaled. "Good. Well, we won't talk about it anymore. Have you spoken to Sean? How is she?"

"She's fine."

"I brought something from Springfield for her, a nice sweatshirt with a hood for her to jog in."

"Sean doesn't jog, Daddy."

"Well, she walks, doesn't she? It'll look good on her. She always looks good in red."

Michael walked away from him and began to gather up the things she had brought with her from home. When she finished, she carried her overnight bag to the door and sat it down. Her father smiled at her. "Thank you for coming over and looking after the place. I appreciate it. I've always known I could count on you, Michael."

Her smile was brief. "Anytime, Dad." She bent down to pick up her bag and her father said, "About what we were talking about, I really do think it's a good idea if you wait to jump into any relationships. People would talk if you didn't, Michael, and I think we've all had our share of that business. I didn't want to say anything before, but Sean's been embarrassed a number of times by references to you made at the school. I've even heard things in the shop that I was too embarrassed to tell you about. We haven't said anything because we love you, and we know you haven't done the things people are saying you have."

Michael straightened. "For instance?"

Her father's smile was patient. "I know you haven't slept with Guy Driscoll, although much of the town seems to think you have. It's all his fault, I realize, after the stunt he pulled to get you out of jail. But it's made many people think unsavory thoughts about you."

Michael had to smile. "Dad, people have been thinking unsavory thoughts about me since I was twelve years old."

Her father bristled at her humor. "They've never called you a whore before."

"Are you saying they're calling me one now?"

"And worse. Some people believe you actually are mentally unbalanced."

His anger suddenly enflamed her own. Her hands curled into fists that she held tightly at her sides. "Maybe I *am* unbalanced. While you were gone I brought Guy over here and tried to get him to sleep with me. I sat on his lap and did everything I could think of to make him give in, but he wouldn't touch me. He said he loved me and he didn't want me to do anything I would feel guilty about later."

Her father was staring at her. "You mean to tell me you brought him into my house and—"

"I wish we had made love," Michael continued. "The man makes me tremble, Daddy. He causes me to shake when I'm near him. I've never felt anything like it, not with Oliver, not with anyone, and part of it is the way he looks at me. I don't think anyone has ever felt about me the way Guy Driscoll does."

"What is there to feel?" her father snapped. "He doesn't even know you."

"Oh, he knows me. Maybe better than I know myself. And I go on hurting him." She stooped to pick up her bag.

"Don't go," her father commanded. "You stay right where you are and talk to me."

"No," Michael said, and she opened the door.

"This is simple physical attraction," her father said heatedly. "You've said he loves you. You can't possibly have grown to love him. Not so soon after Oliver."

Michael looked at her father. "I didn't know how I felt about him until the moment he said he was leaving. Then I knew. I don't want him to go, and I'm going to do all I can to make him stay."

Her father snorted. "Go on. Get out of my sight. I can't talk sense to you. Maybe Sean can. I give up."

They were familiar words. Michael shook her head as she exited the house and knew her father would be on the phone to her sister within seconds, recounting every word of their conversation. She didn't care.

She drove home by way of Guy's house. His Volvo was gone.

At home she left a message on his answering machine to please call her, but she knew he wouldn't. She didn't know what she could say to him to make him change his mind, but tonight it would be enough just to hear his voice. The moment she hung up the phone, it rang. She picked it up and said hello to her sister Sean.

"How did you know it was me?" Sean asked.

"A lucky guess. What's up?"

"You know very well. Daddy's worried sick about you."

"Is he?"

"Michael, don't be that way. He said you were talking strangely, and that you seemed kind of spacey. He asked me if you were taking any kind of medication."

Michael held the receiver away from her mouth while she laughed. "Isn't that typical," she said. "When you say something he doesn't like, he thinks you're on drugs."

"He said you'd had Guy Driscoll over to his house and that you claimed you tried to seduce him."

"Yes," Michael confirmed. Then she sobered. "If I remember correctly, it was you who suggested I sleep with him."

"As a means of physical gratification, nothing more. It really is too soon for you to be seen in public with anyone, Michael. You know that."

"Sean, you're a hypocrite," Michael said, and she hung up the phone. She expected her sister to call right back, but Sean didn't. Michael went into the kitchen to prepare a pitcher of iced tea. After she poured a glass for herself, she went into the bedroom to change. As she peeled off her uniform she thought about how happy she had been to put it on again after so long. But that was yesterday. Today it was old business again, with everyone saying they were sorry about Oliver and then proceeding to ignore her, the lone female on the active force. Everyone but Bob Birzer, who had lost the draw when it came to receiving Michael as a partner. She didn't know why she had been so anxious to return.

She didn't know anything anymore, she decided as she finished dressing in a blouse and shorts and made her way to the patio, where she could see Guy Driscoll's backyard. Her father and sister had said everything she was prepared to say to Guy, and it all sounded so ridiculously trite and just plain selfish that she was appalled at her own shallowness. She imagined Guy felt the same. He was probably asking himself how he could have been so wrong about her.

Michael had no excuse, really, other than confusion and a desire to do the right thing. Which usually meant doing the thing that would please her father and sister. Now both of them were upset with her, and rather than make her frantic with anxiety, as it always had in the past, she felt calm and sure of her position. They were wrong this time, not her.

She saw a light go on in Guy's kitchen, and she nearly fell off her chair on the patio. He was home. Had he listened to his messages yet? she wondered. She waited for the next fifteen minutes and glimpsed his form twice as he moved about his house. When her phone didn't ring, she knew he was going to ignore her plea to call. She left the patio and headed for the door, grabbing her purse on the way.

When Guy opened his door he was dressed in jogging clothes. He glared at Michael and then stepped outside. He closed his door behind him.

"We need to talk, Guy," said Michael. "Please."

"No, we don't," he replied, and he took off across his yard. Michael ran after him a few yards.

"Guy, I was wrong! Please come back and hear what I have to say!"

He kept moving away from her, his gait awkward as he strove to find a rhythm with his injured hip. Michael sat down on the curb in front of his house and put her head in her hands for a moment. Then she got up and went to sit on his porch. She would wait.

Two hours later she rose from his porch and walked dejectedly back to her car. He was deliberately staying away to avoid any contact with her.

She drove home and called the paper to ask if the rumor about Guy Driscoll leaving was true. The night editor told her yes, it was true, and that Guy would be going back to Chicago at the end of the month. When the editor asked who was calling, Michael said thank you and hung up.

It was official. He was really leaving.

Michael went into her bedroom and stared at the uniform hanging on the back of the closet door. She opened the closet and looked at the contents. Then she went into the basement for some boxes.

There was no guilt or remorse this time as she packed Oliver's clothes and other items. There was nothing but calm acceptance and a willingness to go on in a different way.

It was late by the time she dropped her boxes off at the Salvation Army. Some things she had taken to Oliver's mother and sister, and their treatment of her suggested that they too had heard rumors. Michael dismissed their coolness and went on her way. After emptying her car, she drove home and entered the house in time to hear the phone ring. Hoping it was Guy, she rushed over and snatched up the receiver. "Hello?"

"Have you cooled off?" asked Sean.

Michael sighed. "I wasn't angry. What do you want?"

"To talk some sense into you. Oliver's sister just called me and said you'd brought a lot of his things over. Didn't you keep anything?"

"Of course I did," Michael snapped.

"I'm just surprised at how quickly you've abandoned his memory," Sean continued. "You're ready to jump into bed with Guy Driscoll and forget all about what Oliver meant to you."

"I can't believe I'm hearing this," Michael said. "You were the one who kept urging me away from his bedside. The man was dead for all means and purposes, you claimed. What is this, Sean? Aren't you happy I listened to you?"

"I was wrong, Michael. People are talking, and the things they're saying aren't very nice."

"People will always talk about me, Sean. I'm used to it."

"This time it's hurting us," Sean admonished. "After the article Guy wrote about David Eulert, people are coming up with things you wouldn't believe. They're speculating about the source of his information, and some are saying you and he cooked up the whole story to paint David as black as possible and to cover up the real reason for his death."

"Neither of us had anything to do with his death," Michael argued. "We weren't anywhere near when he died."

"People believe want they want to believe, Michael, and they don't want to believe David Eulert was a homosexual who paid male prostitutes for sex. Guy Driscoll didn't realize what he was doing when he wrote that story. He doesn't know the people of Colson. But you do, and you should know you're asking for trouble by running around with him so soon after your husband's death."

Michael grew exasperated. "I haven't been running around

with him. For crying out loud, he's been running *away* from me. He won't even talk to me. Besides, he's leaving at the end of the month. He's going back to Chicago."

"Good," Sean said with a sigh of relief. "Maybe things can get back to normal around here."

"Meaning me?" Michael asked.

"Meaning everything. It seems like things have been crazy ever since he came to town."

"Oliver was shot long before Guy showed up. Don't blame Guy out of convenience. It's not fair."

"To him, no. But Colson needs a scapegoat right now, and he's been elected. When he's gone, people won't have anyone to blame but themselves again."

Michael listened to her sister and realized for the first time that Sean had accepted the small-mindedness of their town. Had perhaps even contributed to it by accepting it. Michael emitted a rueful sigh of her own, then she said, "I've been trying to see him again. I have to explain to him, Sean."

"There's nothing to explain. He's got eyes and a brain in his head. He knows the score. Leave him alone, Michael. We'll all be better off if you do. We haven't got anywhere else to go. We have to live here with these people. Which reminds me, did you find any sign of Arnold Dupree?"

"Nothing," said Michael. "It's as if the man simply vanished."

"That's odd," Sean commented.

"Very."

"Well?"

"Well what?"

"Are you going to leave Guy Driscoll alone or not?"

Michael gave up finally and told her sister what she wanted to hear. It was the only way she would get any peace. Then she said goodbye. As she hung up, her thoughts returned to the missing Arnold Dupree. Soon an image of Elma Voycheck and Vernon Diest surfaced. There had been a flicker of something in Vernon Diest's eyes when Michael asked him about

the old man. She was certain of it. But perhaps it was para-
noia about Diest that made her think so. It was entirely possible, she admitted. Every time she looked at Vernon Diest she
saw him holding a gun on her.

She thought back and remembered the possessive way he
placed his arm around the deaf Elma's shoulders as he led
her out of the garden. There was definitely something going
on between the two of them.

"And I thought I had problems," she murmured to herself.
She could only hope Elma knew what she was doing.

CHAPTER
THIRTY

GUY SAW ELMA the next day when he went with Adam to help harvest some of Arnold Dupree's garden. The cabbage and beans had long been ready; the tomatoes were ripe and falling off the vines. Adam knew Arnold would have hated to see any of it go to waste. While they were picking, Guy happened to look up and see Elma peering at them through the fence. "Hi," he said, and gave a little wave with his hand.

Elma jerked back into the cedars, but at Guy's smile she slowly emerged again. She poked her face and then her body through the trees to stand and look at what they were doing. Adam straightened and looked at her. "We're picking it so it won't go to waste. Arnold is my uncle."

She nodded and pointed to some of the vegetables on the ground. Guy and Adam looked at each other.

"I know who she is," Adam said finally. "She can't talk. She can't hear, either. I've heard about her. I think she wants some of the stuff we picked."

"Looks like it," Guy said, and he made some motions with his hands. "Do you sign?"

Elma shook her head and pointed to her eyes and then her mouth.

"Okay. You read lips. Do you want some of what we've picked?"

She nodded. After a moment of hesitation, she made a writing motion with her hand and looked questioningly at Guy.

"Are you kidding?" he said with a smile. "A good reporter always carries something to write on." He took a small pad and a pencil from his pocket and walked over to hand them to her. She took them from him and smiled her thanks before she began to write.

She wrote: *Arnold gave me vegetables and seeds for my garden. Always very kind to me. Did man with you say he was Arnold's nephew?*

"That's right," Guy said after he read it. "Adam lives next door to me."

Adam nodded shyly to Elma, and Guy saw his cheeks redden slightly. He turned away and began to pick beans again. "Adam's on the quiet side," he explained to Elma.

Elma wrote: *I am, too. Tell him he looks like his uncle— probably just as nice. Has there been word about Arnold?*

Guy read the note and said, "No, nothing." Then he recognized her. He stared at her face a moment. "I saw you in the mortuary, didn't I? You work for Diest."

She nodded and began writing again.

Vernon and I will be married on Saturday. We'll run the mortuary and chapel together.

"Married? You're going to marry Diest?" Guy said, and Adam looked up.

Elma's wide smile was her answer. Adam looked down again and concentrated on the beans.

"Congratulations," Guy said, though his heart wasn't in it. Elma nodded happily and handed the pad back to him. Guy placed it in his pocket and then stooped down to gather some of the produce they had picked. "Do you have something to put them in? I think we have an extra sack."

She skipped away and was back in seconds with a large basket. She pointed to the garden and then over the fence.

Then she pointed to herself. Guy understood. "Your garden is on the other side of the trees. In the cemetery."

She quirked a brow at him and spread her hands, as if to say, *Where else?*

Guy filled the basket with vegetables and handed it back over the fence to her. She looked different than she had the day he saw her, he observed. She was fuller, and had color in her cheeks. Her brown eyes were moist and lively, not sad and drawn as they had been the day he went to the mortuary to see his dead daughter. Elma was a pretty woman.

"Ask her if her dad is going to give her away," Adam said, and Guy frowned at him. "What?"

Adam looked timidly at Elma. "I saw your father yesterday. The man who married Mrs. Diest. Will he be in your wedding?"

Elma stared at Adam until the brown in her eyes was almost covered with black. Her mouth opened and began to tremble. Adam stepped back from the shock he had given her.

"I was just asking. It's none of my business, I know. I was only curious. I heard he was gone again, but then I saw him downtown at the bus terminal as I was coming home yesterday and—"

The basket tumbled to the ground, spilling vegetables everywhere. Elma turned on her heel and ran away from them, her dress flapping against the branches of the cedars. Guy looked at Adam and blinked. "What did you say?"

"I don't know," Adam said. "I guess she didn't know her dad was in town." He paused then and said, "I don't think she likes him."

"That may be an understatement, judging from her reaction. I can't believe she's actually going to marry Vernon Diest. Maybe the old man came home to try and stop her."

"Maybe." Adam's face colored again. "That's what I get for opening up my mouth. She ran off without taking any vegetables."

"I'll fill up the basket again and put it in her garden," Guy said. "Maybe she'll come back out to get them."

"Think we should take them to her?" Adam asked.

Guy had a brief memory of the moments spent in the bottom of a grave in the cemetery, the panic he had experienced as he tried to breathe life back into Michael.

"No," he said. "I don't want to be anywhere near the place."

"Yeah, you're right. I've caused enough trouble for one day."

"I didn't mean that," Guy said.

"I know. I know you didn't." Adam's face turned beet red then. "Just for a minute there . . . looking at her, with her pretty dress and her pink face, I actually thought I could feel something . . . down there."

Guy stared at him. "You did?"

"It must have been my imagination. I've seen lots of women."

Guy grinned and opened his mouth to make a comment, but the pain on Adam's face caused his grin to fade. Guy made a decision then. "Come to think of it, if we leave the vegetables sitting out all day they'll probably rot in the heat. Let's fill up the basket again and run it up to the mortuary on our way home."

Adam turned his back on Guy. "You take it up to the door."

Guy blew out his breath in frustration. "Do you want to see her again or not?"

"She's getting married," Adam said flatly. "Stop what you're doing. I don't need to know if I felt something or not. I don't want to know. All right?"

"Fine," said Guy, and he hopped the fence. "I'll fill up the basket and leave it in the shade."

Adam turned to watch him. When Guy hopped the fence again, Adam picked up the sacks he'd filled and started back to his truck. Guy picked up the remaining sacks and went after him. Once in the cab he said, "I'm sorry. I thought I saw a chance to help."

"I don't need help," Adam said, and the bitterness in his voice took Guy by surprise.

"I'm the same as you," Adam said after a moment. "I'm only different in that I don't have sex. I like to live quiet, Guy. I have my dog, and I have my television. People always think bad things about me, but if they knew I couldn't do anything it wouldn't change their minds. I'd still be that weird old guy who lives on the corner. They'd just think I had a basement full of videotapes and magazines and other stuff to make up for what I can't do. They don't know that I read books and watch soap operas and comb Baby every day. No one cares if I feel anything or not, Guy. They say my mind comes and goes, and maybe it does, I can't tell if it does, but it won't make a damn bit of difference if I ever *feel* anything again. Do you know what I mean?"

Guy wasn't certain, but he thought so. "Yes," he said, and he reached over to lay a hand on Adam's shoulder. "I'm going to miss you when I go."

"I'll miss you, too," Adam said with a grudging smile. "I like having you for a neighbor. We do things together."

Guy gave a short laugh. "You're my bodyguard this week. The phones were ringing like crazy at the paper. Seems people want me strung and quartered for the bit on the local boy wonder. Glasstock rapped my wrists and sent me home for the day."

"He didn't know about the article?" Adam asked.

"I substituted it for another one I'd written. Same word length, same everything. He left early the afternoon I turned it in, so he didn't see what was going in for the next day. He usually checks, so it was a big surprise for him. For everyone, evidently."

Adam shook his head. "You like to shake people up, don't you?"

Guy smiled and looked out the windshield. "That's why I

got into the newspaper business. Small town sinisterness was something I didn't count on. They don't want the news, they want a pretty cake with icing on top. They want heroes to remain heroes, even when the charge is attempted murder."

"It's annoying isn't it?" Adam said in a mild voice, and Guy turned to look at him.

"Annoying? That's not the word I'd use."

It was Adam's turn to laugh. "It's the only word you'd use if you lived here long enough. Some of the meanest people in the world live in small towns just like this one. You can't let 'em make your choices for you."

Guy looked at him. "You have."

Adam shrugged. "Maybe I have. Maybe I haven't. I have what I want. You don't have what you want, and that's why you're leaving."

Guy's voice was dry. "Her choices were made long before I came around. I was incidental."

"What's in Chicago?" Adam asked. "Can you get your old job back?"

"I don't want it back. I've got an appointment with some magazine people. I've never edited a magazine before. It might be just what I'm looking for."

Adam pursed his lips and nodded. "Send me a subscription?"

"If I take the job, sure."

Adam smiled happily, then he turned serious. "Guy?"

"Yeah."

"Don't feel bad, all right? Sometimes I don't think we were meant to be happy. Not for longer than a few minutes, anyway. I don't think we're capable of sustained happiness. Do you know what I mean?"

Guy looked at him. "I know exactly what you mean, Adam. Let's get home and get these vegetables in the refrigerator."

"We'll have to blanch some and freeze them. Do you know how to blanch?"

"I'll leave it to you. I won't be here to eat the frozen ones."

Guy helped Adam get started in his kitchen, then he took his small sack of vegetables home and let himself in the door. Michael was on his answering machine again, and he hit the erase button after hearing her identify herself. He didn't care to listen to anything she had to say. It would only be excuses meant to rationalize and justify her actions, and he was sick of rationalizations and justifications.

He hoped he would never fall in love at first sight again. The experience had been nothing but painful. In fact, his entire experience in Colson had been an exercise in frustration and futility. These people weren't ready for progress of any kind. They weren't ready for anything but what they already knew. He didn't know why he had ever thought he could get along here. The fact that he was born here meant nothing. The memories he had were all tinted and made rosier with the patina of age. Adele had been right in thinking he was crazy for bringing her here. He *had* been crazy.

His phone rang and he stared at it, waiting for the machine to answer. After the recorded message and the beep, he heard a familiar voice:

"Guy, this is Dr. Spantzer. I called the paper, but they said you were home. I heard you were leaving us, and I thought I'd offer to buy you a drink. If you can make it, meet me in Corby's Bar around five."

Guy smiled and looked at his watch as the message ended. Corby's Bar was downtown, about two blocks from the paper. Five o'clock was several hours away. He had time to get started on packing a few items, things he would give to the movers he had hired. He took the boxes he had saved from the first move and began putting them together again and taping the bottoms so they would hold more.

At four-thirty he abandoned his packing and went to take a shower. At ten to five he stepped out the door and got in his Volvo to go to Corby's Bar.

The interior was well lit, unlike most bars Guy had been in. A game of pool was being played in the back room, and two men were hooting over a point on the shuffleboard table. Guy saw Dr. Spantzer sitting at the bar and he went to join him.

The doctor smiled and stuck out his hand when Guy sat down beside him. "Glad you could make it, Guy. Good to see you again. How's that hip?"

"Okay. I ran for the first time last night. It was sore as hell at first, but by the time I finished it was fine."

"Good. Don't rush anything. You're a quick healer, but your body needs time. Did I hear correctly that you've decided to leave Colson?"

"That's right. I'll be leaving at the end of the month. How did you know?"

Spantzer smiled. "Word travels. Sorry to hear it. Did I ever tell you I knew your family? I knew you, too, when you were just a boy. You probably don't remember."

"I do," said Guy. "You set my arm when I broke it."

The old man's smile widened. "I sure did. I didn't know if you'd remember that or not, since I wasn't your family doctor. Hell, I didn't remember myself until the day you came to get your release to go back to work. Your parents were fine people, Guy. I never knew any finer."

Guy nodded and ordered a beer from the bartender. Before the man could fill his order, a voice barked at him from across the room to draw two more beers. It was one of the men playing shuffleboard. The bartender ignored him and went on to get Guy's beer. Guy thanked him and laid some money on the bar. The doctor shoved it away. "I invited you. I'm buying."

"Thanks," Guy said, and he opened his mouth to say something further, but the man playing shuffleboard shouted at the bartender in a loud voice that obscured Guy's words.

The doctor frowned at the shouting man. "I thought that worthless fool was gone for good. Too bad he didn't stay gone."

"Who is it?" Guy asked.

"His name is Voycheck. He used to be married to Alissa Diest, Vernon's mother. Vernon runs the funeral home."

"I know him." Guy went on to tell the doctor about seeing Elma that day, and her reaction to the news of her father's return.

"Doesn't surprise me," Spantzer said, and he leaned close to Guy. "Alissa once brought Elma to me for a visit. She had a rash all over the lower half of her body, and it seemed to be worse in the genital area for some reason. I never did figure out what the rash was—hydrocortisone took care of it—but I'll tell you something I suspected after examining that poor deaf mute. Her body was being used sexually by someone, and if I had to guess who, I'd say it was that witless idiot in the corner over there."

Guy looked at the man in question and felt disgust harden his stomach. "Did you say anything to Mrs. Diest?"

The doctor clasped his hands on top the bar. "As a matter of fact, I did. She looked at me and said, 'As if you wouldn't do the same thing, given half a chance.' Mrs. Diest had a notoriously low opinion of men. Since then I've come to realize that people with such fatalistic attitudes were often victims of abuse themselves, either physical or sexual. It's a pervasive thing."

"So she knew about it and let it go on."

"That would be my guess, yes. Alissa Diest was a strange, hard woman. Not an ounce of tenderness in her that I ever saw. Except for the girl, which made the abuse even harder to understand. Elma was like a toy or a pet that she liked to dress up and play with. Vernon always got the sharp end of her stick, and I do mean *stick*. She carried one for years, swinging it just like she was Teddy Roosevelt. She got it from Vernon's father, who swung the stick just as often, though probably not as hard."

Guy looked at the man called Voycheck again. "Why did she marry someone like him?"

"I figured she married him because she needed some help

around the place. Someone to help Vernon with the coffins. He was a big boy, but he needed help. He still does, I hear, now that Arnold Dupree is missing."

"What's your opinion on that?" Guy asked. "Did you know Dupree? Was he the type to just disappear?"

"He saw me for years for hypertension, and when a younger doctor came to town he switched allegiance. He figured the younger man would have newer information. I never forgave him for that. But no, Arnold Dupree didn't seem like the type to just get up and go. Something happened to him that someone's not ready to have us know about yet."

"Foul play?"

"About as foul as you can get. My guess is he's lying dead somewhere. He'll be found eventually. They always are."

"You're a cheery guy," Guy said with a laugh.

Spantzer grinned. "I'm too old to be any other way. Drink up and tell me your plans for the future."

"My immediate plan," Guy told him, "is to get out of Colson in one piece."

"Might not be easy. Had any burning crosses on your lawn yet?"

"No. Only some nasty phone calls."

"Threats?"

"The usual. 'Don't let me catch you on the street.' That sort of thing."

"Ah. Well, they seem to be taking it better than I thought. When I read your article I expected to be setting both your arms and your legs as well."

Guy laughed and the doctor laughed with him. They went on talking and Guy drank another beer. When it was time for Spantzer to leave, Guy walked him out of the bar and said a fond farewell. The doctor clapped him on the back. "Colson doesn't know what it's letting go, my boy. Send me a card sometime?"

"I will," Guy promised, and he shook the doctor's hand and walked away, over to his own car. As he started his engine he saw Voycheck lurch out the front door, take two steps forward, and then fall face down onto the sidewalk. Guy kept his foot on the brake and watched as Voycheck staggered to his feet. The drunk took two more steps and then fell again. Once more he got up, and he stumbled down the street to the corner, where he held onto a white Buick while looking dazedly around himself. Soon he pushed himself away from the Buick and headed toward the middle of the street, where he began to walk in an unsteady gait. The blare of a car horn made him jump, and he was nearly struck by the fast-moving vehicle.

Guy cruised out of the parking lot, and after arguing with himself for several moments, he pulled up beside the man and asked if he could give him a lift somewhere.

Voycheck looked at him with bleary eyes and said yes, he wanted to go to the mortuary.

Guy sighed and opened the car door to let him in. When they reached the funeral home he nodded away the man's thanks and sat and watched while Voycheck reached the porch and rang the doorbell. After what seemed an eternity, the front door opened.

CHAPTER
THIRTY-ONE

VERNON WAS THOROUGHLY exasperated with Elma. She really was trying his patience. He had asked her to marry him, poured it on thick, the way he knew she would like it, and here she was reverting to her scared little rabbit act. He didn't know what to do or how to get her to stop. He hated her when she acted like this. She was nothing that he wanted or needed when she hid behind him and cowered at every thump in the house. When he asked her what was wrong, she only shook her head and buried her face in his shirtfront. Vernon had to shove her away from him to go to the bathroom and pee. That made her mad, and she glared at him before she disappeared onto the second level. Vernon felt better after that. The glaring he could live with.

It was her own fault, anyway. If she refused to tell him what the problem was, how could he be expected to know what to do? Vernon smirked to himself as he remembered something his father told him long ago. He had said, "The secret to women is that there is no secret. What you see on their faces is usually in their hearts. It's the ones with no heart that you need to look out for."

Elma was definitely in the former category. Her emotions

were as easy to read as her expressions. Vernon's mother had filled the latter bill, but his father had loved her for her very heartlessness. He loved her coldness and admired her calculating mind. And she didn't coddle Vernon, which Alfred Diest found extraordinary in a woman. She beat Vernon even more than Alfred did, and when Alfred's time came, she took over his stick and carried on for both of them.

Vernon didn't think about his father very much. He didn't like to think about his mother, either. Not anymore. She wouldn't have approved of the changes in him. She would have laughed at his emerging sexuality and made him feel ashamed and embarrassed of his choice for a mate. She wouldn't have acknowledged the changes in Elma, how beautiful she had become, or how confident. Vernon wanted that Elma back, and if being mean to her was the only way to have her again, then he could be a real sonofabitch. Just like his father.

At suppertime Elma still hadn't emerged, so Vernon fixed himself a sandwich and sat down in front of the television. It was almost six-thirty when Vernon heard someone pressing on the doorbell downstairs. Once, twice, three times the bell sounded. He buttoned his shirt and hurried down the stairs to the front entrance. When he pulled back the curtain and saw who was standing outside, his lip curled. Saylor Voycheck saw him through the glass and gave him a wavering salute. Then he half-stumbled, half-fell down the steps and landed on the ground below.

Vernon opened the door and stepped outside. First David Eulert, then Arnold Dupree, and now Saylor Voycheck. Who else was going to turn up to try and sabotage his plans?

Elma, he thought suddenly. Somehow she had known he was back, and that's what was wrong with her. He had never paid much attention to the Voychecks when his mother was alive. Saylor had probably beaten Elma, and that's why she was so terrified of him. Well, she didn't have to worry. No one but Vernon would lay a hand on her now. He would see to it.

"What do you want?" he asked, as the grinning Voycheck struggled to his feet.

"Want? What do I want, boy?" The grizzled old man looked incredulous. His greasy hair and yellow teeth sickened Vernon. "I want what I always want. To see my little girl. She still lives here, don't she? She did the last time I looked, anyhow."

"Go away," Vernon **said** tersely, and he gave the man a shove before he turned to go back inside.

A thick, calloused hand caught his arm. "Are you saying she don't live here anymore?"

Vernon looked at the hand on his arm and shook it off. "She doesn't want to see you. Neither do I. Now go away and find somewhere else to sleep tonight."

"A man's got a right to see his daughter if he wants to."

"I told you," Vernon said grimly. "She doesn't want to see you."

"Let her tell me that, you stupid piece of walking shit. I want to see her. Bring her out here."

The old man's eyes were filled with as many broken blood vessels as the skin on his face—the trademark of a drunk. He wanted a fight tonight. He was begging for a fight. Vernon wanted to give him one. He wanted to jump off the porch and tear the bastard's throat out for calling him a stupid piece of walking shit. He forced himself to be calm. He didn't need this. Voycheck had called him names before, plenty of them. He had taunted him often, always behind his mother's back. Vernon could handle him now. Vernon was a better man, no question about it.

He stood aside and opened the door. "Come in. I'll find Elma."

Voycheck looked surprised. He swayed a little, then he mounted the first step. "You already had supper?"

"I'm afraid so," said Vernon.

"Think she could rustle up something for me?"

Vernon chose not to answer. He led Voycheck into the mortuary's sitting room and asked him to sit down. Then he went upstairs in search of Elma. He stood on the landing of the second floor and stamped his foot twice. He waited several minutes, then he stamped again. Finally she poked her head out of one of the casket rooms. Her expression was cautious but quizzical.

"Come down here," Vernon said. "You know who's here. I want you to tell him to go."

Elma shook her head vigorously. *No.*

"Yes," Vernon said forcefully. "He says he won't leave until you tell him to go. Now come down here and do it."

Her look turned frightened again and Vernon lifted his arms and walked toward her. "Do you honestly think I'd allow him to lay a finger on you? Elma, don't be afraid. I'll be with you the whole time. We can't get married with him around. I won't. I want him gone."

Elma closed her eyes for a moment as if in pain, then she edged slowly out into the hall. Vernon strode toward her and frowned at her instinctive flinch. "What's wrong with you? I've told you I'll protect you from him. Come on. He's in my sitting room and he stinks."

Vernon alternately dragged and pushed her down the steps to the main floor. When Elma saw her father, Vernon felt her body begin to quiver. Voycheck stood up and held out his hands.

"Elma, baby! Come see your daddy!"

Elma promptly stepped behind Vernon.

"Is that answer enough for you?" Vernon said coldly.

Voycheck sneered. "She ain't seen me in a while, is all. Why don't you leave the two of us alone for a spell, let us have a chat."

"What is it you want, Voycheck?" Vernon asked. "What exactly are you after?"

"What am I after? Hell, I ain't after nothin'. Just a place to sleep for a few nights, is all. Maybe some decent food. You can do that much for me again, can't you, Vern? I can't sleep in the bus station."

"Why do you keep coming back here?"

"For no good reason. Just a yearnin' to see my sweet darlin' girl. What do you say, Vern? Let the old man bed down for a few nights, huh? Hell, I might be able to help you out around the place. Just like old times."

Elma's nails dug into Vernon's arm. Vernon said, "Get out, Voycheck. Get out now."

Voycheck smiled and rubbed his greasy face. "Okay. But I'm takin' Elma with me. If I go, she comes along."

"What?" Vernon said in complete surprise. "You must be joking. You have no claim on her. She's a grown woman."

Voycheck looked at him queerly. "I figured you'd be glad to be rid of her. I'm wonderin' now why you ain't. I think I can guess, though. Oh yeah, I'd say little Elma been spreadin' her legs for big Vern, is that right? She's lookin' awful pretty these days, Elma is. She been treatin' you right, Vern?"

Vernon opened his mouth to snarl a reply, but at that moment Elma stepped out from behind him. Her face was white with fear. She pointed to her father, and then she pointed to the door. *Go.*

Her father laughed. "Hell, sweetie, what if I don't feel like it?"

"Leave," Vernon said, his voice hoarse and strained. He was going to have to kill Voycheck. He knew it. He was going to have to get him out of the house somehow and kill the drunken bastard. There was no way he was coming to live with Vernon and Elma. No way he was going to stay alive to keep coming back to Vernon's house whenever he felt like it. Voycheck had to die. How? was the question. How was Vernon going to kill him?

Vernon found himself looking around for something he could use as a weapon. Anything would do. Perhaps even his bare hands would suffice. At that moment he felt they would.

"Yeah, sure, you kids need someone to help you around the

place. Elma's been helpin' you in other ways, I'm sure, Vern, but there's things I can do. Hell, I used to do all kinds of things for your mother. 'Lissa was a wonderful woman, and she thought a lot of me.''

"She thought you were a drunken fool, same as I do," Vernon responded. "Now get out of my house before I come and throw you out."

Voycheck's hairy brows rose. "Think you're man enough to do that? You're man enough to poke Elma, sure, but hell, anyone can do that. I—"

Elma rushed forward and beat at her father with a fist. He fended her off easily and sent her crashing to the floor with the back of his hand.

Vernon's nostrils flared. His fists clenched and his knuckles turned white. "You don't know what you're doing," he warned Voycheck in a still, deadly voice. "If you don't leave here, I will kill you."

"Ooooh," Voycheck said, and raised his hands over his face. "Vern gonna kill me. Oh, man, am I scared now. You little pissant. I watched you pee your pants when your mama spoke your name. You're gonna kill me?"

Elma scooted away and ran from the room. Vernon advanced on Voycheck. His eyes were black as midnight.

"I'll kill you, and I'll enjoy it, Voycheck."

The smile began to fade from the older man's face. His cheek twitched as he watched Vernon approach. "You worthless shiteater. What, are you a man now? Is that it? You gonna make me pay for all the shit I done to you when your mama was a—"

He stopped and sucked in his breath. His reddened eyes rounded. His hands reached up in an attempt to grasp at his back. As he twisted around, Vernon saw the letter opener from his desk protruding from the middle of Voycheck's back. Voycheck lurched away, and Elma followed him. She had disappeared and come back, slipping up unnoticed, the way she always did. She lunged for the letter opener in her father's broad back and snatched it out of him only to plunge it in again. Vernon stepped back and stared in amazement as she stabbed him over and over again. Voycheck rose and fell a number of times, coming up off the carpeted floor of the sitting room only to fall with each downward arc of the long, daggerlike letter opener. He crawled across the room on his knees, his red eyes bugging out and his mouth working as soundlessly as his daughter's, until Elma jumped on his shoulders and stabbed him in the back of the neck. His greasy head arched up, then he dropped, quivered, and finally was still.

Tears rolled down Elma's face as she climbed off of him. Dripping with blood, she walked a few steps away and then sank to her knees to begin retching. Vernon went to her and picked her up to carry her to his bathroom. He placed her in the bathtub and turned on the water. Then he went back to her father.

He found himself smiling as he picked up the carpet and attempted to roll it around the dead man.

Elma, he thought. My sweet, wicked little Elma, oh, the things you do.

When Voycheck was safely in the middle of the carpet and waiting by the front door, Vernon went to check on Elma. She was naked in the bathtub. There was no sign of blood on her or on the porcelain. Vernon stared at her nude body and felt himself grow erect. He reached for his collar and undid the buttons of his shirt. She looked up at him, and surprisingly, there were no more tears. She was calm. Vernon took off his clothes and got in the tub. They were made for each other, he thought. Suddenly he was sure of it.

CHAPTER
THIRTY-TWO

ELMA LOOKED AT THE HAPPINESS radiating across Vernon's features as they drove away from the house and knew he would marry her as planned on Saturday. He would stand up beside her and say the words, and she would wear a veil and a white dress found in Alissa's closet. Only the pastor and two witnesses were to be present, but soon the whole town would know they were husband and wife. Vernon and Elma Diest; two murderers, married to each other.

She looked down at her hands in shame. Never in her life had she experienced such a complex riot of emotions as she had in the moment before she plunged the letter opener into her father's back. Rage and fear and anxiety like she had never known roiled inside her until the mixture exploded. All she could see was how he was going to ruin things for her. All she could see was his filthy yellow smile, his fat, hairy belly and spindly, naked legs.

And then she had done what she knew Vernon was going to do. She had killed him, and killed him, and killed him.

Vernon was so proud of her. She could see it in his eyes, and she had read it on his lips as he made love to her in the bathtub.

"You wouldn't have recognized yourself," he had said to her. "You were beautiful. You were . . . glorious."

Elma made no kind of reply. She didn't have to. The sex was wonderful. It was as if the act of killing her father had charged her to her sexual core. She had been wild and uninhibited and insatiable.

That's why Vernon was so happy. He claimed his legs were so weak he was barely able to drive.

Elma was settled against the door in the front seat. In the trunk was the carpet with her father inside. She tried not to think about him. She tried not to think about killing him. Instead she attempted to focus on the life ahead of them. They wouldn't kill anyone else. Never again, no matter how bad times were, or who came to threaten them. They would never kill anyone ever again.

With that resolved in her mind, she turned to look out the window. She had no idea where they were going. Vernon told her he knew of a well they could dump her father's body in. He swore it would never be found. Elma had no choice but to leave it up to him. She knew nothing of the country surrounding Colson. She knew very little of Colson, for that matter. She had been out only a few times with Vernon in his van, and had gotten herself lost twice the night she had taken his pistol and run with it. What she knew was the house, the chapel, the mortuary, and the cemetery. She had been to the doctor with Alissa once, and a few times Alissa had taken her along to the grocery store, but for the most part, the stone house and its contents were Elma's world.

Before that there had been a small three-room house she shared with her grandmother. Grandma had the television and her phone, and she needed nothing else. Elma had done all the shopping and cooking and cleaning. Then Grandma died, and Elma's father came to collect her . . . and what was left of Grandma's money. It didn't last long. Then he left town for a while, and when he came back, he said he was married. He and Elma moved to Colson and became part of the business of dealing with the dead.

Is that why killing had come so easily? Elma wondered uncomfortably. Had she become somehow inured to death?

Perhaps, she thought. Perhaps she had indeed grown accustomed to the presence of death in her soundless existence, much as Vernon had. Vernon had known death all his life.

While she was looking out the window, he turned down a dirt road and sped up. His gaze was fixed on the rearview mirror for a while, causing Elma to touch his arm and give him a questioning look.

"Nothing," he said. "Just antsy, I guess. For a minute there I thought someone was following us."

Elma turned around and saw nothing but the blackness of the night. Vernon concentrated on his driving once more, and soon Elma settled back against the seat again. She must have dozed off, because Vernon's hand on her shoulder startled her. She looked at him and he said, "Almost there. Just up this draw. Are you all right?"

Elma nodded. It was hard to read his lips in the poor light from the dash, but she managed to catch every other word.

"Good," Vernon said. "Can you hand me the flashlight out of the glove compartment?"

She opened the glove compartment and took out the flashlight. She flicked it on in the car to check the batteries and then turned it off again and handed it to Vernon.

"Thanks," he said, and he stopped the car. Elma looked out the window and saw nothing but darkness.

"Do you want to stay here?" Vernon asked her, and she immediately shook her head. *No way.*

"All right. Get out and stay close to me. It's so dark out here I wouldn't be able to see you if you stepped away." He opened the car door and got out. Elma opened her door and got out to go and stand by the trunk. Vernon didn't turn on the flashlight until the body was out of the trunk and on the ground. When the beam came on, Elma looked at everything but the blood-soaked carpet at their feet. Vernon was breathing heavily. He turned to her and said, "Can you get one end of it? It'll be heavy, I know, but we don't have far to go."

Elma's stomach churned, but she nodded. She picked up the end he pointed to and followed his lead, her arms straining under the weight of the body and the carpet. Soon Vernon stopped and pointed the beam; Elma saw nothing but brush and more brush. Vernon put down his load and began to pull away the limbs and debris. After a moment Elma saw wood— or splintered pieces of it. Soon a peculiar smell drifted into her nostrils. She looked at Vernon to see if he noticed, but he was hard at work clearing away the remaining limbs. The odor she smelled was unmistakably that of putrefaction. Elma moved to take the flashlight from Vernon. She wanted to look in the well.

"No," he said sharply, when she reached for the flashlight. "There are dead things down there. You don't want to see them."

Dead things? Elma backed away from the fierceness of his glare. How would he know there were dead things in the well?

Suddenly Elma knew. She knew what was in the well—had known it, really, from the moment he turned up missing. The nausea rushed up her throat, and she pivoted away from Vernon to throw up in the trampled grass. Poor Arnold. Poor, poor Arnold.

A rough hand grabbed her arm and spun her around. She looked into Vernon's face, and he put the light to his lips to say, "We're in this together, Elma. We don't need a vow to tell us that. Now help me get him up over the edge."

Elma felt too weak to help him anymore. Her quivering stomach couldn't handle it. She shook her head and looked at him through eyes blurry with tears. Vernon took a deep breath and then slapped her. The blow snapped her head back and made her look at him in shock.

"I'm sorry," he said gruffly. "You can fall apart in the car on the way home. Right now I need you to pick up your end and help me."

Elma picked up her end of the carpet and nearly shoved her father into the well herself. Then she turned her back on Vernon and started for the car. Her eyes had adjusted, and the moon had risen enough for her to see where she was going. Vernon wasn't following her. She didn't look to see, but he was probably busy replacing the brush. Elma had the urge to keep on going once she reached the car. Just keep walking and see where the dirt road led her. Get away from Vernon, get away from everything. All of it.

She felt a touch on her arm, and she whirled to see Vernon smiling at her. He put the light to his mouth and said, "That pistol I told you I got rid of? I decided to toss it in, too. It wasn't in a very good hiding place. People are always messing around with graves. So that's it. It's over. We won't talk about it anymore. We won't even think about it. We can concentrate on the future now, with no interruptions, no one to worry about. We can go home."

Elma stared at him. His black eyes were even blacker here in the dark. His smile was confident.

Home, he had said.

The word chimed in Elma's brain. It rang of longing and hope and some heretofore unreachable harmony. All her life she had wanted a home of her own. Always.

Her eyes found the moon in the sky again. A white moon, white as could be. It looked different from the way it did at home, from the windows of the house. It seemed brighter. The moons of summer were spectacular moons, bathed in the warmth of day and surrounded by cluster upon cluster of stars, particularly here in the country, where the only light was the moon's, and the heavens appeared to be a very busy place indeed, with all manner of tiny multicolored objects zigging and zagging across the night. The moons of summer made all things seem possible to Elma. They were moons to dream by.

She put her hand in Vernon's and allowed him to lead her to his car. Once inside and on the road again, he didn't let go of her hand. Elma loved him for that.

CHAPTER
THIRTY-THREE

IT WAS LATE, nearly one in the morning, when Michael's phone rang. She picked it up and said hello, and then she shot up in bed when she heard Guy's voice. He said, "I need to talk to you. Meet me in front of my house in fifteen minutes. And bring your gun."

"My gun?" Michael echoed, but he had already hung up. She sat for a stunned moment, then she threw the covers away and got out of bed. In ten minutes she was dressed in jeans and a blouse and reaching for her holster. She went swiftly out to her car and drove as quickly as she could to Guy's house. He was walking out to his Volvo when she arrived. She left her car, and he gestured for her to come with him.

"What is this?" she asked as she approached him.

"Did you bring a flashlight?" Guy asked.

"There's one in my car. Don't you have one?"

"A small one. Would you get yours?"

Michael nodded and turned around. In seconds she was back, flashlight in hand. "Would you mind telling me what this is about?"

"This is about Vernon Diest. Are you coming, or do I call the police and tell them?"

Michael's pulse speeded up. "What have you got?"

"I don't know yet. I'll know when we get where we're going, if I haven't forgotten how to get there."

"Are you being cryptic on purpose?" Michael asked.

"Get in the car. I'll fill you in on the way."

Michael breathed out through her nose and slid into the passenger seat. Guy got in, buckled his seatbelt, and started the engine. He drove quickly through town, and when he left the town limits, Michael looked at him. "Well?"

Guy kept his eyes on the road. "Earlier this evening I gave a man called Voycheck a lift to Diest's place. Voycheck never came out again."

"He used to live there," Michael said. "Maybe he's moved back in."

"I don't think so. I was getting ready to leave when I saw Vernon shove Voycheck. Voycheck grabbed his arm and they exchanged words. Vernon finally let him inside, and I left to go over to Arnold Dupree's place to see if Elma had picked up the vegetables Adam and I left for her. I thought of taking them to her at the house, just to see what was going on with her father and Vernon, but I got to poking around Arnold's place and didn't leave for maybe half an hour or more. As I was leaving I drove by the funeral home in time to see Vernon and Elma putting something very large into the trunk of Vernon's Continental. I followed them to the place I'm taking you now. What they did there I don't know, but they were there only a short time. They came directly back to town."

"So what are you saying?" Michael asked. "You think they drove out here to dump a body?"

He finally looked at her. "Why else would someone drive forty minutes into the country and then turn around and come right back?"

"Where did you meet Voycheck?" Michael responded.

"He was in Corby's Bar when I went to meet Dr. Spantzer.

Spantzer told me he thought Elma's father might have sexually abused her. Earlier, when Adam and I saw Elma, she reacted with shock when Adam mentioned that her father was back in town. She told me she and Vernon were getting married. I was interested to see what would happen when Voycheck showed up at Vernon's door."

"So you sat and watched. And then you followed them the same way you followed David Eulert the night he tried to kill me."

"I didn't sit and watch. I went to Arnold's house. Then I came back and saw the two of them heaving something into the trunk. That's when I decided to follow them. I think Vernon did more than argue with Voycheck, but I'm not sure. That's why I phoned you rather than Captain Mawby. If nothing's out here, then nothing is lost. If something is out here, then I've just handed Diest to you on a platter."

"Why would you do that for me?" Michael asked, watching his face closely.

"I haven't done anything for you. People will want to know how you knew."

"And I'll have to tell them you came to me, rather than call the police, which will go that much further to substantiate everything people have been saying about us."

Guy looked at her. "Small towns can be so cruel, can't they?"

"They can. You don't realize what that kiss in the jail started, Guy. In the city it would be nothing, but here in Colson it's drama. Everyone watches everyone else."

"And passes judgment."

"Yes. It's not fair, but that's life in Colson. I've lived here all my life, Guy. These people have known me since I was a child, and I've always cared about what they think. That's the way I was raised, to care what others thought of me. It's not something I can turn off just like that."

"No one's asking you to, Michael, so stop trying to explain. I'm leaving, remember?"

"I don't want you to go," she said.

He looked at her with raised brows. "Oh, you want me to stay, but you're asking me to hang loose for six or seven months until your period of Colson-approved mourning has been completed. Then we can start dating, right?"

"Yes . . . no, dammit, I'm asking you to understand what I have to do to get along."

"You'll get along just fine without me," said Guy.

"You said you loved me," Michael said angrily. "If you really meant that, you'd be willing to—"

"Wait for you?" Guy interjected, just as angrily. "I'm not some lovesick pimple-faced kid, Michael. I'm thirty-eight years old, and I'm not going to let anyone in this town or any other dictate what happens in my personal life. If you were half as mature as you like to think you are you'd know it's impossible to please anyone in this life but yourself."

Michael was silent for some moments. Finally, she said, "I'm sorry. I'm truly sorry. I should never have become involved with you while—"

"We're not involved, Michael. We're not anything."

The words stung her deeply. She had been about to tell him she was willing to face all of it, defy her father and sister and everyone, if only he would stay, but she remained silent. She clasped her hands in her lap and forced herself to concentrate on looking out the window to note landmarks.

Soon she knew where they were going. When Guy finally turned onto the dirt road, she said, "There used to be an old Quaker farm on this section. The man was very rich, but he was ridiculed for his religious beliefs. He finally took his family and left the county. When I was a kid my grandfather still used to talk about the 'quackers.' They've been gone for years."

Guy drove off the road and up a draw before he stopped the car. "This is where they pulled over. I had to hang back, so I couldn't see where they went from here, but if you'll give me a light we'll try to find out."

Michael handed a flashlight to him and took one for herself. She turned it on and pointed the beam at the ground. There were tire tracks in the grass beside their own. She looked for tracks made by feet and saw trampled grass just a few yards away. She followed the signs of disturbance for twenty feet or more and found herself staring at a large, brush-covered pile of debris.

Here we are, she thought, in the middle of nowhere. The nearest farm was five miles away. It was the perfect dumping ground.

"Guy," she said softly; then she cleared her throat and said his name louder. He walked over to her. His eyes met hers in the glow from their combined flashlights.

"Do you smell anything?" she asked.

He nodded and turned away from her to begin pulling at the limbs and debris. Minutes later, the well was exposed. Guy shined his flashlight inside and leaned over to peer down. He quickly straightened and came to Michael.

"One large blood-stained carpet and what looks like an arm."

Michael stepped forward. "I have to look."

"Are you sure you want to?"

"I have to know what I'm talking about when I call Captain Mawby. I'll be fine." She took the large flashlight and went to point it down the well. Slowly she leaned over the edge. She saw a stained and muddied carpet at the bottom of the well. Beneath the carpet was a human arm, veined with dirt and slime. The smell was so powerful she had to throw her head back and suck in fresh air. Guy came to steady her, and she leaned on him for an instant before she stepped away from the well.

"What do you think?" Guy asked her.

"I think there may be two bodies. One in the carpet and one beneath it."

Guy nodded. "Are you ready to call the captain?"

"I'm ready to get Vernon Diest. We have to be careful not to disturb his tire tracks when we leave. We may need to take a mold.''

"Why take a mold? I'm an eyewitness.''

"The captain likes to be prepared for anything.''

They walked back to Guy's car and climbed inside. The ride back was mostly silent, with both thinking their own troubled thoughts. Finally, Guy said, "Do you think Arnold Dupree was one of the bodies?''

"I don't know," Michael answered.

When they reached town, Guy drove directly to the police station. Once there they contacted Captain Mawby and drank coffee from the station's coffeemaker until he arrived. Mawby's hair was tousled and his face flushed when he walked in the station door and saw the two of them. He frowned at Guy and then turned to Michael. "All right, let me see if I copy. Mr. Driscoll here hauled Voycheck to Diest's house, and then he followed Diest out to the old Quaker place later and saw him dump something in the well.''

"No," said Guy. "I didn't see them dump anything. I was too far back.''

"He came home and got me," Michael said, "and we went out and found what appear to be two bodies in the bottom of the abandoned well. There are tire tracks to take molds from, and Guy can place Vernon Diest there.''

Mawby put a hand to his head. Then he turned to stare at Guy. "Why did you come back and get her? Why didn't you call the police right away?''

Guy shrugged. "I didn't know what I had. I didn't know if I had anything. I thought it was better to have a cop along if I did find something.''

"Aren't you just a handy guy to have around," Mawby said with a frown. "You sure like to follow people, don't you?''

Guy said nothing and the captain turned to the desk sergeant on duty. "Get me three squad cars and call the medical examiner. And get me a tow truck with a winch." He pointed at Michael. "You come with me, Mike. Driscoll, you can go home now."

"Can't do it," Guy told him.

"You can, or I'll throw you in—"

"Captain," said Michael. "He does work for the paper. And he did give us the tip."

Mawby eyed him a moment then nodded. "Fine. Just keep your story accurate."

Guy met the captain's look and said, "My stories are always accurate."

Mawby's mouth tightened. He looked at Michael and said, "I'll send two squad cars out to the well to verify what you saw. Tell me the location as exactly as you can, and as soon as they radio us, we'll move on Mr. Diest. I want you to go out and keep surveillance on his place, let me know if he's gone, going, or if he's sleeping peacefully and doesn't suspect a thing."

Michael nodded and told him how to find the well. She started out, then stopped. "I'll need a car with a radio."

Mawby patted his pocket and took out his keys. "Take mine. I'll be right here until I hear from the boys going out to the Quaker place. I'll radio you when we're on our way to Diest's. Right now I need to call a judge." He turned away and didn't see Guy follow Michael out the door. Michael got in the captain's car and saw Guy get in his Volvo and slam the door. She didn't know what he was doing until she started the engine and left the parking lot. When he pulled in behind her she realized he was coming to Vernon Diest's place with her. That made her feel better.

She parked on the curb across from the darkened stone mansion and radioed in to the captain. The van and the Continental were in the garage in back, and all the lights in the place were out. The house was quiet.

"Stay on it," said the captain's voice over the radio, and Michael signed off. In the next second, her passenger door opened and Guy slid inside the car.

"We've got a while," Michael said to him. "To wait, I mean."

Guy nodded and brought a deck of cards from his hip pocket. "Can you see by the street light?"

Michael thought she could. "Knock poker?"

"Is that the only game you know?"

"No, it's the only one I can win at."

"All right. I was a nice guy last time."

"Are you saying you let me win?"

"No, I'm saying I was a nice guy and just didn't try very hard."

"What a jerk," Michael said under her breath.

Guy laughed.

Fifteen minutes later he was on top by three games and looking for a fourth. When he laid down a full house after her knock, Michael nearly threw her Ace-high straight into his face.

"What's wrong?" he asked. "Your game let you down?"

"No, you have," she said in a tight voice.

"Me? What did I do?"

"You're trying to punish me."

"I'm playing cards, Michael."

"You're playing cards and trying to punish me. It's subtle but you're doing it. Admit it."

He raised his hands and then began to gather the cards. "All right. We won't play anymore. I'll even go back to my own car if you want me to."

"I want you to."

"Fine." He put the cards in his hip pocket and moved to open the car door. Before he could pull back the handle, Michael put a hand on his arm. "Guy . . ."

He turned to look at her. In the darkness of the car her pupils were large and dark.

"I don't want you to go," she said. "I don't want you to leave me. Not now, not ever. Please stay."

Guy stared at her. His breathing became shallow as he

watched her face. Finally his lips moved. He said, "I'm going."

"Don't," Michael begged in a whisper, and she reached forward to put her arms around his neck. His hands came up to her forearms, but he didn't resist her as she kissed him. After a moment of hesitation he began to respond, and as the kiss deepened, Michael felt an ache begin in her lower half. His hands splayed out across her back and hips to pull her against him and within seconds she was nearly writhing. The heat came quickly and the need in her was sudden and fierce. She half-pushed, half-pulled him into the backseat and reached for the belt on his trousers. He did nothing to help her, concentrating instead on her mouth and neck and the exposed tops of her breasts in her bra. Michael finally freed him from his trousers and briefs and moved his hands to the top of her jeans, where they undid the snap and unzipped the zipper and tugged the denim away from her hips and over her legs.

Michael pushed her panties down herself and then reached for him. He held himself above her and paused, staring down at her with inscrutable eyes and panting breath. Then he made some decision within himself and drove into her, grinding her backside against the cool vinyl seat and causing her to moan aloud. He was punishing her still, she knew, as he continued to push himself ever deeper inside her. She wrapped her arms around him and held on, loving the sensations he created within her. Michael came close to passing out as he sucked the breath from her and brought her to a rocking orgasm at once. As she gasped for breath, he stopped, shuddered, and quickly withdrew himself, so that his seminal fluid flowed across her thighs rather than inside of her. Michael felt the warm fluid and looked at him in surprise.

Wordlessly he lifted himself away from her and sat up to begin wiping her thighs with the tail of his shirt.

Michael watched him and whispered, "Why did you do that?"

He turned to look at her. "We've never talked about sex or protection."

Michael went on looking at him. After a moment she whispered, "I do love you, Guy. I'm almost sick with it."

His hand squeezed hers until she thought the bones would break. His voice was thick when he said, "I've been sick over you for some time now. That's why I'm leaving. I'll never get over you if I stay here. I'll never be able to play by Colson's rules and make compromises where you or my work are concerned. I'll never forget that Adele was murdered here, because of me. I have to go."

Moisture fill Michael's eyes. "Guy, please. It will get better. We—"

Guy cut her off with his lips as he reached for her and pulled her up close to him. "What if I asked you to come with me? What would you say?"

Her mouth opened, but nothing came out.

"I guessed as much," Guy said. "I know what your answer will be. You have family and a career here. Colson is your home. It's not mine."

Michael put a hand up to touch his lips. Then she replaced her fingers with her mouth and kissed him deeply. When the kiss ended, she said, "It can be your home, too. The people in Colson will get used to us. I promise."

Guy opened his mouth to reply, and she kissed him again, twining her arms around his neck and pouring her heart into the kiss. Suddenly the police radio in the dash crackled to life, causing Michael and Guy to break abruptly apart and stare into the front seat.

"Mawby, here," said the captain. "Come in, Michael."

Michael leaned over the front seat and grabbed the microphone to respond.

"The boys found two bodies and a pistol in the well," the captain went on. "Saylor Voycheck and Arnold Dupree. We're on our way out to you now. Don't make a move without us."

Michael signed off and replaced the microphone. She

leaned back in the seat and began to button her blouse and pull on her jeans. Guy was already dressed again. He noted her stunned face and said, "You knew he was dangerous, but you never realized just how dangerous."

"Right," she said softly. "Speculation is always easy, but facts make a different picture." She shook her head and looked at Guy. "What do you suppose his motive was?"

Guy couldn't say. "Maybe one day he woke up pissed off at life and never got over it."

Michael stared out through the windshield. Suddenly she looked at Guy. "Do you realize if you hadn't driven by tonight, Diest would have gotten away with it? The location of that well was the perfect dumping ground. No one has been there in years. Voycheck would never have been missed, and Dupree was already missing. They—" She paused as she saw the clench and release of a muscle in Guy's cheek. His eyes were fixed on Vernon Diest's stone house.

"Guy?"

He glanced at her. His eyes glittered. He said, "That sonofabitch shot my daughter."

"We don't know that yet," said Michael.

"I know," Guy said darkly. "Mawby said there was a pistol down there."

"Let us handle it," Michael said, suddenly worried at the look on his face. "We'll arrest him and take him in."

Guy was still focused on the house. "I want to be there. I want to hear what he has to say to the charges."

"All right. We'll see what Mawby—" She paused and saw approaching lights. "Here he is now. Let's go."

She left the car as Captain Mawby and another officer arrived on the scene. Guy stepped up beside her, and Michael asked about the pistol. "We think it might have been the gun used to kill Adele Driscoll."

Mawby looked at Guy. "Maybe it was, and maybe it wasn't. We won't know until we run some tests. Let's go get Diest."

CHAPTER
THIRTY-FOUR

VERNON CAME AWAKE WITH A START. Someone was ringing the bell downstairs, over and over again. Elma sat up as he left the bed, and he turned to tell her he was going downstairs. She probably couldn't see his mouth in the dark, but he was too lazy to turn on the light and tell her again.

His eyes rounded and became instantly alert when he saw his visitors. There were perhaps thirty seconds of hesitation while Vernon decided what he would do. Finally he opened the door. "Good evening, Captain Mawby. What can I do for you at this late hour?"

"You can come with us. I have a warrant for your arrest, signed a half hour ago by a judge who doesn't like being awakened any more than you do. He came around a bit when we told him the reason why."

"How about telling me?" Vernon said coolly.

Mawby stepped back and pointed a thumb at Guy. "Our Mr. Driscoll there saw you take a ride tonight. He followed you out to the old Quaker well, and sometime after you were gone, he took a look and found two bodies in there. One of them was your neighbor. The other was a man who entered your house tonight and never came back out again. Shall we go, Mr. Diest?"

Vernon half-turned away from them and murmured something under his breath. Mawby took out his cuffs. "What did you say?"

"I told her it would come to this," Vernon said, his innards churning as the panic built up inside. The words came quickly, pouring out of his mouth as his frantic brain worked. "I told her you would come to arrest me, thinking I had done everything. She is brilliant, wouldn't you say? She knew all along no one would suspect a poor deaf mute. Oh, yes, Elma definitely is brilliant. Go on and arrest me, but I'll tell you now what happened. Elma claimed Arnold Dupree attacked her one day in her garden, so she hit him with a brick and killed him. She came flying up to me then, begging me to help her hide him. I knew better, but she was terrified that she would be taken away if the truth were known.

"So I helped her hide Arnold Dupree's body. I should have known it wasn't the first time, especially after she killed David Eulert, but I wasn't seeing clearly. She was only Elma. Sweet, dumb Elma, who needed my help to survive. Then last night her father showed up. He had been drinking, and he was happy to see Elma after so long. I left them alone together for one minute, and when I came back she was riding around on his back and stabbing him while he screamed and begged her for mercy."

Mawby's hands paused in the handcuffing. "Why didn't you call us then?"

"It was my turn to panic. I know the police have been watching me since the incident with Officer Bish. I know I'm suspected of wrongdoing. All I could think about was getting him out of my house." He exhaled then and looked at Captain Mawby with weary eyes. "You won't believe this, but I'm relieved it's over. She was beginning to frighten me, living in the same house with someone capable of doing what she did to her own father."

Guy looked at Mawby. "You're not buying this, are you?"

Mawby ignored him. "Where is Miss Voycheck?"

Vernon lifted his shoulders. "I'm never sure. She sleeps in a different place every night. Sometimes she sleeps in the coffins on the second floor."

Michael made a face and looked at Guy. Guy was shaking his head in disbelief.

Mawby turned to the officer with him and gestured for him to go and find Elma. As the officer started up the stairs, Vernon said, "Go to the second landing and stamp your foot twice. That might bring her out. She might even be on the third floor, where I sleep. She has this notion in her head that I'm going to marry her, and she keeps crawling into my bed."

"You bastard," Guy muttered under his breath, and Vernon turned to look at him. "Excuse me?"

"You *told* her you were going to marry her. Arnold Dupree was her friend. You killed him and Voycheck, and you stood on Michael's patio and shot my daughter in the back."

Mawby stepped forward. "Put a lid on it, Driscoll, or remove yourself. We didn't come for discussion. I want to know where Elma Voycheck is and if there's somewhere she can go while Mr. Diest is in custody."

"She can stay with me," Michael offered, and Vernon's lip curled the tiniest bit.

"I wouldn't advise it," he said. "Elma has some peculiar habits. She steals things, and she's made a mess of my mother's closet. I let her stay because she has a certain talent for styling hair, but believe me, I've often questioned whether she's worth the trouble."

"How strange to hear you to speak of her this way," Michael said. "The two of you seemed very affectionate the last time I saw you."

All affinity for Elma was swept away as Vernon stared at Michael Bish. Self-preservation took precedence over any passion he might have entertained. Vernon knew this as well as he knew his own name, as the three police officers and Guy

Driscoll stood waiting for his answer. He cleared his throat and looked sheepishly at the captain. "The woman fancies herself in love with me. I told you, she believes I'm going to marry her."

The officer appeared at the top of the stairs again. "I don't see her anywhere. It's a big house, Captain. Do you want to call for some more men?"

Guy noticed Vernon's frown. "Where did she go, Diest? Or don't you know?"

"Of course I don't," Vernon snapped, and he swallowed the last of his guilt over the lies he was telling and said, "I've just told you, she sleeps in a different place every night. She could have seen you and decided to hide. She's like some wild, witless animal, I tell you. I've hardly had a minute's sleep since the day she shot David Eulert."

Elma saw Vernon say that. From her position on the stairs behind the officer, she saw Vernon call her a wild, witless animal.

At first she couldn't believe it. He had to be talking about someone else. But no, his next words confirmed her first impression.

She knew why he had said it. The looks on the faces of the police around him told her why. They had found evidence of some kind and they had come to arrest Vernon. Only now it looked like he was trying to implicate her. She should have known he would do this. She should have known he would betray her in an effort to save his own miserable self. Instead she had believed him. Loved him.

Elma looked at him again and saw him saying she could be anywhere in the house, and she would most likely be armed, so caution would be necessary.

She smiled bitterly and uttered a silent sob. Just hours ago he had been laughing with her, telling her how beautiful she would look in the dress she had chosen. He had asked her again about her deafness, and if it would affect any children they might have. No, Elma told him. She was deaf because her father had beaten and severely injured her when she was four years old. Any children they had would be able to hear.

Vernon hugged her then and kissed her and asked if she wasn't glad then that the filthy drunk was dead.

Elma had nodded yes, she was glad.

She was glad he was dead and glad she was alive, alive and with Vernon, the only man she had ever loved.

Her face wet with tears, she rose up and moved soundlessly toward the officer on the stairs. Gently, she touched the man's arm, and he whirled in shock, his revolver drawn. She saw his eyes, round and startled, and she felt a hot, terrible pain in her abdomen and a strange vibration in the room. She looked down and saw smoke rising from the barrel of the policeman's revolver. Then she saw blood rushing down the front of her nightgown. She opened her eyes wide and looked for Vernon. She saw Captain Mawby, his mouth a round oh of dismay, and she saw Michael Bish, her blue eyes suddenly filling with tears. Then she saw Vernon. His nostrils flared and his spine stiffened as he stared up at her. His black eyes were cold.

The officer in front of her was still staring at her in horror, holding his gun limply in his hand. Elma ripped it away from him and pointed the revolver at Vernon. Vernon's eyes rounded in alarm as she squeezed the trigger, and at the last moment she swerved the barrel. Captain Mawby went down, his shoulder spurting blood. Elma turned and shot the officer who had shot her, hitting him in the side of the head as he ducked. He fell unconscious to the floor before her, and she stepped over him and aimed at the man behind Michael Bish. It was Guy Driscoll. She saw him, and for a second she faltered, long enough for Michael to draw her gun and fire.

Elma jerked away and the round plowed through the meaty part of her left upper arm. She aimed at Michael and fired. Michael rolled and Guy grabbed her and shoved her toward the doorway. Elma fired again, but they moved out of sight.

Vernon went for Captain Mawby's pistol. The captain opened his eyes and tried to sit up, but just as he rose, Vernon grabbed his wounded shoulder from behind. Mawby's eyes rolled back in agony and he fell down again. Vernon lifted his gun and looked up at Elma. She watched him, her brown eyes riveted, and saw his lips form the words: "Thank you, Elma. I love you." Then he pointed the pistol at her and squeezed the trigger.

The shot went astray. Vernon's black eyes locked onto Elma's, and for a moment he stared at her in pained surprise before he fell face forward onto the floor. There was a bullet hole centered in the middle of his back. Elma looked at the doorway and saw Michael Bish staring at her, waiting, her revolver held ready. Michael's eyes pleaded with her to put the gun down.

Elma looked at Vernon. He was already dead. The keeper of the dead, the preparer of the dead, was dead himself. Her abdomen burning, Elma sat down on the top step and put the barrel of the revolver in her mouth. Michael Bish lunged forward, her lips forming one word: *No!* Elma smiled around the barrel and pulled the trigger.

CHAPTER
THIRTY-FIVE

GUY FINISHED LOADING his Volvo and went in the house to drink a final cup of coffee before heading out. The daily edition of the *Colson Beacon* was on the kitchen counter, and he opened the paper to the editorial page, where the managing editor had written a special letter to Guy, bidding him a fond farewell. Guy read the letter again and smiled at the note on the bottom that read: *This letter was signed by everyone in the newsroom.*

"Because everyone is happy to see me go," Guy said to himself with a wry smile.

He put the paper away and took his cup out to the back to look at Michael's house one last time. He thought she would come around during his last week to say goodbye, but she hadn't made it over. He hadn't spent any time with her since the night of the shootings at Diest's Mortuary. Michael was given new respect around town after people learned the truth about Vernon Diest and his assistant, Elma Voycheck. Diest had, in fact, killed Guy's daughter. The ballistics test had proved it, and the prints on the pistol found in the well were all Vernon's. It was never established exactly who had killed Arnold Dupree and Saylor Voycheck, but all bets were on

Vernon. Guy had testified in two informal hearings. He wouldn't be needed for any other testimony.

He had seen Michael several times in public, and talked to her once on the phone, but the conversation was brief and hurried. She was in demand now, to speak at this function or that one and tell all she knew about the story of the murderous Vernon Diest and his deadly consort. Guy was saddened and amused by the attention she received. Saddened because she obviously loved it, and amused because people's memories were so short. Only two weeks ago Michael had been the town pariah. This new regard for her stank of hypocrisy. Guy, on the other hand, was treated even more poorly than before by the people he encountered, almost as if they blamed him for all that had happened.

He dumped the coffee out of his cup and got up. With a last look in the direction of her house, he went inside. It was time to go.

Guy went through the house and checked every room one last time. The movers had come and taken everything he brought with him. The house was empty but for a chair and a table that were there when he moved in. He locked the back door and the front, and put the key on his dash, so he would remember to drop it off at the realtor's on his way out of town. He was tempted to drive by Michael's house, but he talked himself out of it. It was probably better if he didn't see her again.

When he walked outside, Adam Dupree was standing beside the car. Guy went to him and held out a hand. Adam took it and shook it twice, hard. His features were ridged with sadness. "You said you weren't going until Saturday."

Guy smiled. "No reason to wait. I'm packed and ready to go."

Adam nodded. "Yeah. No reason to hang around another three days. Don't forget to send me a subscription to that magazine you're going to work for."

"I won't forget," Guy promised. He handed him a slip of

paper. "Here's where I'll be staying when I get to town. I'll give you my new number when I get one. I want you to call me and keep me up on the latest around here."

The corner of Adam's mouth lifted. "I'll do that. It's been an interesting summer so far, hasn't it?"

Guy looked at him. "Adam, you have a wonderful gift for understatement. Take care of yourself and that dog of yours. Maybe you can come up to Chicago and visit me sometime."

Adam looked doubtful. "We don't get away much. But thanks for the invitation. You heading right out of town or will you be stopping anywhere?"

"I'll be going downtown to the realtor's office."

"Anywhere else?"

"Where did you have in mind?"

Adam lifted both shoulders. "Nowhere. I was just curious, is all. Thought you might stop by Michael Bish's house on your way out. It's not good to leave things undone."

"Things are okay, Adam," Guy told him. "At least they're as okay as they're going to get."

"If you say so," said Adam.

"I do." Guy opened his car door.

"I bet she comes up there looking for you," Adam told him.

Guy smiled again. "Bet she won't." He got in his car and stuck his hand out the window. "Goodbye, Adam."

Adam shook his hand again and smiled back at him. "Goodbye, Guy. I'll talk to you soon."

Guy nodded and started his engine. He drove slowly through town to the downtown area and parked in front of the realty office. The woman inside saw him coming and met him at the door. She took the key from him, checked to make sure he had signed everything he needed to sign, and told him to have a safe trip. Guy thanked her and returned to his car.

In fifteen minutes he was looking at Colson in his rearview mirror. With only a glance, he looked forward to the road ahead. It was going to be a long time before he stopped thinking about Michael. But he was glad to be going.

* * *

Adam Dupree walked around to his backyard and let his dog, Baby, out of the house by opening the sliding glass doors off his patio. He sat down on the glider he had purchased last spring and patted one thigh. Baby jumped up beside him and automatically licked his hand. Adam smiled and patted the little dog's head. She was such a sweet thing. The very best of companions, was Baby. He didn't know what he would do without her.

People were so complicated, so fragile. But dogs, dogs were always the same, day after day. Dogs were constant in their affections and in their devotion. Just the way people would be in a perfect world.

Adam heard someone pounding on wood somewhere in the neighborhood, and he looked around until he saw some people standing in Michael Bish's backyard. He got up and carried Baby with him to the left side of his yard, where he could see Michael's yard better. From where he stood he could see part of her front lawn, where someone was putting up signs. One sign was a realty sign, with the words *For Sale* across the top. The other sign was a large homemade job, written in purple marker. It read: *Moving Sale—Thurs & Fri.*

Adam shook his head and looked at Baby. "What did I tell you? I guess we'll have to go see her today."

He took Baby's leash from the house and attached it to the poodle's collar before opening the gate at the side of his house. Adam took his time walking around the block, and by the time he reached Michael's house, the realty people were gone and she was heading back inside. Adam called to her and she stopped and turned around. She smiled when she saw him and came out to meet him.

"Hello, Adam. Out for a walk?"

"No, I came to see you. Guy just left, Michael."

Her smile fell. Her eyes looked stricken. "He left? He just left for Chicago?"

"That's right. He was all packed, so he figured why wait."

Michael's mouth opened and hung there. Finally she said, "He told me he wasn't leaving until Saturday. I've been trying to get everything ready. I've told my family and my friends goodbye and—"

"You should have said something to him," Adam told her. "He didn't know."

"I wanted to surprise him," Michael said.

Adam nodded. "He would've been surprised, all right. He hasn't seen you in a while."

"I told you," said Michael, "I was saying goodbye."

"Try here." Adam fished the piece of paper out of his pocket and held it out to her. "He said he'd be staying at this address for a while."

Michael turned and stared at the slip of paper. Then she threw her arms around Adam's neck and kissed him on the cheek. Adam's face grew warm and he tugged at his shirt collar in embarrassment. Michael ran in to copy the address, then she brought the slip of paper back to him. As he turned and shuffled off for home, Adam patted his little dog.

"I win the bet," he told Baby.